THE FORSAKEN AND THE DAMNED

BY

ELIZABETH REVILL

DEDICATION:

'For Dad who was a profound and loving inspiration in my life. I miss you.'

INTRODUCTION

Life before the Cultural Revolution in China was harsh, particularly for women. Baby girls were frequently left to die after birth and those that survived were undervalued. But spiritually, the Chinese people have always maintained an enviable faith and indomitable spirit for survival.

Recently, I went to Singapore and I was excited by the vibrancy of the city and the uniqueness of its multicultural society and its inescapable links with China. It was such a safe environment for women and this also impressed me.

While I was there I read several books; true stories of life in China before the Revolution leading up to the Second World War. I found these fascinating especially as I had taught Twentieth Century History at examination level, which included the First World War, Second World War, and the Cultural Revolution. I was touched by the oral history from comfort women and anecdotes of the unendurable life of young girls in orphanages, which motivated me to write *The Forsaken and the Damned* as a screenplay.

I felt a powerful need within me to write the story that had formulated in my head and heart, and I used other elements close to my heart like the use of "Lily" as a spiritual Guardian Angel. I know in Chinese cinema and stories that this role is often attributed to mothers who have passed, but in this case our heroine's mother is not dead. Therein lie the roots for a sequel to *The Forsaken and The Damned.*

My Great Aunt told me many touching anecdotes about her visits to the Orient to reunite with a friend who had lived and worked in a remote part of China. This served to feed my curiosity of what it must have been like for a young girl who had no one. Putting that together with my own life experiences ignited my imagination to write something, truthful, engaging, powerful, and moving.

So, although it began life as a screenplay, I felt it needed a much bigger canvas, so I tapped away and the novel was born.

Other titles by Elizabeth Revill

DCI Allison Thrillers:

Killing me Softly
Prayer for the Dying
God Only Knows

Llewellyn Family Saga:

Whispers on the Wind
Shadows on the Moon
Rainbows in the Clouds

Stand Alone Novels:

Against the Tide
The Electra Conspiracy
Sanjukta and the Box of Souls.

Acknowledgements

My first thanks must go the well-respected award winning NY producer Lee Levinson who optioned this as a screenplay and has always encouraged me in all my writing endeavours.

To my delightful Commissioning Editor, Sarah Luddington who is an inspiration to me and I am sure all the other authors she has under her wing and her great team at Belvedere.

To my long suffering husband Andrew Spear, my gorgeous son, Ben Fielder with whom it is a joy to discuss ideas.

My supportive extended family, and my dear friend, Hayley Raistrick-Episkopos with whom I share all my joys and tears.

To Hajni Blasko of Substance Books Online Publicity and for all her help in promoting my novels.

Finally to all my readers, without you, there would be no reason to write. I hope you enjoy this offering and here's to the next!

If you do like my work please visit my Facebook page and give me a like:

https://www.facebook.com/pages/Elizabeth-Revill/221311591283258?fref=ts

Check out my website:
http://www.elizabethrevill.com

My publisher's pages:
http://www.elizabeth-revill.co.uk

CHAPTER ONE

In the beginning

The scorching sun pounded down relentlessly and dazzlingly from a seemingly perfect cloudless azure sky. The searing heat was unbearably debilitating leaving those out working in it, sticky and drained. Sweat poured down the faces of the Chinese peasant women working in the rows of verdant, mulberry bushes, which stretched for miles just within the southern border of Kwangtung at a place called Siu Laam. They loosened and hoed the sprouting weeds in between the bushes to prevent them from becoming choked with rampant undergrowth. It was hard work akin to slave labour. The year was 1926.

Nuo Low, a care worn but nevertheless beautiful nineteen year-old grimaced in pain. Her long dark hair was twisted back into a ponytail and the tufts, which had liberated themselves from this constraint stuck in slick strands on her face. Nuo was at a distance from most of the female workers and in the company of her friend, Bo Yap, who was five years older. The two had deliberately kept themselves away from the rest of the work party. Every now and then Bo would glance across at her friend with concern and watch her.

As Nuo straightened up from her backbreaking work her silhouette against the burning sun revealed that she was heavily pregnant. Her loose but damp tunic instead of hiding her condition now clung fast and appeared to strain against her middle. Nuo doubled over in pain and tried to stifle the cry that rose so readily to her lips. Bo looked anxiously across at her, "Has it started?"

Nuo's dark, almond eyes widened, then she screwed them tightly closed, as another wave of pain contracted her stomach. She groaned aloud. She felt as though the pains of hell were upon her.

Bo glanced around watchfully ensuring they were unobserved, and whispered, "Are you sure this time?"

Nuo let out another grunt of pain as she asserted, "Yes… Arrgh! It's coming. I can feel it. We know the head's engaged and I want to push." Her last words were torn from her as she moaned in agony.

Bo took Nuo's hand and they ran awkwardly through the field and to a place where they knew they couldn't be seen. Bo helped Nuo to squat behind a tree and supported her. She removed a stick from her pocket and thrust it into Nuo's mouth as the young woman bore down in an attempt to prevent her from screaming out with the intense pain and the constant urgent need to push.

All of the time, Bo kept a look out and tried hard to still her friend's cries, whilst encouraging her to push and breathe through each wave of contractions. She peered under Nuo's sarong, "I can see the head, it's crowning. One more push and the shoulders will be through. It will soon be over. Go on, try again. More! Count and breathe through the contractions. Another one, a big one now; push!"

Nuo struggled and forced herself to push as hard as she could. There was a strange sound like pigs slopping at a trough and a wet sucking noise. The shoulders were through and the baby slipped out into Bo's arms. Bo's eyes filled with tears as she saw the gender, "I'm so sorry… It's a girl."

Nuo nearly collapsed with the shock and pain of childbirth but she managed to remain conscious. Bo took out a small pocketknife and sliced through the umbilical cord separating mother and baby. "Another push, Nuo. You must expel the afterbirth. Try."

"I can't. I'm exhausted. I just want to rest. Leave me. Go back. There is no need for both of us to be caught. I will stay with my baby."

"You can't, we must get back if we don't want to be beaten. Please." Bo set down a small cloth taken from around her waist, which had been tied like an apron and she placed the infant on it in the shade of the tree. She hurriedly tied the umbilical cord, "Quickly now, push once more. It will poison your body if you don't get rid of it. You could die. Hurry."

Too weak to argue Nuo grunted with exertion again and again, until the liver like placenta left her body, which Bo immediately covered with leaves and debris knowing that in the night wild animals would seek it out and devour it, destroying all evidence of the birth.

Bo continued, “Please, Nuo. We must return and quickly. There’s nothing more we can do.”

“But, my baby,” cried Nuo in despair. “I can’t… my little girl.”

“It’s no good, Nuo, believe me, we have to leave her. We have no choice. They’ll only kill her and us, too, if they catch us.”

Bo grabbed her reluctant friend’s hand and dragged her back to her workstation. Nuo shrieked out in abject misery as she was tugged back through the field where they had been working and her cry echoed miserably around them.

A white bird flew up from the shrubs and called shrilly. Female workers stopped their arduous toil and stood up shading their eyes against the glaring sun and watched the snowy bird as it circled in the now bright cobalt sky before it flew off toward the mountains. One woman muttered, “It’s a sign, a spirit of our ancestors, come to watch and bless us.”

The peasants resumed their exhausting labour and Nuo shed tears of sorrow at her plight and loss. Her chest heaved uncontrollably and her breathing was unsteady. She and Bo struggled to continue with their punishing tasks and time clicked on.

The sun had moved from the midday point and began to sink in the afternoon sky. A few small clouds traversed the blue ceiling and one wizened elderly woman, Jien Rum stood up, rubbing her aching back. She had sharp bright eyes and few teeth. She sucked in a mouthful of air and shook her sweaty head when the cry of a baby assailed her ears. Jien stopped and looked about her. She heard the lusty cry once more. No one else moved or looked up.

Jien threw down her hoe and made her way toward the sound, stumbling through the shrubbery and undergrowth to the back of the field where behind a bush she saw the tiny naked baby girl laid on a small, blood stained cloth. Her heart filled with love and pity. She made soothing noises to the child, removed her outer tunic and wrapped the little one in the rough, coarse cloth before walking back to the rows of women workers.

She stared piercingly at each young woman she passed but none would hold her gaze or speak. Bo glanced at her friend. She nodded to reassure her and warned her with her eyes and expression to keep silent. She looked again and it was then that she noticed with horror the birthing blood, which stained the front of Nuo's work clothes. Bo hurriedly grabbed a handful of dirt and smothered it over the stain and then, rubbed soil up her own arms and hands to disguise the confession of blood, which had dyed her skin. Again, she put her fingers to her lips to instruct Nuo to be silent as Jien passed them with the infant.

Nuo looked longingly, and in anguish, at the tiny baby, as Jien walked on and Nuo felt her breasts seep with milk. Her pain wracked eyes filled with tears and she bit her lip to stop herself from crying out. The taste of coppery, warm, salty blood filled her mouth and in despair she hung her head in sorrow and helpless resignation.

Bo slowly moved toward Nuo and placed a restrictive arm around her to both comfort her and restrain her. Finally, Nuo collapsed to her knees and Bo struggled to haul her back to her feet amid the whispers of some of the other women, but fortunately, Jien didn't hear them and continued to walk through the rows until she reached the overseers in charge of the work force who immediately fell into deep discussion. One of them pointed toward the track leading from the field and Jien was allowed to go on her way and she began the long walk toward civilisation.

The sun was setting now, and there was little respite from the heat, but Jien stoically marched on toward an official looking building, which fronted many rows of long sheds that lay behind, hidden from prying eyes and the outside world. A wooden sign with letters burnt into it read, Wing Fong Girls' Orphanage.

Jien placed the swaddled baby onto the steps and scurried back the way she had come without looking back. The tiny baby hungry for nourishment screwed up her face that was now turning red with both temper and the heat, and she began to cry. She had a fine pair of lungs and a lusty wail, which soon alerted those inside who came to investigate but they could not see who had deposited the small bundle on the steps and abandoned the infant.

The child was picked up by a woman in a guard's uniform and taken indoors, to what fate, no one would know.

Chapter Two

Six Years Later 1932

Rows of dilapidated sheds stretched behind the stark orphanage building and in front of these sheds were low rustic bamboo cages with numbers above each of the prison type cells. Inside each cage a girl was curled up and asleep. They were thin and scrawny and clearly malnourished. They wore identical thin cotton tunics like a slave army and ranged from six to thirteen years old.

Outside the cages on a rickety boardwalk patrolled a forty-year-old fat, masculine looking female guard, Lien, who had short, cropped hair. Her uniform was tightly fitting and fought against her bulk and rolls of surplus flesh, her face was plump and doughy and her small, mean eyes were like currants in the folds of flesh that were her cheeks. She had a razor thin white scar that showed up in her olive complexion, which ran down the side of her nose to her top lip. Her lips were thin and curled with a cruel twist. She looked formidable.

Lien carried a brass gong and stout wooden baton. She swaggered along the boardwalk and began to bang the gong as an alarm call, waking the girls. She laughed as she watched them trying to sit up but the space in the cage was limited and there was no room for them to sit comfortably. They moved around their cage with difficulty and all had an aura of fear about them. Some, in an attempt to look alert, crouched on all fours. Their faces were upturned and forward. None of them wanted a beating. They were silent and sad, and waited.

A second guard, Mee, stick thin and considerably younger stooped down and opened each cage, but although the young ones were cramped, and yearning to stretch their muscles, not one child moved. They knew better. On a given signal, Lien battered the gong in quick succession and the girls crawled out and sat silently in front of their cages. Although tempted to rub their aching limbs they resisted, such was their rigorous training. They each picked up a small metal bowl from the ground in front of them.

One girl squealed as she saw a cockroach that had settled in her dish and tipped it out. Lien's eyes snapped onto the child and she trembled in fear. Lien strutted up to the small girl and rapped her hand with her baton. The little girl's eyes welled with tears but stoic in her punishment she remained silent not wanting a further beating.

Lien shouted out, "Up, now." The girls, as one, lifted their bowls aloft and an elderly woman in her seventies struggled with an old iron cauldron on wheels along the boardwalk and as she passed each girl she slopped a ladle full of watery rice and chopped yams into each bowl. Lien screeched another instruction, "Eat."

The girls hungrily gulped down their meagre rations and then placed the empty bowl in front of them and crawled back into their cages to wait; that is, all except one girl known as Number Eleven who called herself, Lily. Lily was thirteen and she hadn't quite finished eating. Lien swung her baton across the cages, which was the signal for the girls to emerge and line up with their bowls. When she saw Lily still sitting and eating she scowled sullenly and strode across to her and dashed the bowl from her hands. It flew up in the air, spinning around before it tumbled into the latrine ditch.

Lien viciously prodded Lily with her baton and forced the girl to her feet, ordering her to retrieve her bowl. "Go, fetch! Now! Do it!"

Lien pushed Lily forward hitting her across the backs of her legs with the stick until Lily was coerced into jumping into the ditch of raw human sewage to fetch her dish.

Once retrieved, Lily climbed out with her basin and lined up with the other girls. She was splattered in human excrement and soaked in urine. She struggled to keep her face expressionless, as she knew this would only attract further punishment. The other girls wrinkled their noses in distaste but they didn't murmur and Lien laughed scornfully.

Lily was a strikingly beautiful girl with long, straight dark hair that flowed down her back and had eyes that had seen much sorrow and pain. Her skin in spite of lack of food and care had an ethereal hue. Her developing breasts were pert, firm and upturned like ripening plums. Her young body toned through hard work was lean and she was long limbed for her age. She had a quality about her that none of the other girls possessed, possibly due to the fact that Lily had been well educated and brought up with love until her parents had died so tragically, in a freak boating accident, and her uncle had swindled the family's money and her inheritance and she had been deposited at the orphanage with a note and some money for her care. The Chinese Yuan Renminbi was greedily taken by those that ran the home and no questions were asked. Lily was just another lost soul, forsaken by the Gods. But Lily still had her dreams and her strong heart and no one could bludgeon that out of her no matter how hard they tried. And try they did. To survive Lily had kept herself to herself only choosing to communicate with a much younger child in the next cage who listened avidly to all of Lily's stories and dreams in complete awe.

Lily was daydreaming now as the girls marched along the boardwalk to a rough wooden table, where they collected their baskets and small rice shoots. Those that were lucky were provided with raffia hats to shield them from the heat of the sun before they were herded out into the rice fields to begin another gruelling day of work. They toiled in the glare of the abrasive sun planting multiples of the small rice shoots in regimented rows. Occasionally, some girls collapsed and died, drowning in the muddy water with no one to pull them out or save them, or some suffered with such damaging heatstroke they would faint with exhaustion. There was no respite, no love, just the constant battering of their wills into complete submission.

Lily took the opportunity to immerse herself in the murky water to try and cleanse herself of the latrine debris that covered her clothes, hair and skin. Somehow she managed to achieve this without being hauled from the field and beaten.

There the children laboured without shade or cover except for the old coolie raffia hats provided by the overseers. More were given out to those who had not been fortunate enough to receive one with their tools as they paddled in the field.

Now the sun had begun to set. Like a burning ball of orange fire in the heavens it sunk rapidly to the horizon and bled out into the dusky sky. The guards on patrol shouted their orders and gathered the girls together to trek back to their solitary prison cages to wait for their evening, meagre, watery rice rations.

As soon as the girls lined up they were ordered to sit and wait but Lien marched up to Lily and dragged her to her feet. She pointed in the direction of the big house and the guards' quarters and ordered her, "Go to my room and wait for me there. Now!"

Lily hesitated. That slight pause earned her a smack on the back of her legs with Lien's baton. It left a big red weal on her calves. She stumbled forward and reluctantly made her way to the house.

The little six-year-old girl with large haunted eyes and who sat in the next cage to Lily known as Number Twenty-Six looked anxiously after her friend. She whispered to the ten-year-old girl housed on the other side of Lily, known as Number Eighteen but who called herself Ah Moi, "Poor Lily. What's going to happen to her?"

Ah Moi whispered back, "She's going to be used by the guards."

"Used?"

"After cleaning her they'll play with her before sending her to the big house to live and be fattened up." Ah Moi smirked as she teased the younger child.

"Fattened up?"

"Didn't you know? Once you get to a certain age or size, they feed you up to make you fat and then you're slaughtered like a pig and your meat is sold at market."

The little girl exclaimed in horror and curled up tightly into a ball to make herself look smaller, "What? No… It can't be true…"

"That won't work," sneered Ah Moi enjoying the little one's discomfort, "And if, as you get older, they consider that you're really pretty they'll sell you to the highest bidder."

"Why?"

"For jiggy, jiggy."

"I don't understand. What does that mean?"

Ah Moi giggled disdainfully and then stopped abruptly as she saw one of the guards on patrol turn her head.

It was Mee, the thin guard, who spun around trying to detect where the whispers were coming from. She spotted the two girls interacting and noted with a modicum of pleasure Number Twenty-Six's frightened expression. Mee hurried across and cracked her whip hard in front of the two girls' faces. She yelled at them, "No talking or we beat you. Then, you die."

The girls flinched in horror and went quiet. Mee laughed inanely there was a touch of madness in her face and a manic glint in her eyes. The girls were left in no doubt that she meant it. They dared not speak again that evening.

Chapter Three

Night Travels

The night sky was velvet black with pinpricks of light that pierced the heavens in a celestial display. The moon hung low that night, a golden orb of shining promise. The burgeoning dark was filled with the sound of thrumming cicadas that called for mates to sing and join in harmony.

The crickets and grasshoppers fell silent as a strange scraping was heard moving along the rough track from the house to the confining cages. Lien dragged Lily along the path and thrust her into her cage. She pushed the girl's limbs inside the prison and rammed the door shut and pegged it closed.

Lien guffawed in sadistic glee as she swaggered away, and returned to her quarters. Her mocking laugh echoed hollowly in the night air and faded into the distance. Only then did Lily adjust her position in the cage and the child sat up as best as she could.

The little girl in the next cage whispered to her friend, "Are you all right?"

Lily opened her dusky brown eyes and gazed up at the starry heavens, a serene expression on her face. "As long as I have the stars and the moon, I can live and dream."

Number Twenty-Six hesitated before speaking. She sighed nervously and finally managed to ask, "Did they hurt you?"

Lily turned her face to the child and smiled with love, "Only on the outside. They are not able to touch me inside. They will not break my soul. Inside, I travel. When everyone is asleep I leave this cursed place and fly over the mountain to a beautiful land."

The little girl listened in rapt wonder. She loved to hear Lily talk.

"There's a lush green valley with rainbow clouds. The

scent of Jasmine is on the air. It is my favourite, such a wonderful perfume. There the animals roam freely and children laugh and play happily without fear. It's paradise."

Number Twenty-Six continued to listen to Lily's soothing voice. She had a warm tone that conjured such beautiful images and the child drifted off into a world of imagination as Lily continued to speak.

"If I want to I can fly like a bird, soar high in the sky. I can go anywhere. I'm only telling you this because you are my closest and dearest friend. I trust you with all my secrets."

"Tell me more, please."

"Beyond the rainbow valley is another place with a wondrously calm blue lake and such beautiful people. It's surrounded by restaurants and bright lights such as you've never seen. And the food… the food makes me drool to think of it. It's delicious and sets your taste buds tingling."

"How do you know?"

"Because I've smelled and tasted it. I've hidden and watched those folks enjoying themselves and eaten the leftovers before they're thrown to the dogs. You should learn to fly and come with me," urged Lily.

"I'm afraid," said Number Twenty-Six in a small voice.

"Fear is here in this place, but not in your heart." Lily paused and studied the angelic face of the small child adjacent to her, which was bathed in silver moonlight. "What is your favourite name?"

The little girl stopped and thought for a moment, "I'm not sure…" She was puzzled by the change of direction in the conversation.

"Think of it and I'll call you that. Better than Number Twenty-Six. You should have a proper name. It makes you a person who'll have respect."

The little girl bit her lip as she thought before she blurted out, "Mai Lee. I like Mai Lee"

"Then I will call you, Mai Lee and you may call me Lily. Together we will dream what our lives will be and make those dreams a reality."

"Really?"

"If you believe, really believe then anything is possible. Just think we could be waitresses in one of those wonderful restaurants. We'd get to eat the same delicious food. This will be our shared dream. You must learn to dream. We all need dreams to survive. If we're very lucky we may get sent to the same slave camp or brothel."

"Then we'd meet every day," smiled Mai Lee.

"Every day. We'd save enough money and escape together. Somewhere far away where they'd never find us. Of course, first I'll have to teach you to fly. It's quite easy really."

"But, I've never seen you leave your cage."

"We can get out if you like. The latch can be worked free. I've done it many times before when everyone's asleep. But even in here I fly. My spirit flies. Oh, how I'd love to be a bird. To fly free." Lily sighed with longing, "Everything looks so beautiful from up there." She gazed up at the heavens a serene expression on her face.

Both girls fell silent as Mee marched toward them. The girls feigned sleep as Mee halted outside their cages and stared hard at them. She hissed in scorn, "You, two. Ha! You pretend to sleep so soundly… Good, you'd best not speak. Something special is in store for you. Just you wait!" Mee started to whistle as she strolled away but Lily caught the supercilious look on the guard's face as she turned away from them. Lily took a deep intake of breath and lifted her eyes to the night sky and fixed them on the shimmering moon. She appeared to go into a deep trance and said no more. Mai Lee opened her eyes and watched.

"Lily?"

But there was no answer and Mai Lee settled down in an attempt to sleep, but her heart was filled with an inexplicable joy, such as she had never known. The curtain of night had now drawn to a close embracing all in its shaded cover. Stars shone from the velvet black sky that was once a lovers' ceiling as the gentle silver light of the moon caressed the curve of an upturned face that gazed in hope and longing for the dawn of another day.... For the first time in her life she felt hope and she had a name, a name to be proud of. She was Mai Lee.

The following morning instead of being marched to the rice fields after their morning ritual of wake up and food, Mai Lee was made to follow Ah Moi to the guards' quarters by the big house.

They entered a treatment room where Lien lay on a trolley type cot with her back bared. Ah Moi, spoke quietly to Mai Lee, "This is an honour for you. You have been selected to learn the art of massage. Watch and learn."

Mai Lee observed wide-eyed as Ah Moi poured a little aromatic oil into her hands and rubbed them together, "So the oil is not cold when it touches the body, see?"

Mai Lee nodded and edged closer. Ah Moi used the palm of her hands to vigorously massage the healing oil into Lien's back. "This gives you the feel of the muscles and relaxes her. You find the knots in the muscles and the aching trigger points and pay special attention to them. Always keep one hand on her. Never stop touching the back once you have begun, understand? Now you try. Firm strokes remember, oil first."

Mai Lee did as she was asked and began to knead the pressure points where she found tightness. Lien began to groan in pleasure and satisfaction and Ah Moi, nodded as she watched, "That's right, good. Now to finish use big sweeping strokes and cover the whole back and lightly tap, here and here like this." Ah Moi took over and demonstrated and Mai Lee remembered to keep one hand on Lien's flesh, as Ah Moi took over. "Well done! You have learned well. Now, your test will come as another will take Missy Lien's place. And I will observe to see if you have got it right."

Lien rose, her mountains of flesh wobbling. She was unashamed of her nudity and seemed to enjoy the spectacle she created in front of the impressionable child. "You have good hands," she said to Mai Lee. "Like little pads of velvet. It bodes well for when you are older." Lien smiled lasciviously and chortled as she gathered her clothes and left the room, where another guard came to take her place and laid down for Mai Lee to begin the same ritualistic massage.

Mai Lee was an eager pupil and developed further

techniques, learning how to walk on the backs of her subjects exerting and using her weight on various acupressure points. It was better than working in the fields every day. She was learning an art that would prove useful to her in the future. But, sadly she was unable to spend every day doing this and was soon back taking her turn at working in the blazing heat in the rice fields.

The blisteringly hot sun beat down on the row of cages making the girls shift uncomfortably inside them. Mee rattled a baton across the bamboo slats at the front to rouse them and she stopped at Lily's cage. Lily was dragged out and forced to stand in the full glare of the sun without shade or cover and no coolie hat on her head. "Stand up tall, don't move. You stay there. No slouching, No squinting. Understand?" shrieked Mee.

Lily said nothing. She stood there with dignity. Her bearing was proud and defiant in spite of her fatigue and weakness. Physically she was tortured but her spirit was indomitable. It shone through in her face and the irrepressible light of her soul glowed in her eyes.

Mai Lee looked on in horror as she watched her friend begin to sway as if she was near collapse. She opened her mouth to shout and protest but Ah Moi silenced her, "Hush! You cannot help her. If you try, they will beat you like a dog. Say nothing and live."

"But this will kill her. It's the fourth day she's been made to stand in the sun."

"You don't want to join her," insisted Ah Moi.

Mai Lee sighed, "But it's her stories that keep me alive. They give me hope."

Ah Moi, scoffed, "Huh! That's all they are. Stories, just stories. Not worth losing your life over."

Mai Lee bit her lip and stifled back her tears. What could *she* do? A small child like her? But she so wanted to do something. She whispered again to Ah Moi, "But she's had nothing, no food, nothing. She will die."

"Then that is her fate," murmured Ah Moi, philosophically.

Mee summoned the girls and they crawled out of their cages. The signal was given and they held their bowls aloft as the elderly woman trekked before them, as she did every day, slopping the thin watery rice and yams into their bowls.

Mai Lee watched surreptitiously, trying not to attract any undue attention, as Lien arrived and dragged Lily away from her spot and forced her toward the building. Mai Lee's face was creased in concern for her precious friend and she was chided for not eating quickly enough.

The girls lined up and trooped toward the open rice fields where there was no respite from the sun's searing heat. She began planting the rice shoots bending double and struggling to concentrate on the task in hand. She continually stood up and scoured the trail looking for any sign of Lily, hoping against hope that she would see her arrive to work with the rest of them. But always, Lily was nowhere to be seen.

Mee's eagle eyes were on the workers and when she saw Mai Lee stopping, yet again, she strode forward and smacked her hard across the back. "You, girl. Keep working. No slacking!" Mai Lee bit back a cry and continued her arduous work without complaint. She was discovering an inner reserve of strength, strength she was sure that had been implanted by Lily.

The long day stretched on before it finally faded to dusk and the girls were regimentally marched back to their bamboo prisons, fed and shut in for the night like dogs. Mai Lee saved some of her yams and hid them in her tunic pocket. The moon shone full and silver, its gentle beams washing over the sleeping girls. The crickets chirruped in a carefree buzz. They sang in insect harmony calling for a partner to come and dance.

Mai Lee cast her eyes towards Lily's empty cage. She could not sleep, although her small body ached and her skin burned. Her eyes filled with tears as she thought of her lost friend, her inspiration, and the light in her life.

Sounds from the big house blew on the wind and Mai Lee became more alert as a door slammed and shuffling footsteps were heard. Mai Lee closed her eyes tightly and pretended to be asleep. She waited hardly daring to breathe but knowing that if she was seen to be awake then that could attract a beating.

The footsteps approached and Mai Lee heard Lily's cage door squeak open. Something was shoved roughly inside and the cage door creaked shut and the peg locked it. Mai Lee's heightened senses listened to ensure the footsteps walked away, footsteps she recognised as the flatfooted stomp of the fat guard, Lien.

An agonised groan compelled Mai Lee to open her eyes. She was relieved to see Lily struggling to find a comfortable position in her ramshackle cage, "Lily?" she whispered trying not to wake the other girls.

Lily rolled over in obvious pain. Her body was blistered and burnt, bruises and welts were raised on her body from some horrific brutality. Her eyes shone brightly with unshed tears but she mustered a smile for Mai Lee. "Mai Lee?"

"Are you all right?" asked Mai Lee in a tight, frightened voice. "I saved you some of my yams. Here."

Lily took the offered fruit and devoured them. "Thanks, I was starving. I have had nothing to eat all day."

"They can't keep doing this to you," said Mai Lee.

Lily sighed and turned her sorrowful eyes on her young friend, "I've had enough. I'm going."

"What?" gasped Mai Lee fearfully. "What do you mean?"

"To escape. I can't take anymore."

"But, why? What's changed? We've got plans and dreams. You can't go without me…"

"Oh, Mai Lee, if I stay here then my life is over."

"Why? What has happened?"

"I wouldn't do it. I couldn't do it."

"What?"

"Live with that fat pig of a woman in her bedroom. I'd rather die."

"Is that why…?

"They beat me and made me stand for hours in the sultry heat without food and water? Yes."

"Please, Lily. Don't run away without me. Please not without me," begged Mai Lee, her beautiful eyes filling with tears.

"Oh my sweet angel, you will be fine. You will."

"But girls who have tried to escape before have… have…" she choked back a sob. "They did unspeakable things to them. Tortured them before butchering them like animals."

"I'll kill myself before they kill me. I will. I swear I will. Look." Lily lifted her tunic. "See what that bitch did to me." Lily's stomach was red raw and blistered. "She poured boiling water on me because I took too long to fill her bath. Because I was not a willing sex slave."

Mai Lee flinched at the horrific sight and the bubbling blisters defacing Lily's skin. She hesitated before she spoke again, "But, I don't want you to be caught and tortured."

Lily smiled beatifically through her pain and her face took on an unnatural but heavenly light. "They won't torture me," she said with authority and determination.

"How can you be so sure?"

"Because I'll slit my own throat first." Lily painfully lifted her arm and revealed a small knife secreted in the sleeve of her tunic jacket. "I have spent hours sharpening this blade on a stone. It is razor sharp and will do the job quickly, I won't even feel it."

"Oh, Lily, no. I am so afraid for you. I cannot imagine being without you. Please think again."

"You must be strong. I know you can do this, Mai Lee. Listen, if you are questioned, you know nothing; you saw nothing. Do you understand?" Mai Lee nodded slowly and sniffed back her tears. "Good, now you must try and sleep."

Mai Lee shuffled back down and struggled to do as Lily asked but her sleep was fitful and broken in spite of her exhaustion. She felt as if her reason for being was ending. Now with Lily gone she would have nothing. She prayed in her head, who to, she didn't know. She didn't want Lily to suffer or be killed and she could not bear the thought of her impending loneliness without her.

A whisper floated to her ears, "Fight on, Mai Lee. Live on. I will give you my strength. My time is come but you are stronger. You will rise above all the pain, all the ills, I just know it."

With those words swimming around her head Mai Lee drifted away into a sound sleep as peaceful as could be in those circumstances; along with the rest of the orphaned slaves who all resided in the world of dreams, but the soft magical dreams of hope turned into a nightmare as strange and ugly sounds permeated the dark. Cruel fingers reached in and plucked them from their dreams.

A huge hullabaloo broke out and harsh floodlights plunged on rousing the girls in their cages to sleepy wakefulness. Chaos surrounded them with guards who screeched and shouted, and who chased into the shadows and undergrowth with flashlights. Dogs yapped and barked ferociously. Guards had beasts on chains tracking something or someone.

Mai Lee knew. She hardly dared to show she was awake and she was afraid of what she would see when she opened her eyes. She had been riding on a black devil of a stallion with blazing red eyes that had reared and bucked, throwing her to the ground. The demon horse had reared and was about to pound out her brains when she had been roused from this bleak and horrific nightmare. Mai Lee's frenetic breathing became slightly easier and she knew she had to be alert and she had to see.

Mai Lee sat up as best as she could in her cramped conditions and stared at the empty cage next to her, the door squeaked crazily on its hinges in the night air and the latch peg dangled free. Mai Lee bit her lip. Her biggest fear was upon her. Lily was gone and she was alone.

Chapter Four

Lily's peace

The guards scoured the hillside, thick with lush vegetation, tangled undergrowth and trees like broccoli tops that merged together to make an almost impenetrable forest. The searching officers shouted and poked in the brambles and bracken with sharpened sticks. Small creatures flushed out, by the dogs and guards, broke cover and fled. The women, relentless in their pursuit, left no bush or large stones unexamined; they moved on doggedly before they finally headed toward a rocky outcrop of boulders that housed a number of caves. The fierce fighting dogs barked and yelped, as they strained against their leashes, in their hunt for Lily.

The cacophony of sounds filtered through the mountains and foothills, and through the valley and rice fields to the orphanage. Tortured sounds carried on the wind as the dogs became more and more excited. Their barking became more vicious and ferocious as they arrived at the entrance to a deep dark cave. The dogs tugged and pulled, leaping up and anxious to break free. They salivated like ravenous wolves, their eyes bulged with hate as they had been bred purely for this purpose to punish and destroy.

Lily sat huddled in a corner and shivered. Her coarse cotton but worn tunic was now shredded to rags and she was filthy. Her long dark hair was matted and her face dirt streaked, and dried salt tears carved a track through her mud-spattered cheeks. As she heard the approach of the terrifying animals and the footfalls of the guards who prepared to release the crazed canines she took a deep breath and slowly removed her knife. She tested its blade on a lock of hair. It sliced through it without difficulty, which boded well for Lily but still she honed the steel on the rock next to her. There would be no mistakes. The scrape of the metal on the damp rock was almost comforting. Water dripped down the side of the cave wall and tree roots dangled like the tentacles of some giant alien creature intending to strangle and suffocate.

A dog yelped angrily and she tremblingly placed the knife at her throat and felt for her carotid artery, which pulsed frantically in her neck. The first of the enraged creatures, now free, bounded into the cave. It snarled at Lily, drew back its lips and bared its teeth; its massive bone crunching jaws dripped with saliva in anticipation of a blood feast. A terrifying growl rumbled into another savage snarl as the creature drew closer.

Lily closed her eyes to the coming onslaught and said a quick prayer before she took the knife and rested it against her neck. Her hand shook almost uncontrollably and she closed her eyes, pleading with herself in a quiet whisper, 'to do it'. The arrival of another murderous canine gave her the final push and Lily's trembling hands found the power and she slit her own throat quickly, cutting from side to side.

The arterial blood spurted in rapid pulsing bursts as if to keep time with some tribal beat. Her body slumped down and twitched involuntarily as her life's blood drained away in a surging crimson fountain.

Mee entered with torchlight and flashed it on the ground where it picked up the dying body of Lily who looked more like a cloth doll or bundle of foul, tattered rags. She shouted out, "She's in here! Quickly now."

Mee strutted across to Lily and kicked her dying body as the pack of dogs surged forward and raced to tear at her young flesh and devour her steaming innards as the needle sharp teeth ripped at her skin and muscle. The other guards arrived at the scene and laughed cruelly as they watched the animals feast on Lily's bloody intestines, which protruded from where she had been disembowelled.

The guards called back the blood-crazed dogs and left the remains of Lily on that rocky cave floor. They scrambled out, and negotiated the steep mountainside, which led back through the thick undergrowth to the track that returned them to Wing Fong Orphanage. They laughed and chattered together as if they were on a holiday outing.

"The wild dogs in the hills will finish her off. There'll be nothing left of her by tomorrow," said Mee.

"Not even her bones," said another guard.

"What sport! That was more exciting than anything I have ever seen, better than a cock fight."

"Or dog fight," agreed the guard.

When they got back, Lien made a point of striding past the cages. She ran a bamboo cane across the slats, which made a raucous rattle, waking the girls, who in their fear pretended to slumber, and Mai Lee reluctantly opened her eyes.

Lien shrieked, "Listen and learn. Number Eleven is dead. Her filthy body has been left as fodder for the wild dogs that maraud the hills. Anyone else want to escape?" She laughed hideously and swaggered back to the building.

Mai Lee wanted to shriek back that Number Eleven had a name, a name she would never forget but she waited. She waited until she had watched the last of the guards as they retreated to their quarters and the floodlights were extinguished. She wriggled to the front of her cage and fiddled with the peg in its catch. She muttered in frustration before she finally succeeded in slipping the peg out. She pushed open her door and crawled out.

Ah Moi heard her scratching around and she looked up. She pushed herself up on one elbow and watched in stunned horror as Mai Lee opened the cage, "What are you doing?" she whispered. "If they catch you they'll break your legs and beat you."

"I don't care. Lily was my very best friend, she told me stories and gave me a reason to live."

Ah Moi tried to stop Mai Lee again, "Don't. You'll be punished severely and we may get beaten, too."

"I'm sorry…" Mai Lee crawled out, stood up and stretched. She tiptoed along the boardwalk, very slowly; all the while she kept a wary eye out for guards or the sign of any movement from the big house.

Ah Moi shook her head and muttered, "You're a fool."

Mai Lee ran to a stone track, which led to the woods. She hurried on toward a clearing and sat on the dusty ground, where she flung herself down and sobbed. "Oh, Lily, Lily, why? Why did you go? Now, I have no one." The tears coursed down her cheeks as she allowed herself to cry and mourn her dead friend. She shook her hair from her face and peered down at the ground in despair when she heard a strange sound like a rustling on the breeze. She sat up properly and wiped away her tears wondering if some animal was approaching, but none appeared. Mai Lee gazed up at the night sky where the moon and stars shone brightly bathing the dell in its silvery light.

A few small puff balls of clouds began to swirl together. Mai Lee gulped and watched in wonder as the clouds in the sky took on a form. She blinked, rubbed her eyes and stared again. In the heavens above her, Mai Lee clearly saw the face of her friend, Lily. She whispered in awe and wonder, "Lily?"

An inexplicable calm and warmth flooded through her. Mai Lee could feel the presence of her friend. Her throat closed up with emotion and she struggled to clear the very physical lump that had manifested and just managed to speak, "Lily? Oh, Lily, is that you?"

Lily's voice came to her like a myriad of tinkling silver bells, as she said softly, "Yes, it's me. Oh, Mai Lee, please don't cry." The scent of jasmine was in the air.

Mai Lee felt loving, invisible hands, which stroked her hair and tenderly caressed her face. She was filled with an overwhelming feeling of fond affection and her eyes no longer streamed with tears. She sniffed loudly and focused on the vision in the clouds.

Mai Lee's eyes fixed on Lily's face, whose ethereal countenance looked beautiful. She was radiant and glowing with a godly, white light. Lily smiled serenely and again the ghost hands ruffled the hair on Mai Lee's head and gently stroked her forehead.

"But, I've lost you. How can I learn to fly without you?" protested Mai Lee.

The cloud form took on more substance and Lily's angelic psyche floated down to Mai Lee's side

The two girls gazed deeply into each other's eyes. Time

seemed to have no meaning and they sat in silence. Lily lightly brushed her lips across Mai Lee's downy cheek. Mai Lee sighed, closed her eyes but shivered involuntarily and Lily vanished.

Mai Lee felt the loss and opened her eyes but Lily was gone. She cried out in pain and sorrow, "Don't go. Come back, please. Lily!"

A soft breeze stirred the leaves on the trees and Mai Lee rose. She turned around and her eyes searched the dark for her friend but there was no one. She sadly began to retrace her steps. As she approached the trail to the cages there was a sudden rush of wind, which swirled the leaf detritus and twigs up in the air like a mini tornado. Mai Lee stopped, as that same feeling of love embraced her and her face lit up with joy, "Lily? Are you back? I can feel you. You are here aren't you?"

A shimmering shape that danced in the moonlight became clearer and once more, Lily, her friend, stood before her. She whispered, "Oh, Mai Lee, you trembled so, when I kissed you that I thought I had frightened you and so I left."

"Oh, Lily. You could never frighten me. I wish I were a spirit, too, and we could play and talk together forever."

Lily raised her arms, a sublime expression on her face, and she began to levitate. She rose to the very tops of the trees and ruffled the leaves gently. Her voice came to Mai Lee as a thought, "There's one more thing I have to do. Now, I know that you do not fear me I will try and return. Go back and be safe. Life maybe difficult for you now and in the immediate future, but it will not always be that way. I promise you. I have seen what is to come, Mai Lee. But most importantly, now, they mustn't discover you have gone. Hurry back now." Lily dissolved into a ghostly mist and Mai Lee heard her laugh, which blew on the wind surrounding her with warmth and love before it dissipated into silence and the sound of the leaves soughing in the warm night air.

Mai Lee smiled and scurried back to her cage. She settled back inside and refastened the latch, a blissful expression on her face, as she closed her eyes and drifted into a welcome but dreamless sleep.

The cloying breath of the dark wrapped around Mai Lee and enfolded her in its uneasy embrace. Even though she was in reality imprisoned in a cage, in her heart and mind she was free and that feeling was down to Lily. For that reason alone Mai Lee slumbered more peacefully.

Suddenly and dramatically the relatively comfortable silence of the night was ripped apart once more by the agonised screams of a woman in unspeakable pain and terror. The sounds shrieked on the whispering breeze emanated from the guards' quarters.

Many of the other girls awoke in fright at the horrifying screeches of tortured screams, which travelled to them on the boardwalk. They sat up uncertain of what was occurring. The cries were dragged out as if stretched from a gallows and then stopped as abruptly as a hanging man ended his dance of death. The girls shivered miserably in fright uncertain what to say or do.

Ah Moi released her catch on her cage and wriggled out, "I'll go and see what's happening."

"I'll come with you," volunteered Mai Lee.

"No!" insisted Ah Moi. "You stay here."

But Mai Lee would have none of it and persisted stubbornly, "No. I will come, too."

"Quickly then."

Mai Lee undid her latch and followed after Ah Moi who sprinted toward the big house and the buildings that housed the guards' accommodation.

They ran silently and Mai Lee tried to still her wildly beating heart as they forced their way through to the guards' residences. A group of the warders stood silently and numbly at the entrance to one of the rooms. The two girls pushed their way through the shocked women who stood stock still, their eyes glazed with the dullness of horror. No one spoke or stopped the children who pushed in front of the two guards inside the room. One was vomiting violently and groaning whilst the other had her eyes averted. Her breathing was laboured and in snatched gasps as if trying to still a rising sickness in her throat.

"I've never seen anything like it," whispered one guard at

the door and she explained to another what she had witnessed.

"Lien was running as if chased by some unseen entity. She batted at something with her hands and I truly thought she had lost her mind. She was jabbering like a lunatic."

"What then?"

"Bite marks and nips appeared on her arms and she fled into her room and bolted the door, but it flew open and the sound of flapping wings like a hundred birds filled the air. Lien crouched fearfully in a corner but she was lifted as if by magic and flung onto the bed. Her arms were wrenched up and her legs splayed. She struggled but she couldn't move and her jaw was ripped open, then she began to cough and retch as her insides were torn from her and pulled out through her mouth. It is the devil's work. You can be sure of it."

The girls listened to the exchange and glanced at each other. What were they to see? Ah Moi stepped forward and gasped. Mai Lee's jaw dropped in shock and horror at what lay before her. The grossly fat guard, Lien who had made Lily's life such a misery was spread-eagled on the bed her arms were stretched out like a crucifix. Protruding from her gaping mouth were serpentine coils that streamed out in tangled knots and steamed bloodily over her chest. Her entrails had, indeed, been wrenched from her mouth and throat and now dangled over her chin to her stomach. A dog had its paws up on the bed and was ravenously gobbling up the woman's intestines.

Mai Lee stifled a scream and turned away. Ah Moi took her by the hand and they hurriedly fled back to their cages and wriggled in as if the devil himself was chasing them. Mai Lee's breathing was laboured and in shock. Neither girl had ever seen anything like it before.

One of the other orphans whispered fearfully, "What is it? What did you see?"

Ah Moi was breathless with horror, "It was horrible. The fat guard, Lien, the one who tortured Number Eleven…."

"Lily. Her name was Lily," insisted Mai Lee.

"She's dead. The ogress is dead. She won't hurt anyone ever again."

"Her insides were hanging out as if someone had put their hand down her throat and pulled them out. I think Lily had her revenge," said Mai Lee.

"Someone said Lien was walking to the Latrines when she began screaming. She tried to escape to her room. The guards said she was being attacked by something invisible. But, no one… nothing was near her."

"It was Lily. Lily did for her. She deserved it," said Mai Lee stoically before she settled down to sleep. The girls were restless that night, some afraid to sleep in case the demon that murdered Lien would visit them and take their lives, too. But Mai Lee felt no such fear. She knew it was Lily and Lily would not hurt her, ever.

The following morning a small girl of about four years old called Number Fourteen was pushed into Lily's empty cage. She whimpered and turned her huge dark eyes filled with sorrow and pain on Mai Lee. Mai Lee pushed her fingers through the bamboo slats and entwined them with those of the little girl and whispered, "Don't be afraid. I'll be your friend, as the one who had your cage before you was to me."

The days and nights were to continue as they always had but without the ruthless, swaggering cruelty of Lien and without the loving support of Lily. But Mai Lee knew in her heart that she would see Lily again and that she would survive whatever ordeals were brought to face her.

It was much later in that fateful month when the girls had been put in their cages for the night that Mai Lee found it hard to settle. Her stomach churned with an almost excited anticipation and although weary from working in the hot sun she tossed and turned in the cramped cage as she restlessly tried to sleep. A nervous apprehension filled her waking thoughts and disturbed her tangled dreams.

Even the usual comforting thrum of the chirruping cicadas did little to soothe her troubled mind. From nowhere in the cloying still air a breeze began to blow up around the line of cages. It travelled like a mini tornado and paused at the front of Mai Lee's cage. There was a sudden rush of whirling wind that blew up the dust and detritus that littered the rough and grainy boardwalk. It sounded like the flapping of wings, the sound of a bird trapped and confined, or bats looking to leave their cage and forage in the night and Mai Lee stirred. But, no one else moved, no one else heard and no one else awoke. The surrounding girls slept on but Mai Lee sat up and rubbed her tired eyes.

Mai Lee stared ahead and out of her prison bars as a dark shadowy shape began to take form. Filled with an inexplicable calm Mai Lee continued to stare as the form developed eyes and recognisable features. It was Lily but her spirit form had changed. Gone was her ethereal angelic glow to be replaced by a darker countenance with shining eyes, which flashed red. Her smile, too, was different. Her black lips gaped thinly and her teeth appeared sharp and pointed like that of a demonic vampire that is, had Mai Lee known what a vampire would look like. Yet, Mai Lee was unafraid and whispered almost happily, "Lily?"

The spirit that had been her friend, stretched out her hand now clawed with long talons, "I've come to say goodbye."

Mai Lee pleaded and sobbed out one word, "No!"

"Look at me. I've changed. I'm being punished for killing Lien."

"But..."

"Hush now and listen. I have been given permission to speak with you one last time before I descend into Hell."

"Noooo..."

"The Death Shadows will come and take me. They will keep me until I have paid penance for my wicked deed. I don't know when I will be allowed to leave or when I will be given redemption. Spirits who have been evil must be punished. It is our fate."

"But, Lily..."

"Goodbye, Mai Lee, my sweet friend. I will think of you often and pray for your soul." A lonely tear of blood travelled down Lily's cheek and dropped onto the floor. Mai Lee was surprised to see the blood spot congeal and stain the wood. It was very real.

Lily's face and form began to disintegrate into pearl drops of light that lit with fire before dissolving and sinking into the ground. Strangely enough Mai Lee remained calm and unafraid. She brushed her fingers across her lips in the semblance of a kiss and blew it out through the slats as she whispered, “Goodbye, Lily.”

As she spoke those words a voice came to her on the wind and fell like honey on her ears, “I will watch over you when I am free. This I promise. Know that I will see you again. This is my oath and my salvation.” Her voice drifted into a sigh that was caught by the breeze, which ruffled Mai Lee’s hair and Mai Lee felt strangely at ease and serene, a feeling that she would remember in the years to come.

Chapter Five

Six Years Later 1938

Removed from the confines of their cages some of the girls from that fateful night, now years older, were gathered in a dormitory and sat on a dirt floor cross legged; each one bore a plaque around their neck on a cord with their number. They whispered quietly together, afraid of attracting the attention of the guards who chattered amongst themselves in the doorway.

Evening approached and the dusky hues of night shielded the terrible secrets to be shared in dreams that would come.

Tao, a thin raven-haired thirty-eight-year old warder, gossiped with the older guard, Mee. Neither took any notice of the assembled girls now ranging in age from between twelve to fourteen years. Mai Lee was sitting next to another girl, Ting Ling who seemed to be very knowing about what was to befall them. Mai Lee was singularly and naively innocent. She ventured to ask quietly, "Why are we here? Why have they brought us to this room?"

"We've reached the selling age. It's now that they'll get the best money for us. We are their personal possessions and whoever gives most will have us first," replied Ting Ling. "Men pay well to be first."

"Have us first?" questioned Mai Lee not understanding the lewd inference.

Ting Ling shushed Mai Lee as two rough looking men arrived and interrupted the proceedings. They strode in and looked the girls up and down. Tao clapped her hands and shouted, "On your feet. Stand tall, shoulders back."

The girls obediently scrambled to their feet and the two men addressed them, "I am Fu Yap and this is Shun Kyiang." The other man nodded his acknowledgement. "We are here to inspect you. If your number is called step forward and turn around slowly. Understood?"

The girls nodded as one. Fu Yap pulled one pretty girl forward. He nipped her adolescent breasts with his fingers and spun her around, before lifting her tunic and examining her legs. He yelled her number to his companion who scribbled it down on a piece of paper. The procedure was repeated with several more.

Mai Lee held her breath as Fu's finger pointed at her, "This one, Number Twenty-Six. Tell me about her," he asked Tao. "We have an order for twenty girls. We want only the best. What is her history?"

"Number Twenty-Six was abandoned in a mulberry field shortly after she was born. We could not find her mother, who we presume is dead, or enslaved elsewhere. She was very lucky to have been found or she could have died and been left to the rats or wild dogs that maraud the hillside."

"Hmm," murmured Fu as he considered the information. "How old is she?" His voice was like gravel on the ears.

"From our records, she must be twelve nearly thirteen. She was barely a day old when she was left on the orphanage steps. She's healthy and pretty. She should fetch a very good price."

Fu grunted again and passed down the line to another child where more questioning continued.

Mai Lee's heart beat wildly like a frightened bird as she was singled out with a group of other girls and Mee marched them back to their cages. Mee instructed them, "You are the first. Now sleep. Difficult and joyous times are ahead and you will need to rest."

The girls crawled back into their cramped confined spaces and laid their heads down to try and escape into slumber. Mai Lee finally succumbed to a kind of rest. Sleep came and went like waves hitting the shore; dreams although intermittent were colourful and both odd and exciting. The thought of what morning was to bring, possibly conjured by the strange meeting and assembly in the dormitory that day, lingered about her being like a vengeful spirit and made her think of her friend. "Oh, Lily. Not a day goes by that I don't think of you," she murmured to herself.

The fear of the unknown and what was to come played

tricks with her mind. Her imagination created many scenarios and she wondered what would be. Tossing in a fitful sleep the moments ticked by but her weary eyes caught the strange distracting flashes of light from dancing fireflies prior to drifting once more into confused dreams of distorted borderlands and streets of Technicolor houses and smiling pavements, such as she had never seen, with people who turned into statues of long dead memories of Lien and Lily.

Mai Lee awoke with a start. She stifled a small sob and as the dawning light permeated through the bamboo slats and the day sounds became alive once more she lay still for a time in the half sleep of a soul filled with discontentment. She finally permitted her body to slowly unwrap itself from the tormented chrysalis of a very restless night as she knew her life was to be changed forever. The morning light heralded the signs of yet another crazy day being born. The truth of this was to be proven sooner than she expected.

Most of the girls still slept. Mai Lee tentatively opened her eyes once more as she heard gentle footsteps approach the boardwalk. Tao was followed by Fu and Shun and two other grim looking men with pigtails and wispy beards. They carried rope and pieces of rag, which Mai Lee somehow knew was for them.

Tao undid the latches on the selected cages and as the rough bamboo gates swung open she shouted out the numbers of the selected girls. One by one they crawled backwards out of their cages and stood uncomfortably, too terrified to rub their aching numb limbs, which fizzed and sparked with pins and needles.

As each girl emerged and stood, the rags were thrust in their mouths and tied, effectively gagging them. Their hands were roughly pulled behind their backs and bound tightly. There was to be no escape.

"Number Twenty-Six," called Tao in a voice like shredded iron. Now it was Mai Lee's turn. Mai Lee shuffled out of her cramped space, which she was to never see again, and was hauled to her feet as she did not move quickly enough, and received a rap from Tao on the back of her legs as punishment.

Fu shouted angrily at the guard, "Leave no marks. It will reduce her price."

Tao responded, "A little redness that is all. It will quickly fade."

Mai Lee was bound and gagged like the others before being herded away with them like cattle.

The girls stumbled clumsily forward as they were pressed to march from the familiar Orphanage grounds along a hot and dusty track to a stone pebbled road where two bullock carts awaited. A pile of rough bags sat on the ground by the carts. Each girl was thrust into an empty rice sack and forced down inside the Hessian bag where bits of rice husk and small grains lodged in their hair and nostrils. A few weevils skittered inside and explored the skin of the girls and crawled around their ears and face. The top of each sack was loosely but securely tied and then thrown into the waiting cart as if they were just bags of meal and grain.

Fu instructed the men, his tone like grit scraping along a rocky surface, "You have been warned. Be careful, no marks we don't want them bruised. You will lose money for your work if you disobey. Gently, now."

Mai Lee's turn came. She was lifted off her feet and pushed into a sack. Her heart jumped in her chest as she struggled for air. She told herself to calm down and that the men didn't want her to die. She would be worth nothing. She just had to try and keep a cool head. She felt herself being placed onto the cart alongside the other girls. Some began to wriggle and murmur feeling suffocated in the sultry heat and Shun cried out his warning, "Be still! If you cry out or make one small sound we will beat you to death."

Mai Lee trembled inside the sack, she could hardly breathe. The filaments and fibres from the Hessian tickled her nose and skin. It smelled musty. She had an unpleasant taste in her mouth and her tongue felt furred. She was terrified that she would never again breathe fresh air and she gasped through her gag, which dryly clung to her mouth soaking the little saliva, she produced, which no sooner dribbled than it was absorbed by the rag. The taste was bitter and the threads from the material stuck to her tongue. The rice husks irritated her throat and lips but she was too scared to move or complain and suffered in silence.

The cart trundled along the bumpy track in the blistering sun and Mai Lee felt her hair stick to her face in slick sweaty strands. The child in the next sack, wriggled violently as if to effect an escape. Strange murmurings were emitted from the girl's throat and muffled cries of terror escalated before an elongated cry of pain was ripped from her belly. Then the sack was still, unnaturally still, and in spite of residing in the burning cocoon of heat Mai Lee knew she must restrain herself and no matter how uncomfortable she was she had to remain still or punishment would rain down upon her.

Time ticked on. Hours passed as the oxen plodded slowly through villages and open countryside. Weary and tired, Mai Lee tried to rest, afraid to panic or draw attention to herself and she did as Lily had taught her. She transported her mind to another place, a safe haven of her own making and imagination to the rainbow valley and lake that Lily had so beautifully described. The journey was then passed less fretfully and time drifted into an eternal vacuum of misty space and became indefinite and meaningless. She was jolted abruptly from this deep trance as the oxen stopped their persistent tattoo of their stout cloven feet on the road. Mai Lee sighed and once more tasted the filthy rag in her mouth. Her body was cramped and she ached all over. The restraining bonds cut into her wrists and she longed to free them and ease her pain.

Men unloaded the sacks and Mai Lee felt herself being lifted out and her sack was dumped on the ground. She strained her ears to listen for any clue of where she might be but she heard nothing, not even the song of a bird or the whistling hum of crickets. The trapped girls resisted movement and speech. They all waited patiently before they found themselves hauled up in the air and bundled onto the shoulders of men workers.

Like bags of grain they were carried up a path and Mai Lee could just see through a small hole in the sacking that there was a battered building ahead. They were carted up a weed-covered path and unceremoniously dumped on a stone floor inside the dwelling. Mai Lee grimaced as she thudded onto the floor but she knew better than to cry out. One or two girls found their voices and squealed. They received a sharp kick from the booted foot of someone.

Mai Lee struggled to see through the tiny tear in the Hessian. She could see that she was in a large empty space like a hall and the sacks were all heaped together. She waited patiently as someone began untying and cutting open the necks of the bags. Fu and Shun dispassionately freed the exhausted girls. Eventually it was Mai Lee's turn and she slid out gratefully onto the floor and squinted in the oily linseed light from a rustic lamp.

One bag had no movement. Fu sliced through the sackcloth and a young thirteen-year-old girl tumbled out. He face was blue and her tongue, also blue, protruded awkwardly from her mouth where she had struggled to cry out and had gasped for air. There was blood on her neck, which had snapped and lolled to one side. Her eyes were wide open and staring as in her final death throe. She was undoubtedly dead.

Some of the girls began to cry when they saw the horror of their dead companion and the expression fixed on the corpse's face. Fu swore loudly and struck his fist into his hand in exasperation. He grabbed one of the empty sacks and indicated the dead girl, "Quickly now. Pack her body up and remove her. Now. Take her away!" he ordered gruffly.

The rest of the girls ignored their own discomfort and huddled together in a corner, too frightened to move or speak.

Fu growled, his voice as brittle as ice, "That has cost us!"

"Not to worry. We will make it up on the next batch," assured Shun.

The two men strode out of the hall, but the girls continued to hold onto each other in an attempt to draw some comfort from their dreadful state. One girl Number Thirteen started to sob. The girl next to her, Number Nineteen surreptitiously removed a small knife from her tunic. She hissed at Number Thirteen, "Shut up! If they come back and beat us because of your racket, I'll cut your tongue out." She waved the blade menacingly in front of the girl's face before replacing it in its hiding place.

Mai Lee tried to quiet the sobbing child, "Hush, Thirteen. I think she'll do it. I really do. Please, calm yourself."

The girl attempted to stifle her sobs and buried her head in her lap as three women entered carrying steaming bowls of rice and placed them in the centre of the floor. They left silently. To begin with the girls looked at the offerings with suspicion as if it was some trick to kill them. But Mai Lee stepped forward and picked up a bowl. She ladled some into it and smelled it and nodded. "If we are to be poisoned then better to die on a full belly," and she began to eat it. The girls watched her and when nothing untoward happened to her they all dived into the food and devoured it greedily. They were ravenous; it had been a long time since any of them had eaten or drunk anything, and nothing as good as this had passed their lips in a long time. Some yelped in pain unused to piping hot food and burnt their mouths. They grinned in pleasure at what was to them a sumptuous feast.

"This tastes so good," exclaimed Number Nineteen.

"This is better than I have ever tasted," agreed Mai Lee.

The other girls nodded in agreement and rapidly ate their fill. There were ravenously hungry and this was manna from heaven and out of their experience. They had never tasted rice like it. As they scoffed the most ample meal they'd ever had, one of the women returned. She clapped her hands and the girls all turned to look expectantly.

She smiled at them, "I am Heng. Remember my name. You will get to know me as I will know you. But now that you have eaten, I want you to follow me and I will take you to your dormitory. Once there you will sleep comfortably for as long as you like. Come."

There was a sudden rush of whispering amongst the girls as they stood up. They exchanged glances not understanding what was about to befall them and were suspicious as they marched out after Heng.

Mai Lee whispered to Number Nineteen, "Why are they being so kind? I don't understand…"

"Huh! They want to fatten us up like pigs before we're

slaughtered and our meat sold at market. You mark my words."

Heng overheard the frightening words of Number Nineteen and contradicted her, "No, no. We need you to be fit and healthy. We can only do that with good food and rest."

"But why?" questioned Number Nineteen.

"Because you are going on a long journey across the sea. You will need to be fit to survive."

"And what will happen to us then?" asked Mai Lee.

"You will be sold to brothels." Heng laughed cruelly, "Then you will be raped and beaten." She guffawed again, "And there you will be made to do the work of slaves."

"No change there, then," muttered Number Nineteen.

Heng stopped and opened a door, where there were proper beds, which were clean and soft, "Make the most of it, while you can."

The girls ceased their frivolous chatter and became silent. The prospect of what was to happen filled them all with trepidation and fear. They were feeling confused about their situation but Number Nineteen tried to rally them, "Look, we don't know what is going to happen but for the moment let us enjoy the food, the kindness and the proper beds. It could be over all too soon."

"She's right," agreed Mai Lee and flopped down on a soft cot, and luxuriated in its simple comfort. She sighed and snuggled up. "A bed! A proper bed!"

The others followed suit and threw themselves on their bed of choice and unusually for the girls, they laughed, a rare sound amongst them but one, which filled Mai Lee's heart with hope.

Chapter Six

Preparations

Gradually the girls were beginning to relax. They were less nervous than they had been previously in their young lives. Instead of gruelling work in the debilitating humidity, dissipating their energy in the abominable heat and uncomfortable sleeping conditions, they each had food, decent beds and were allowed to socialise. They had rarely been allowed to speak to each other at the orphanage let alone chatter and laugh. It was now that their limited vocabulary was beginning to expand.

Mai Lee drank in the words like a drug. She yearned for language and knowledge. She loved the sounds different syllables made and the music and tone of language and expression. It gave her a feeling of power, of poetry, and Mai Lee realised that language development was indeed the key to improving herself and her life. She determined to learn all she could.

Mai Lee was to enjoy two more weeks in this paradise, for paradise it truly was in her eyes. But the heavenliness was about to end that morning. The door to the dormitory crashed open shortly after dawn and Heng entered with another woman who carried shaving equipment and a bowl of foul smelling sulphur paste diluted in kerosene oil.

Heng set everything out on a table together with a pair of scissors and set of brushes and combs. She nodded to her companion and indicated Number Nineteen. The woman dragged the girl up and forcibly sat her in a wooden chair. She lifted the girl's long locks and hacked at them with the scissors leaving a fine shock of hair spiked like a crew cut. Heng proceeded to soap the girl's head and began to shave the remaining hair from off her scalp. Once done, the tender skin was dried and the disgusting foul smelling paste was plastered all over her bald and now very sensitive head. The choking fumes caught the girl in the back of her throat and she began to cough.

The rest of the girls wrinkled their noses in distaste and watched in horror as the girl was stripped naked and the evil ointment was smothered under her armpits and in her groin.

Heng laughed in demented glee as she explained to the dumbstruck girls, "To kill all the lice and free you from parasites."

The other woman, Chyou pointed a crooked finger at Mai Lee and announced, "You next."

Mai Lee replaced Number Nineteen in the chair and was made to suffer the same humiliating cleansing ritual as she had witnessed. The lightness of the last few days disappeared into gloom and as each girl went through the same barbaric treatment, clouds of despair descended on them, and they huddled miserably together as Chyou collected all the fallen hair and carefully placed it in a bag. They did this sacrilegious deed silently, as if they were ashamed of the act and then left the room without so much as a backward glance.

Number Nineteen rubbed at her stubbly head and cursed angrily before muttering, "Nothing's wasted. Nothing... All of our hair, they will sell to a wig factory."

"But why?" questioned Mai Lee, "Why have they done this? What are they preparing us for?"

"I don't know. This time, I truly don't know."

Mai Lee frowned and her eyes smarted with tears in humiliation, "They will not make me a lesser person. They will not steal away my soul. I am not their chattel. I am not their property. I am ME."

"Brave words, Twenty-Six. I hope you will live long enough to see your next birthday."

"I have a name," said Mai Lee proudly. "It is Mai Lee. Even the beasts on the road have names, why should we be any less? Come Nineteen, choose a name to give you dignity. Be you and express yourself."

"You have high ideals for one of such humble beginnings. But then, I like that. Why not? Yes, I will choose a name. A name to remind me of freedom and the few days we have had here. I am… I am… Ming Hua, tomorrow's flower because I have yet to grow into the person I want to be."

Mai Lee blinked back her tears and smiled. Her face shone with something akin to pride and the two girls embraced. The rare touch of a fellow human being filled them both with warmth and for a moment they clung to each other, giving each other strength. Together they walked back to the dormitory for their last comfortable night of sleep not knowing what would befall them the following day.

Morning came all too soon for Mai Lee. The golden dawning of the sun slipped in through the shutters of the dormitory and splashed its honeyed hues on the wooden floor and bathed the girls' faces in warm light rousing them from slumber.

The main door opened and Heng clapped her hands, "Up now, come on get up and dress yourselves. The girls obediently threw off the cotton sheet covering and slipped into their tunics. "Wash rooms now," Heng ordered. They filed into the ante room where jugs and basins were laid out and splashed their faces in the tepid water and dried their faces and hands on the rough towelling cloths before hurriedly returning and lining up in their sleeping quarters.

On each girl's bed was a board with new numbers painted in red and fixed with twine. "Go to your bed and take the newly numbered board. Hang it around your neck. Now."

The girl's meekly did as they were asked. Mai Lee's face registered her disgust at the number placard. She was now Number Sixteen and Ming Hua was to be Number Twelve.

"This is all so confusing," murmured Mai Lee. "We should have names, proper names," she grumbled.

Heng snapped her head around, "You dare to criticise?" she shouted.

"No," said Mai Lee bravely. "Just saying it would be simpler if we had proper names."

Heng snorted cruelly, "In time, when your new owners decide on a label. For now, keep your mouth shut and your eyes down. To engage eyes is insolence. You have been fed too well it has made you bold. Remember, you are like the bug that has crawled out from the grain. If you wish to live be silent. If you continue to talk, I will cut your tongue out."

The reprimand served to quell any dissension amongst the girls and they remained silent. Mai Lee bit her lip and stood defiantly but she did not respond. The girls were then marched from the dormitory and out into the growing heat of the sun and escorted along a roughly beaten track to the bullock carts.

There they were loaded onto the back of the wagon and forced to stand together like a herd of animals. One girl slipped and missed her footing. She cried out and was rewarded with a sharp crack on her back from a stout cudgel. The girls crowded together and waited as four new women guards took over from Heng and Chyou who returned to the building. Heng and Chyou had been harsh but these women looked as vicious and cruel as the ones from the orphanage.

One of the women called Genji climbed into the cart and slapped each girl across the face, and yelled, "I am Genji. Now you will obey me and sit. We start as we mean to go on. You will listen and do as you are told."

The subdued girls sat. Genji jumped down from the first wagon and climbed into the front. She pulled on the oxen's halters and reins, and instructed them to move. The beasts began to plod away from the small hamlet and out onto the open road. As the cart trundled and rolled along the thoroughfare the girls remained still and silent. Mai Lee took Ming Hua's hand and squeezed it. The two girls took comfort in the contact and smiled gently at each other gradually nodding off to sleep on the rolling cart in the glowing heat of the day.

The oxen hooves ate up the miles and the smell of salt air mixed with the odour of putrefying rubbish, which assailed their noses and they awoke and gazed down at a small seaside village. The beasts plodded down the hill to the harbour side where the girls were herded off the carts and forced to the quay.

Sampans littered the water and the girls were transferred to the crafts and rowed out to a much larger vessel moored in the water. Ming Hua swallowed hard and courageously tried to speak but her mouth was dry and no sound would come she just croaked. Mai Lee finally questioned, "Where are we going? Where are you taking us?"

The coolie, a gnarled old man with few teeth, grinned. He was amused by the comment and chortled, "You are to board a tongkang. Then you journey."

Mai Lee looked out to sea and wrinkled her nose in disgust as she saw and smelt the foul water heavily polluted with sewage and the floating dead bodies of cats and dogs bloated with gaseous vapours and smelling putrid. No seabirds swam in the muddy brown water that was filled with flotsam and jetsam and other filth, the stench of which made the girls feel nauseous.

The sailing vessel arrived at the side of the junk. A wizened, toothless old man threw a rope ladder down the side. The coolie grunted, "That man, Chan. He will help you up. Climb aboard now."

None of the girls moved. They were filled with fear, fear of being on the boat, fear of falling in amongst the rotting, floating garbage, fear of what was to come and what was expected of them.

The coolie shouted again, "Move! You go, now!"

Genji pushed her way through the girls and the sampan swayed crazily. She prodded Mai Lee and urged her to her feet. Genji smacked Mai Lee's backside hard with the cane until she grasped the rope ladder, which swung wildly against the boat and she began to climb.

Genji goaded the rest of the girls to queue up and climb the unstable ladder. Mai Lee focused on one rung at a time. She gripped the thick fraying twine and inched up the side of the boat. She felt the ladder pull below her as another girl began the ascent and it was with great relief that Mai Lee reached the top and Chan tugged her onto the deck.

Mai Lee's relief turned to horror as she saw large brown rats, which scampered fearlessly across the wooden boards. One dashed between her legs and Mai Lee froze in terror. She didn't like the creatures and even in the orphanage had never been so close to them. There they would run in the latrine ditches but they were timid creatures. These animals were bigger and bolder. Chan took a swipe at one that ventured too close and the creature sat up defiantly and revealed its yellow gnawing teeth. Mai Lee shuddered as the rodent fixed its eyes on her. She was convinced it possessed the spirit of one of her earlier tormentors, like Lien, such was the creature's unusual behaviour.

The rat scuttled away as Mai Lee was joined on deck by another girl. They were made to line up once the last child had climbed aboard. Genji patrolled before them and counted her cargo of human misery. Genji divided the girls into two groups, which were taken to different parts of the ship.

Mai Lee and nine others were forced down the stairs to a lower deck. They were crammed into a small space. In the corner was a large wooden tub with water to be used as a communal toilet. Genji indicated the container with her cudgel, "When the tub is full, two of you will take it up to the top deck and dispose of the contents into the sea. You will pair up and take turns with this chore. Do you understand?"

The girls nodded dumbly as one.

"Good. Now sit quietly. We want no fuss. Those disobedient to my instructions will feel the weight of this." She slapped the cudgel into her hand and the girls flinched at the sound. Genji returned to the top deck and away from the stuffy air that the girls were condemned to endure.

Terrified and not knowing what was to happen to them they huddled together when a fearsome rat moved toward them and Number Thirteen cried out. The rat took no notice and ventured closer. This time Number Thirteen screamed.

Ming Hua hissed at the girl, and warned her, "Hush! You want to bring us all trouble?"

"We're all going to die," wailed Number Thirteen.

Mai Lee looked up sharply, and whispered, "How do you know?"

"Yes," concurred Ming Hua urgently. "Who told you? Tell us."

The teenager fell silent and closed her eyes to the rats and the other girls. Another girl nudged Number Thirteen and removed a needle with thread that was attached to her sleeve.

She held it up and threatened, "Then shut up! Or I'll stitch your lips together."

Weeks passed. The days merged into one with chores of emptying the latrine tub, and washing the deck. The stubble on the girls' heads had grown out and their hairstyles resembled a crew cut of sorts, which stood up on their scalps like black shocks of coconut matting.

The varied members of the crew, who kept themselves to themselves, were not allowed to fraternise with the youngsters although some openly watched and ogled the girls, licking their lips lasciviously as they allowed their eyes to explore the budding innocence of their juvenile bodies.

Some of the girls were on deck being watched by Genji and Jun, another female guard, as the crew worked together to hoist up the main sail to catch the increasing breeze that blew across the water. Number Thirteen and Number Six struggled together with the water tub of excrement and urine and attempted to toss the contents over the side. The smell from this permeated the salt air and filled the noses of those on deck. Number Thirteen attempted to hold her breath through the action but, unused to doing so, ended up inhaling a huge lungful of the fetid, faeces ridden air. She was violently and uncontrollably sick after this and regurgitated all of her gruel type breakfast just as another hag of a guard that the girls had christened Chikusho, which meant 'beast', had emerged from below. As Number Thirteen swung around, the projectile vomit splashed Chikusho's foot. The woman raised her stout wooden baton and began to beat the poor girl who whimpered pitifully and retreated back into the stale smelly hold and shivered in a corner such was her terror.

Mai Lee looked out at the cloudless sky as the boat bobbed along on the cleaner, fresher water of the ocean. She scoured around her for three hundred and sixty degrees but saw no land anywhere. The sun pounded down and she was grateful for the small breeze, which provided some respite.

Mai Lee suddenly squealed in pain as 'The Beast', Chikusho grabbed her arm and spun her around whilst digging her sharp fingernails into Mai Lee's skin. Chikusho guffawed gleefully at Mai Lee's distress and shrieked, "You need to pay attention, not gaze around. For that you will go below, now. All of you!" She laughed raucously again, "You may all hate me. But there is nothing you can do. To me, you are no more than pigs. Pigs to be sold at market. Now get below. Move!"

The girls scrambled below, falling over each other to avoid The Beast's poking, prodding fingers and her cruel stick. They huddled together trying to give each other some form of solace.

Number Thirteen examined her body and her bruised and battered skin, where she had been flailed and dug at by the sharp end of Chikusho's stick. Ming Hua took a small phial of oil that she had hidden in her tunic pocket and applied some to the sore skin. "You must be careful, little one. That monster has it in for you. She will make your life unbearable if you let her."

"What can I do?" murmured the girl in a tiny voice.

"Don't let her get to you?" urged Mai Lee. "Don't let her see that she hurts you. Bullies get satisfaction from inflicting pain. If there is no response then she will tire of trying to provoke you."

"That's hard because she does pain and hurt me."

"I know," soothed Mai Lee. "The trick is to transport your mind. Leave your physical body and let your spirit travel and soar where she cannot touch you."

"How? How do I do that?"

"I will teach you and show you. Just believe and anything is possible."

Number Six snorted derisively, "Believe that and you'll believe anything."

"Mai Lee is right. You have to believe," asserted Ming Hua.

It was then that Chikusho descended into the hold. She immediately pounced on Number Thirteen. She poked her hard with her stick. The girl didn't move. Chikusho stuck her face in front of the teenager and yelled, "I should have thrown you overboard to the sharks."

Still the girl did not move and Chikusho tried to goad her further, "What's this? You are being too quiet. If you are too silent I shall have to up my game. Maybe I will cut you into pieces as fish bait for the sharks, then again I wouldn't have the pleasure of watching them devour you alive."

Still, Number Nineteen sat silently and impassive.

"Do you know what sharks are?" hissed The Beast.

Number Six shook her head and looked alarmed, and Chishuko immediately turned on the girl, "Sharks are big fish, very big fish with razor sharp teeth. They have a taste for human flesh."

Chikusho laughed viciously, "The stench of your fear down here is unbelievable. Your odour and the smell of your blood will bring them cruising around the boat. You had better watch your step." The beast retreated back up the ladder to the upper deck still chortling as she climbed.

Mai Lee turned to Number Nineteen, "You see. I told you. She left you. You didn't react and she found another to plague and persecute."

"You are right, Mai Lee. But I tell you something. I will tell you all, something. I swear before you that I will kill her. I will feed *her* body to the sharks and she will not torment anyone ever again."

Mai Lee turned away sadly, as she remembered her friend, Lily, "Be careful of that. A deed like that could ruin you. It could steal your soul."

"I don't care. It would be worth it." Number Nineteen furrowed her brow and lost herself in wild imaginings of satisfying her vengeful thoughts and a small smile played upon her lips as she planned what she would do and how she would do it. "In fact," she whispered, "Those thoughts of vengeance will keep me alive."

Chikusho screeched below, "Time to empty the slops before the night!"

Mai Lee and Number Nineteen exchanged a glance as it was their turn. They grimaced as they struggled with the container. They moved it to the end of the ladder.

"We can't balance it as we did before," said Mai Lee. "Last time it spilled all over my hair."

"I remember. I was soaked from the waist down. How then do we do it?"

Chikushko yelled again, "Hurry up! What is wrong with you?"

"I know!" said Mai Lee. "We thread this rope through the handles." She picked up a sturdy piece of chandler's twine. "You haul it up. It will be easier to keep steady. I will hold it straight from underneath."

"If it doesn't work, you'll get soaked again," warned Number Nineteen.

"I'm prepared to try."

The other girls watched curiously to see how they fared. All of them had suffered the consequences of the contents dousing them. Mai Lee took the rope and pulled it through securely. She twisted it around and nodded at Number Nineteen, "Okay. Now lift."

The girl tugged and the tub was indeed steadier. She forced a grin at Mai Lee, "So far, so good."

She mounted the first rung of the ladder and Mai Lee came behind her to steady it. "Number Six, can you hold the ladder steady? I will do the same for you."

Number Six ran forward and secured the shaking ladder. The fact it was now rigid helped enormously and they slowly began to mount their way up to the top deck, while Chikushko ranted and railed above them with name-calling and threats. "You are the scum of the earth. Jump to it. Or I will make you jump. Move!"

They reached the opening and miraculously they had both remained dry. Now came the difficult part in getting the tub up and onto the deck. "We can do this," said Mai Lee. "You clamber up above and I will hold it. Then on the count of three you lift and I will push it aloft."

Number Nineteen ensured Mai Lee safely had hold of it before she let go. She scrambled above and took the weight. They counted together; the container was lifted and deposited on deck without spillage. Mai Lee climbed out and they took it to the side and waited for the ship to dip before they threw it overboard but the sea was quite flat with very little movement. They leaned over, depositing the waste into the ocean.

Chikushko looked disappointed that the girls weren't covered in urine and excrement. She scowled blackly and was about to speak when her attention was caught by the Captain. He was gazing out across the water and at the sky. He shaded his eyes and furrowed his brow. Mai Lee and Number Nineteen overheard their conversation as they took the tub back.

"I don't like the look of this," muttered the Captain.

"Why?" asked Chikushko staring at the horizon.

"It does not look good. The colour of the sky, the haze; the stillness of the sea. It is not a good sign."

"Why? We are moving, albeit slowly, and the wind is sufficient."

"The wind is getting up. There are black clouds on the horizon. I feel the disturbance in the air. A storm is coming."

"Pooh! It's miles away," argued Chikushko. "It will blow itself out before it reaches us."

"I don't think so," countered the Captain. "I have seen this before. I just hope I'm wrong."

Chikushko turned on the girls, as they listened, "And what do you think you're doing? Get below, both of you before I push you down."

They didn't wait to hear anymore and both hurried back down the ladder.

Number Nineteen patted Mai Lee on the back, "It worked. It actually worked."

"Yes," said Number Six. "We must all do it that way in future."

That night a fierce wind sprang up and tossed the boat like matchwood on turbulent waves that rose and fell from high, towering walls of water to low troughs and the boat dipped and dived. The clear night sky filled with rolling deadly storm clouds, which bruised the heavens hiding the myriad of stars, which normally lit the way and the path for the vessel. Torrential rain began to sheet down lashing at the sails and mast and lightning flashed illuminating the torrid scene of stormy danger. Thunder cracked, roared and rumbled like an angry monster engaging in war with demonic elementals as the crew scurried around hauling down the main sail and tying themselves to the deck for safety.

The boat tipped and slid over the crests and precipices of the violent white water, which swirled and boiled throwing gallons of furious salt water over the decks, which rushed and flooded into the holds.

Chan shouted, “Typhoon!” His voice was almost lost in the roar of the wind.

A massive wall of water crashed over the side of the ship. There was a splintering crack as some of the decking sheared into bits. Some of the huge rats were washed overboard into the killer sea. More water thundered onto the deck and poured mercilessly into the hold where the girls were kept. The screams from below dissolved and could no longer be heard in the rushing violence of the wind and the now deadly ocean.

The seawater deluged the hold and thundered in where Mai Lee and nine others clung to anything they could in order to maintain a grip. The voracious rats swam amongst them terrified for their own rodent lives. They bit and nipped spitefully as they clung onto the girls’ clothes and they refused to be dislodged. Survival was key to all life both human and animal. The rats were no exception.

The girls screamed again in terror as the water swirled angrily around them. It was now waist high. The powerful sea forced stacked packing cases to tumble. Two girls were knocked unconscious, crushed under the weight and they sank beneath the deadly, devilish, dancing water, which filled their lungs, drowning them and consigning them to a bitter watery grave.

The thunder continued to crack and threaten while the wind howled like a demented demon denied the right to destroy.

Ming Hua clasped Mai Lee and shouted above the cacophony of the boiling storm, “Chan says the howls we hear are the ghosts of the dead who have been shipwrecked in other storms.”

Mai Lee’s face registered her fear, “Knowing what I know and have experienced I believe him. I do… and I’m afraid.”

"Hang on," shouted Ming Hua, "Here comes another wave. Hold tight."

Mai Lee held onto the packing case and put her arm under a leather strap and wedged it. The surging swell of water pushed and then dragged her. She was afraid that her arm would break such was the power of the water. As the wave retreated she unhooked her arm. She didn't want to injure herself and add to her troubles. The water pulled her free and she searched for something else to hang onto as she was tossed in the violent water.

Another deluge of water crashed over the deck and into the hold and the girls that were still conscious screamed in terror. The gigantic swell of water continued to batter the craft and the sea swirled around the frightened and exhausted young girls. Their ordeal seemed unending and the relentless water constantly attacked them. It was as if the seawater had a life of its own, and was possessed by the spirits of the dead, as it tried to prise their grips free from the sides and those youngsters that succumbed struggled to stay afloat, gasping and gagging for air but only succeeded in swallowing mouthfuls of salt water, which made them cough and splutter.

Mai Lee grabbed hold and clung to a barrel, her eyes closed against the turbulent storm. She was losing her strength and energy fast and yearned to allow herself to float free and sleep. But, somewhere amidst the raging sound of the wrecking typhoon Mai Lee heard another sound, a gentle soft sigh and the music of tiny silver bells. A voice called to her in her mind, a voice of love and understanding, "Mai Lee." The feminine tones whispered like a song and Mai Lee forced her tired eyes to open against the salt spray and she saw a swirling mist flying before her. She gazed harder and in the foggy vapour a face began to form, a familiar face that Mai Lee would never forget, a face now shining with a radiant, angelic light. The scent of Jasmine filled the air.

"Lily!" murmured Mai Lee in cracked, painful tones through her salt burned dry lips.

Lily called to her again. "Hold onto the rail. Leave the barrel. Do it now. Trust me…"

Mai Lee immediately released her grip from the barrel, which had kept her afloat and she struggled to the wooden rail highlighted by Lily where a rope was tied and trailed in the water.

Lily continued in a soothing singsong, melodic voice that only Mai Lee appeared to hear, "Tie yourself to the rope. You'll be safe. Hurry."

Mai Lee secured her wrists to the rail with the rope and looked up but Lily was gone.

"Lily?" cried Mai Lee plaintively.

The ship suddenly dipped in the water and the barrel Mai Lee had been clinging to smashed against a crate. It shattered as the crate tumbled onto it. Mai Lee watched in amazement knowing that if she hadn't moved when she did that she would be dead or at the very least, very seriously injured.

The ravaging monster that was at the heart of the storm continued chomping through the night with its wailing winds and banshee howls. The punishing, persistent rain continued to pelt and attack the boat, which bobbed at the mercy of the angry sea. The night dragged on and the typhoon finally whirled on across the vast expanse of water toward other territories before it abated leaving the junk sitting quietly on calm water with the growing light of dawn.

The new day couldn't be more different than the ravaging, merciless havoc of the typhoon. The sun smiled down, the sky was cloudless and blue, the water gentle and tranquil. The crew on deck untied themselves from their positions of safety.

Genji un-strapped herself from Jun and sat back in the sun to allow the warmth to dry her clothes and hair. Chikusho descended the ladder to the lower deck followed by the Captain, a tall imperious looking man. They surveyed the wreckage and damage to their cargo and crates. No one gave the injured girls a second glance. The guards merely counted the number of girls that they could see.

"We're missing two," grumbled Chikusho.

Two guards searched the hold still swishing knee deep in water. They moved a bundle of sacks and discovered the two girls underneath, their mouths open and their eyes filmed over and staring. They were cold and dead.

Chikusho spat into the murky water and pulled a rattan raffia mat from the top of a packing case. She nudged the Captain who took one end and they stretched it out over two cases raised out of the dirty water. Together they lifted the painfully thin girls' broken bodies whose limbs twisted awkwardly and then rolled them up inside the matting.

Chikusho stuck her fingers in her mouth and whistled shrilly as the other prisoners watched cautiously. The two guards waded toward her and she indicated the dead girls, "Get this rubbish up. Toss it over the side. The sharks will have a feast today."

The two guards struggled aloft with the small bodies and disappeared from view. From below the girls heard the splash of the corpses hitting the now still waters.

"I suppose they were dead?" whispered Mai Lee to Ming Hua.

"They looked it, but we'll never know for sure. Still, it's too late now."

"Seems stupid wrapping them up," murmured Mai Lee.

"Hush up!" screeched Chikusho. "Here take these." The beast began to sort out some buckets and pans from the floating debris and thrust them at the youngsters. She ordered, "Bale out this water, now!"

The confused girls tried to remove the water with the buckets. It was an impossible task. No sooner had they filled the receptacles than they lost much of the contents as they climbed the ladder to empty them.

Mai Lee had a thought, "If we work together we can do this."

"How?" asked Ming Hua.

"We form a line from the hold, up the ladder to the top deck and as each bucket is filled pass it along the line."

"Will that work?"

"If we all pull together, yes."

"I'm willing to try," shouted one girl.

"Better than getting a beating," added another.

"We can time ourselves and switch places from balers to handlers," said Mai Lee.

"How?" asked Ming Hua.

"We can all count, can't we?"

The girls nodded their heads and assented.

"Then every ten buckets we move up a place and the one on deck returns to the bottom to bale and so on."

"Won't that cause a jam on the ladder?" questioned Ming Hua.

"No we are small enough to pass each other. We can do it. Let's try. I don't want to be sleeping in water for the rest of the trip, do you?"

The girls agreed eagerly and organised themselves into a working line and the bale out began. The Captain watched with interest as the first bucket passed through the hands and was tipped over the side, then the empty bucket thrown below.

"Whose idea was this?" asked the Captain.

"Hers," shouted one girl indicating Mai Lee.

"Hmm," muttered the Captain, "Bright girl."

They worked constantly for hours until little water remained but their efforts had left them exhausted.

"I just want to sleep," exclaimed Ming Hua.

"I think we all deserve a rest," said Mai Lee. "The sun is hot and the water calm. We are not moving, there is no wind to fill the sails."

"I don't like it," muttered Number Six. "The continual bob, bob in the water makes me feel sick."

"Me, too," said another. "It's all right when we are moving full sail and can feel the wind in our face."

"Yes, even in the typhoon when we were tossed about we were filled with such fear it overrode any bad feelings."

"Then the best thing is for you to go below and lie flat in the centre of the boat," said Mai Lee.

"Why? How do you know? Won't that simply make us feel worse?"

"Think about it," said Mai Lee and she raised her arm from the elbow with a flat palm and rigidly waved her arm from side to side, "The least movement is at the bottom, Most movement is up top. The higher you are the more the boat rocks."

"I see, yes she's right," said Ming Hua. "But why lie flat?"

"Because then you won't move as much. It makes sense."

The girls took Mai Lee's word and they lay down below deck on top of a packing case and closed their eyes.

Although, one said, "I still feel a bit queasy, but it's much better than before."

"Yes, me too. It definitely works," said the other.

The two girls went quiet and tried to sleep."

"I hope when they wake that we will be moving again and they will feel better," said Mai Lee.

"We will soon know," agreed Ming Hua. "And now I am going to take the chance to rest, too."

As the boat continued to bob up and down on the gentle sea, Chikusho began to turn green and feel ill. She clung to the rail at the side of the craft and hung her head over the water and groaned before retching and disgorging her stomach's contents into the water where fish and sea birds landed to devour the mess of vomit.

The boat rocked and bobbed giving 'The Beast' no respite and she continued to bemoan her fate, groaning and spewing until there was no more to bring up. She retched painfully over the side and Mai Lee observed, "At least if she is ill, she is not hounding us. We must be thankful for small mercies."

Chikosho constantly groaned and complained, "Water… I need water." Her moans and feeble cries for water filtered below.

"Let her die," muttered one of the girls, Number Thirteen, who had suffered much of The Beast's brutality and bullying.

"Ssh! She may hear you," whispered Mai Lee.

"I don't care," said the girl. "She is an evil old hag." Number Thirteen paused and her eyes glittered dangerously, "I tell you now, soon she will not bother me or anyone else ever again."

Mai Lee said nothing. She could feel the girl's indignant but very righteous anger and knew she meant what she said.

Time passed and no breath of wind blew. The junk drifted on the ocean bobbing up and down as it floated like a nomad on the gentle swell of the sea seemingly going nowhere.

Moonlight and star shine replaced the heat of the sun as day turned to night. Chikosho's groans continued on, eventually blending with the sounds of the creaking wood of the craft and the snores of sailors and the girls in slumber.

The threads of silver light streamed in ribbons into the lower deck. Mai Lee stirred in her sleep as she felt the movement of the girl lying next to her. She opened her eyes and watched. Number Thirteen moved silently through the hold. She gently removed a coil of rope from around a crate and draped it around her neck. She quietly crossed to the rope ladder and tentatively she began to climb.

Mai Lee watched.

The groans that had drifted on the wind abruptly ceased. Mai Lee closed her eyes tightly. She heard a rustle and opened her eyes to see a rat that had come to nip her. Mai Lee dislodged the creature who looked for more willing fodder in the form of another sleeping girl. Mai Lee was now awake and alert. She kept her body still but her mind was active and she waited and watched. There was a small sound of a splash in the gentle lapping water, then nothing.

In the shadowy moonlight, Mai Lee heard another faint noise and focused her eyes in that direction. She saw the ladder swing and observed Number Thirteen, who descended into the hold and disappeared into the dark to another corner of the confined space. Somehow Mai Lee knew what had happened and said a swift prayer, who to, she didn't know, but surely, she believed, not all of the Gods had forsaken her, had they?

She lay awake a while longer before finally succumbing to very welcome sleep and dreamed of Lily and rainbow valleys and eternal peace. These dreams, she knew, were sent to keep her sane and in her heightened awareness she was sure that the happy visions were implanted in her mind by the one who she knew to be her guardian angel, Lily.

The following morning as the rays of sun broke into the hold Mai Lee awoke, stretched and rubbed her eyes. She saw Genji clambering down the ladder. Mai Lee sat up and blinked herself awake. Genji looked around the hold and noticed Mai Lee was awake she pointed a stick at her, "Hey, you! Have you seen the one you all call The Beast, Chikusho?"

Mai Lee was not going to admit anything and shook her head vigorously and murmured, "No, sorry," but her eyes were wide with fright. She didn't want to be questioned further.

Genji began to poke around in the hold in all the corners and under the matting and sackcloth piles. She grunted in annoyance. "The woman must be here somewhere. She can't have just disappeared." As the heaps of material were disturbed, rats scattered and scurried throughout the hold. Their sharp claws scratched on the wooden planking as they squeaked and skittered. The rest of the girls awoke with the noise and confusion and stared around them. Genji shuddered and swore. "I'll be back." She retreated up the ladder and Mai Lee heard her call for the Captain.

A few minutes later and the Captain, himself, descended the ladder. He screwed up his face and wrinkled his nose in disgust at the appalling, foul odour that filled the confined space. He cleared his throat and struggled to breathe shallowly not wanting to inhale too much of the putrid atmosphere. He coughed and stuttered, "Girls, line up!" He clapped his hands, "Quickly now." The girls moved rapidly and joined Mai Lee against the rail. They huddled together and faced the Captain. "Has anyone seen her? The one you call Chikusho, The Beast?"

The girls shook their heads as one and murmured, "No."

Number Thirteen feigned innocence and asked, "Is she missing, then?"

"Not been seen since sundown," he responded and then sighed heavily. "Hmmm! I don't like this. I don't like it at all." He looked at Genji who had followed him down, "Search again thoroughly." He pulled a silk square from his pocket and put it over his mouth before retracing his steps to the ladder. "This is most odd. It has never happened before." He began to climb back to the upper deck.

Number Thirteen turned to Mai Lee, "She must have died, fallen overboard and been eaten by sharks."

Number Six agreed, "She was ill. We all heard her. She could have easily tumbled over the side."

Genji looked suspiciously at the two girls before moving back to the ladder to go aloft.

Number Thirteen announced, “If she’s dead. I am glad. We should all be glad. She was worse to us than the most vicious of guards at Wing Fong.”

Mai Lee waited until Genji had disappeared from sight and whispered, “Is she dead? Is she?”

Number Thirteen smirked and nodded, “Oh yes, she’s dead.”

Mai Lee pretended to look sad, “Poor sharks!”

The other girls looked at Mai Lee in puzzlement and Mai Lee continued trying hard not to smile, “If they ate her… then they will all die of food poisoning.”

Number Thirteen giggled and the rest of the girls laughed together.

Mai Lee pushed the hair from her eyes and Ming Hua noticed, “Your hair, it’s grown a lot.”

“We have been at sea a long time. We are starting to look like females again not like babies,” said Mai Lee.

“Or bald old men,” said Ming Hua. “I wonder how long we have been on this boat?”

“Months and months, I think. That’s why your hair has grown longer than most,” added Number Thirteen.

Genji shouted down into the hold. “Up on deck, now. All of you. The Captain wishes to speak to you.”

The girls obediently scrambled up the ladder onto the top deck where two of the girls were employed in scrubbing the wooden planking.

“You, girls, stop and line up with the rest of them. You,” he ordered two of his crew, “Take over from them.” The hardy sailors got onto their hands and knees and continued with the cleaning as the Captain walked up and down the line of girls. He studied each one in turn before clearing his throat and then he spoke. “We cannot risk losing anymore of you. You will no longer work on board and we will fill your bellies three times a day until we reach our destination. I do not want any of you to fall sick. We cannot afford it.”

The girls could hardly believe their ears and exchanged surprised glances with each other. Mai Lee gazed out across to the horizon. She turned to Ming Hua, “I can see smoke. I think we must be near land.”

Genji stepped forward and shouted, “Quiet! Depending on the speed of the wind in a few days we’ll be landing. Listen carefully; anyone who tries to escape will be killed. And don’t think we won’t do it. We will, money or no money.”

The girls said nothing but lowered their eyes. No one wanted to be singled out for any reason. Mai Lee sighed and shaded her eyes. She fixed them on the horizon where she had seen smoke rise believing it to be a distant and new land and wondered what her future life would have in store for her. In a few days time she would discover her answers and know her fate.

Chapter Seven

Singapore 1939

The junk was anchored in glorious crystal clear water that sparkled like jewels in the dazzling sunshine. The girls were assembled on the top deck. They drank in the warmth and gazed in awe at the stretch of beautiful white sand, which graced the coastline. It was fringed by graceful palms laden with coconuts such as they had never before seen. The air smelled fresh and clean. The girls each took in a deep lungful of air and sighed.

Mai Lee looked over the side and saw a myriad of highly coloured fish that swam and darted over gently wafting fronds of seaweed and startling, intricate coral reefs and barnacled rocks. Her eyes widened in wonder; it was so beautiful. She could hardly believe they were finally moored and waiting to be taken ashore.

Her friend Ming Hua whispered breathlessly, "It's paradise."

"So beautiful," agreed Mai Lee. "I'd love to touch the water to dip my hands into it and get clean."

"Look! Look over there," urged Number Thirteen.

Mai Lee turned her eyes to where the girl pointed and saw two sampans heading toward their vessel. The Captain and Genji called the girls to order and made them line up in order of their height and Mai Lee was separated from Ming Hua who was so much taller than her.

Mai Lee brushed her tumbling hair from her face that now softly fell half way down her swan like neck and she watched the sampans moor alongside the junk. The girls clambered off the seafaring craft one by one and crowded into the small boats and headed for shore. Mai Lee stepped down and into the boat. She loved the feel of the air on her face. She couldn't wait to set her feet onto dry land and let the soft sand wriggle up between her toes.

Mai Lee looked curiously at the young man, with intense dark eyes and curling lashes, who rowed her sampan. He was older than her at about age sixteen and such as she had never seen. Her only experiences of the opposite sex were the rough sailors and filthy wizened old men, on her journey to this haven. Never before had she seen someone so clean looking and smart. With him was an older woman, who had long willowy limbs and raven hair coiled up onto her head and held with an ornamental tortoiseshell comb. Mai Lee was fascinated.

The muscular, athletically built young man rowed the boat steadily toward the delicate shoreline and Mai Lee leaned over the side and let her hand trail in the smooth, cool, crystal water.

The woman noticed Mai Lee's action and smiled, "Once we are back you can go into the sea. I will bring soap to soothe your itchy skin and sores. It will help you to heal. Number Six ventured to speak, "Please…Who are you? Tell us… Where is this place?"

The woman smiled kindly, "You are in Singapore. I am Su Li and this is my son, Yuan."

Yuan grinned. He had an engaging lopsided smile that made Mai Lee want to smile back.

"Time enough for introductions later. You must be longing to get to dry land and enjoy a bath in our beautiful waters."

The girls hardly dared to speak. They were unused to such kindness.

As the sampan approached the shore Yuan jumped out and dragged the boat to the sand and secured it to a bamboo peg. He helped his mother out and one by one the girls clambered out of the craft. As Mai Lee neared the edge of the boat Yuan extended his hand and helped her onto the shore. He beamed at her and Mai Lee touched by his kindness looked down shyly as she followed the other girls onto the silky sand.

Su Li called out, "Go on, dip yourselves in the sea. I will be back with some soap for you." She made her way up the beach to a dwelling that bordered the sand and disappeared inside. The girls walked fully clothed into the warm sea and delightedly immersed themselves under the water, soaking their hair and swilling the tepid water over their skin trying to rub off the dead cells of skin, which flaked.

Some of the girls giggled and laughed. It was such a pleasant sound. Mai Lee sat at the edge of the shore and allowed the gentle running waves to lap over her and she felt like a princess, if she had known what a princess was; she only knew she felt good, better than she ever had in her life.

The girls watched as big tin baths were dragged onto the sand by a troop of women and filled with clean fresh water. True to her word Su Li returned carrying a cloth filled with slabs of a red carbolic type of soap. She delivered a piece to each bath, which the girls gratefully received. Mai Lee stepped in the bath, slipped under the water and soaped her tired body rinsing the suds off in the refreshing bath. She washed her hair as did the other girls and felt instantly better. So long had they been at sea that it took a while for them to adjust and lose their sea legs.

Mai Lee felt someone's eyes upon her. She glanced around and then at Yuan and saw that he was the one gazing at her, but in a good way. He gave her a mock salute type of wave before shinning up a coconut palm and slicing off some green coconuts with a large machete. He tossed them down and they thudded onto the sand. The girls looked on curiously.

Yuan jumped down and hacked at the outer casing of the fruit, splitting it and revealing the hairy brown shell of the coconut. He took a stiletto type skewer and punctured the eyeholes of the strange fruit and drank.

Mai Lee left her bath and shook her hair shaking off the droplets of water onto the soft sugary sand, as might a dog that had swum in the sea. Yuan strode toward her and offered her some of the fruit to drink. She looked on puzzled not knowing what was expected of her. He demonstrated by drinking again and passed her the coconut. This time she fastened her lips to the pierced hole and drank the sweet liquid. She tasted it and beamed in delight. Never before had she tasted anything so delicious.

Yuan permitted her to drink her fill. She handed it back to him and he laid it down on a flat rock and cracked it open. The fruit came apart easily into two halves and revealed the snow-white coconut flesh. He cut out a piece and gave it to her.

Yuan bit into another hunk and ate it. Mai Lee copied him and tasted it. She clapped her hands in delight. The other girls clamoured around all wanting a taste of this delicacy. Their excited chatter feverishly rose and they giggled and laughed. There was quite a bubble of harmonious sound. It was to this happy gathering that Su Li arrived and tried to attract their attention. It was hard to subdue their girlish enthusiasm, but they finally became quiet and Su Li could make herself heard, but even she was touched by their infectious, child-like delight at something they deemed so simple and ordinary.

Su Li summoned the girls and called them to follow her. She led the way to a large thatched hut. Number Thirteen ran after Mai Lee, "I knew there'd be a catch. I expect we'll be put to work now. You'll see."

Su Li overheard the child and contradicted her, "No. We need to get you all fit and well. I will bring you fresh clothes. Leave those rags you wear now outside the hut. Yuan will burn them."

The girls looked confused at the statement, unused to any such kindness.

"We have always been left to wallow in our own filth, what is this? Why are you doing this?" asked Number Six.

"Yes, what's expected of us?" asked Number Thirteen.

"Nothing yet. Enjoy this peace while you can. I have prepared straw mat beds for you all and you will eat well. No more rats nipping at your toes, no more rice water but tonight you will feast on chicken and rice. Now I will fetch you clean clothes."

As Su Li left them the girls broke into a fevered, excited whispering. They began to undress and Mai Lee gathered the soiled tunics and dumped them outside the hut door. The girls huddled together embarrassed at their nudity but they did not have long to wait as Su Li returned with an armful of flowered clean cotton sarongs, which the girls fell on with pleasure and anticipation.

Each girl put on fresh cotton garb and they paraded in front of each other oohing and ahing at their gay new apparel. They giggled with delight at the freedom they were enjoying and couldn't believe their eyes when Su Li and Yuan entered the hut with comfortable bedding just as had been promised. They laid it out for the girls on the floor and Mai Lee had to pinch herself to see if it was all really happening.

The girls chose their beds and sat on them as Yuan carried in a cauldron of nutritious chicken and fluffy rice with vegetables. Su Li handed out a bowl to each girl and proceeded to fill them from the steaming hot cauldron.

The girls fell upon the food hungrily. They were ravenous. Yuan winked at Mai Lee who blushed and lowered her eyes. She found her voice and called after Yuan, "Where did you say we were, again? I've forgotten."

"Why, you are in Singapore."

"Is it all as wonderful as this?" asked Mai Lee and was rewarded with another beaming smile.

The girls could not believe their luck. Never before had they been treated with such courtesy or gentleness. Number Six muttered to Mai Lee, "It's too good to be true. This can't last."

Number Thirteen grudging replied, "Let's enjoy it while we can. Who knows what tomorrow will bring?"

Ming Hua added, "I don't want to think about it. I want today to last forever."

The girls settled down on their comfortable futons and chattered happily for a while. "Never before have I been so content."

Mai Lee nodded her agreement. She felt for the first time in her short life that she had been blessed. She sighed with pleasure and drifted off on a puffball cloud of pleasant dreams. It was a treat to sleep.

The sun glowed above to make the heavens smile on another glorious day in paradise or so it seemed. Both groups of girls from the ship were playing in the soft, gentle surf and the air rang with their laughter as if they had not got a care in the world.

Yuan had salvaged a coconut pod husk and the girls used it like a ball as it floated in the water. They shrieked and laughed in glee at the game.

The husk splashed on the water in front of Mai Lee and both she and Yuan stretched for it at the same time. Their fingers touched and Mai Lee withdrew her hand quickly. Their eyes met briefly. Mai Lee took a sharp breath, looked away and down when shouts were heard on the shoreline. The Captain and one of his crew approached the lapping waves, which kissed the beach and rushed to remove the footprints pressed onto the wet sand.

Yuan jumped in front of Mai Lee effectively masking her and he spoke quickly, "Under the water quickly. Don't let him see you."

Mai Lee took a gulp of air and submerged herself under the water. She didn't know why she listened to the young man; she just did. The other girls turned to look at the Captain; some shaded their eyes in the glare of the sun.

The Captain did a quick calculation and pointed at ten of the girls, "Hey, you! If I indicate you, step out of the water and line up on the sand, now. And you, and you," he ordered.

The girls instantly obeyed and were marched away and off the beach leaving the other six girls to stay and play in the surf. They stood silently a surprised expression on their faces. The fun had momentarily gone out of the moment.

Yuan pulled Mai Lee up and she gasped for air. Her hair, longer now, streamed down over her face like seaweed fronds.

"Come," called Yuan. "Let's finish the game." The girls rallied around and began to play together again.

Mai Lee whispered shyly, "Why did you do that?"

"I didn't want them to take you to a Death House. If he can't see you then he won't pick you. Simple." Yuan picked up the husk and tossed it to one of the other girls and Mai Lee studied her remaining fellow orphans. Ming Hua was gone as was Number Six. She bit her lip. The only girl Mai Lee knew to speak to was Number Thirteen, whom she was wary of as she felt the girl could be quite harsh. But, her fears were forgotten as the game progressed and they all frolicked in the sea until Su Li called that their lunch was ready. The girls happily waded out of the surf and made their way back to the hut where another good meal was waiting for them.

The seven girls sat cross-legged on straw mats and tucked into some succulent fresh fish and rice. Number Thirteen turned to Mai Lee, "Where have the others gone? What has happened to them?"

"Yuan said they were being taken to a Death House. What *is* that?" replied Mai Lee.

"Death house?" exclaimed Number Thirteen. "Oh no!"

"Why? Tell me. What is it?" pressed Mai Lee.

"It's where Chinese people go to die. It's very unlucky to have a death in a house so the dying are removed and taken away. Those girls will be forced to work as slaves to the sick and dying."

"Poor Ming Hua and Number Six," said Mai Lee sadly. She sighed softly and eventually muttered, "I wonder what is in store for us?"

"Who knows, Mai Lee? Who knows? But anything is better than a Death House," replied Number Thirteen.

The joy momentarily vanished as the other girls contemplated their former companions' fate, especially now, as they realised what the girls were being taken to do.

"It's no good. Don't let us be upset. We must make the most of this kindness while it lasts. Who knows when things will change? Come on and smile. Let us enjoy this while we can," said Mai Lee, sagely.

The girls beamed, "She's right. Come on, smile and live. Live better than we ever have before," said Number Thirteen. One by one the girls relaxed and threw back their heads and laughed. They were going to remember today.

CHAPTER EIGHT

Groomed for sale

The warmth of the golden sunshine washed over the few remaining girls who were sitting and relaxing on the beach. They looked fresher and healthier than they ever had done. Su Li hurried down to the beach with Yuan and captured the girls' attention.

"Girls! I want you to listen carefully. In a moment you are to go to the main hut. There you will find three women waiting for you. They are going to make you look more beautiful than ever, breathtakingly beautiful, so that you captivate hearts and minds. You will enjoy the pampering you will see. Let yourself go in their hands. It will be a wonderful memorable experience."

The girls whispered amongst themselves and some giggled.

"Go quickly now. Don't run. I will see you all later," urged Su Li.

The girls scrambled up from the soft, white, icing sugar-like sand, brushed themselves down and began walking to the main hut. Number Thirteen spoke quietly to Mai Lee, "Well, you wanted to know what would happen to us. Now we know."

"What? What do we know?"

"We are to be sold to brothels."

"How can you be so sure?" asked Mai Lee.

"Why else would they want to make us pretty? she snorted.

Mai Lee bit her lip anxiously, "I think I would have preferred slavery in a Death House to that."

"No, you wouldn't. At least, there will be a chance of escape, for us, when our looks have gone. In a Death House you work until you die from exhaustion."

The girls continued up the beach to the hut and Su Li

hurried after them but Yuan pulled his mother aside. He pointed at Mai Lee and asked, "What will happen to her?"

"Her fate will be the same as the others."

"Is there nothing you can do?"

"My son, I have seen you looking at her and talking to her. This is most unlike you. She is not for you. She is part of a business deal."

"Please, don't let her go to a brothel. There must be something you can do?"

"She is a good looking girl, handsome, and she will fetch an excellent price. Stop mooning over her. Pull yourself together. Come, Yuan, this is not like you."

"I know. Normally it doesn't worry me. But this one, this one I sense is different. I really do like her."

"I know you do," Su Li paused and furrowed her brow. "I can't guarantee it but... There just may be something I can do. I just hope that I won't regret it..."

"What? Anything, anything to stop her being enslaved or sold for sex, anything."

"Well...."

"What? Tell me."

"I do know of a very wealthy woman who is looking to adopt a daughter."

"Then choose Mai Lee, please, Mother."

"It is difficult. These girls are our livelihood and Mai Lee, as you call her is very pretty, very saleable. Many will bid for her."

"Please..." Yuan stared earnestly into his mother's eyes, as he implored her.

Su Li saw the anguish on her son's face, "Oh, Yuan, no matter how many times I say it, I can't help myself. This is not like you. Not like you at all. Has the girl bewitched you?"

"No, she is just... I can't explain it. There is something about her that sets her apart. I feel it."

Su Li sighed resignedly, "We'll see. Say no more now and I am not promising anything."

"Thank you, Mother. Just think about it. That is all I ask."

Su Li grunted and walked on. They followed the girls to the main hut.

The girls waited outside chattering happily. Su Li prompted them, "Go on in. Enter. Go on. You will enjoy this, I promise."

The girls tumbled in through the door laughing, where there were three attractive women in their forties waiting to greet them. The tallest of them had long, flowing dark hair that shone and glistened like wet coal, which was adorned with a fresh lotus blossom. She opened her arms. "Welcome. I am Abi." She indicated the other two women and introduced them, "And this is Ka and here we have Pa-Ru. We are going to make you beautiful. All of you."

Mai Lee's eyes opened wide as she saw the trays of cosmetics, hair ornaments and combs. There were all manner of colours and creams, brushes and artificial flowers, which looked all too real. A rail of silk and beautifully patterned cotton sarongs hung on a rail.

Abi continued, "You two." She pointed at Number Thirteen and Mai Lee. "You go to Ka." She picked another three, you to Pa-Ru."

"Yes, I will dress you," said Pa-Ru. "Dress you to flatter you to make your body look its best."

"And I will do your make-up," said Ka. "I will enhance all that nature has blessed you with.

Number Thirteen looked at Mai Lee and whispered, "I told you so. We are being prepared to be sex slaves in a brothel."

Abi added, "I will do your hair. You will rotate between us until you have visited us all and we have made beauties of you."

"Rotate? What does rotate mean?" asked Mai Lee puzzled.

"Oh I forgot, your vocabulary er… words and language is somewhat limited."

"Not limited just not yet learned," smiled Mai Lee.

"Well, rotate means you move around in your groups between us, when you have had your hair done you move onto make up and then clothes. Go around in a circle. Understand?" She gestured with her hand.

"Yes, yes. We come to you, then to Ka for make up and then Pa-Ru for clothes," they repeated.

"Good. I'm glad we settled that. Now, let's begin."

The girls sat at their allotted stations and Mai Lee had her growing locks sprayed with some fragrant light oil based spray that added gloss and sheen. Abi began to brush and brush; carefully pulling out the tangles and smoothing out the wild strands that misbehaved.

Abi smiled, "You have beautiful hair, lustrous and strong. Surprising on your diet and lifestyle, you must have good genes."

"Pardon?"

"Your parents. They were obviously from good stock, healthy and fit."

"I don't know. I never knew them."

"Take my word for it. They were attractive and strong."

Abi styled Mai Lee's hair, drawing it down one side of her face and over one shoulder. She finished the effect with a tortoiseshell comb adorned with a silk flower to compliment her colouring that contrasted beautifully with her shining hair.

Abi moved onto Number Thirteen and began the process again while Mai Lee went onto Ka who beamed welcomingly at her and sat her on a stool. She placed a cloth like a bib around her neck and began to paint, enhance and nurture Mai Lee's skin. She began with a facial scrub of salt and moisturising cream to slough off the dead cells and give a healthy glow, followed by a soft crème tinted with colour that was smoothed over her face and neck and blended into her décolletage.

Mai Lee gasped as she saw her reflection.

"Wait! I have not finished yet. Next your cheeks." Ka took a pad of soft cloth and dipped it in a rose coloured powder, which she brushed onto Mai Lee's cheekbones. The sides of her face were contoured with a darker colour defining the shape of her face. Next came a black sooty powder that Ka used to line her eyes and fan out at the corners. Her brow bone was highlighted with soft beige ochre. Her eyebrows were shaped and darkened and a soft pink hue dusted under the arch of her brow. In the fold of her almond eyelids Ka placed just the suggestion of colour. In

Mai Lee's case this was a gentle sage green. Her eyelashes were darkened with a type of brown eye paint and brushed with a tiny comb and brush to be clump free. Lastly, her lips were lined and stained with a berry red cream that left a luscious sheen on her lips.

"Now you may look, " said Ka. She held up a mirror for Mai Lee to look at her reflection. Mai Lee's lips parted in surprise and disbelief at the picture she presented. "I hardly recognise myself, " she whispered. "Is that really me?"

"It is. You look lovely and now go to Pa-Ru who will dress you."

Mai Lee crossed to Pa-Ru who held various vibrant silks and cottons against her before finally settling on a violet and gold silk cheongsam that fitted snugly with a high split to the thigh. The keyhole at her neck emphasised her cleavage and the silk clung in places to reveal her tiny waist and full hips.

The girls were soon all dressed, their hair styled and their faces made up. They were ushered to a full-length mirror in the chamber and could not believe their eyes.

"I never dreamed I could look like this," whispered Mai Lee, breathlessly.

The door to the main hut opened and Yuan entered. His eyes widened and his jaw dropped as he gasped admiringly when he saw Mai Lee, "Why, you're beautiful? Truly beautiful."

Mai Lee lowered her eyes shyly and blushed with pleasure at the compliment.

Yuan took Mai Lee by her hands and spoke quickly, "They'll be taking you to the big house soon." He reached into his tunic pocket and removed something on a piece of hemp. "Here, take this and wear it. It will protect you."

He placed it over Mai Lee's head.

"What is it?"

"It's a talisman. A lucky charm. Those are magic symbols inscribed on it. It really will help to keep you safe."

"You make it sound as if I will need protection."

"Whatever happens it will help. Trust me."

"Why should I? Tell me, why should I trust you?"

"Because, I believe in you, and in something better for

you. Let's hope that this will bring you luck.... And..." he paused, "I need you to know that I have never done anything like this before."

Yuan squeezed Mai Lee's hand and withdrew it quickly as his mother entered. Su Li clapped her hands and gathered the girls together, "Come. It is time now for you to meet your destiny."

Su Li opened the door wide and exited. The girls filed out followed by Yuan. They walked away from the main hut at the top of the beach and along a pebbled path toward the big house on the edge of the track, which led to the road. Su Li assembled the girls. She put Mai Lee close to the head of the line. Then, she walked up and down the girls nodding approvingly, placing them in some kind of order. Mai Lee was manoeuvred to the front.

Mai Lee touched her pendant; it seemed to give her strength. It was a source of comfort to her. She soon realised that she would be the first to see what fate had in store and she sighed nervously.

Su Li went to the front of the line after a final check and instructed the girls to follow. They entered the big house and Yuan walked at the back of them. They crocodiled through the foyer and toward a large ornate wooden door. Mai Lee's eyes widened as she saw the intricate carving of strange birds, such as she had never seen, and animals at which she could only wonder. The carving was so neat and so precise she could see each feather in detail. She ran her hand across the honed wood and shuddered with delight the feeling was so lovely and smooth under her fingertips.

Su Li addressed them again but looked directly at Mai Lee, "When I clap, you will enter. After you have been inspected and released, wait back here with Yuan and then the next girl comes in. Is that understood? As each girl leaves the next girl goes in, in the order I have placed you. Do you understand? Answer me."

The girls bowed their heads in acknowledgement and understanding. Su Li grunted in satisfaction and then entered the room. Mai Lee waited nervously. Her heart fluttered inside her and she bit her lip anxiously.

Time ticked by.

Mai Lee, afraid of missing her cue, placed her ear to the door and heard the whispered mutterings coming from inside but the words were indistinct. Then she heard three strong claps. Mai Lee took a deep breath and pushed open the door.

She stepped into the sparsely furnished room. Opposite the door by a large window was a table. Su Li sat at one end and two other women that Mai Lee had not seen before sat next to her.

One with a square face and highly defined cheekbones studied Mai Lee, critically. She stood up and walked around Mai Lee, "Oh, she's pretty. That's for sure. A winner." The woman, Kaci, examined Mai Lee's arm and pinched her flesh. She pushed back Mai Lee's head and lifted her hair before forcing open her mouth and looking inside at her teeth. Kaci grunted appreciatively and returned to her seat.

The other plumper woman, Barra, peered at Mai Lee, snapped her fingers and pointed at her, "Take off your clothes."

Mai Lee looked horrified and stared at Su Li, who explained, "They need to see your body. Undress."

Mai Lee froze in shock. She tried to speak but the words would not come out. She looked at Su Li again pleadingly.

"Come on, child. There is no one else here," said Su Li.

Mai Lee snapped from her apparent stupor and moved her hand to her dress and hesitated. Her hand shook like a fluttering moth trembling in the light. She was unable to do it. Her mouth dropped open in a silent gasp.

Barra tutted loudly and rose from her seat. "Do as you're told," she ordered. "Or I will do it for you."

Mai Lee remained still as if tendrils had grown from her feet and entwined her to the floor. She was rooted to the spot and her eyes were glazed with fear.

Barra thumped her hand on the table and pushed back her chair. She crossed angrily to Mai Lee and began stripping off her clothes. Mai Lee tried to bat away the inquisitive, persistent hands, which pawed at her and uncovered her revealing her nakedness. Mai Lee tried again to stop her but she was no match for Barra's strength.

Su Li saw the pain, embarrassment and humiliation in Mai Lee's eyes. Most girls simply accepted their fate and did or said nothing to complain. She recognised something different in this girl, Mai Lee, and unable to help herself she shouted out, "Stop!"

Barra turned in surprise and Su Li justified her comment by saying, "Careful with the clothes. They're brand new. Nor do we want to bruise her and lessen her value."

Mai Lee looked fleetingly at Su Li and tried to cover her body with her hands and arms but to little effect as both Barra and Kaci walked around her and studied her. Mai Lee felt distraught and ashamed. She tried to remove her mind from what was happening and a vacant expression fixed on her face as she attempted to do as Lily had taught her and take her mind away to a different place. Words of the women's conversation drifted in and out of her head.

"Clear skin and very little pubic hair," said Kaci. "Good. Men don't like a lot of pubic hair," and she chuckled lewdly. "Not for what they want to do."

Su Li flinched at the words and bit her lip.

Barra concurred, "Her breasts are large and full."

"And firm," added Kaci, pinching them. "Just what men want."

Su Li was hesitant, she looked deeply into Mai Lee's eyes and it was as if an invisible thread connected them. She found herself understanding Mai Lee's plight and for the first time in her life she saw a person and not a piece of meat, not a body to be sold to the highest bidder. She cleared her throat and spoke gently as she picked up Mai Lee's fallen garments and handed them to her, "You can dress now." She turned to the other women and spoke more forcefully, "I was thinking. I know a wealthy childless woman who's looking for a slave that she might adopt as a daughter."

"For a good price?" questioned the eagle eyed Barra.

"Why, yes. Better than we would get in the brothels," answered Su Li. "I was thinking this one would be suitable. She's bright."

"How old is she?" asked Kaci.

"Thirteen or fourteen. She's menstruated."

"Hmm!" The women considered Su Li's words and Mai Lee began to redress, albeit slowly as she listened to the discussion. She fingered her talisman and noted carefully what was being said.

"Who knows, if she doesn't get on with the woman, we can take her back and sell her again?" said Su Li with cunning.

"If that happens, won't she want her money back?"

"Not all of it. She will be shop soiled, as a worker, but still a virgin," countered Su Li.

Mai Lee watched the faces of the women carefully as they considered Su Li's proposition.

"I say we sell her to this woman," said Kaci a note of authority in her voice.

"Agreed," said Barra with conviction.

Su Li sighed with relief and turned it into a smile, "Then that is settled."

Kaci put her face up to Mai Lee and called her to attention. "Listen, from now on you will be called by a name. You are a number no more. You are Dandan."

"Please…" said Mai Lee hesitantly.

The women looked amazed that the girl had the nerve to speak.

"What is it?" barked Kaci.

"I have a name," said Mai Lee boldly.

"And how is that?" asked Kaci.

"I have a name already used by my friends. I would like to continue to use it and be known as Mai Lee, please."

The women were stunned at Mai Lee's daring and eventually, Barra snorted, "Ha! I admire your pluck, child. Dandan or Mai Lee, it's all the same."

Kaci added, "All right. You can be called Mai Lee. Now, finish dressing, tidy yourself up and return to your hut."

Mai Lee completed buttoning her cheongsam and hurried out. Her heart was pounding and she felt faint, but a strange feeling of pride had entered her that she had, had the courage to speak out and had overcome the burning humiliation of her body inspection. She knew in her heart that Lily was to thank for this. She could feel her presence around her and the sweet scent of jasmine, which she knew to be Lily's favourite perfume.

Once outside the door, the girls clustered around her, whispering excitedly and asking questions, "What happened? What did they say?"

Mai Lee just shook her head. She was lost for words and unable to speak until Yuan stepped forward and took her hand. She turned to the other girls and said proudly. "I am Mai Lee, I am not a number. You, too, will have names."

The girls looked in surprise as they recognised a change in their companion. The next girl in the queue heard the three claps from inside and feeling somewhat braver now entered the room and the door slammed weightily behind her. The girls whispered together as they waited and Mai Lee walked away, her shoulders back and her head held high.

CHAPTER NINE

Uncertainty

Yuan began to walk Mai Lee back to the main hut, "Come. You must walk back with me and tell me what happened. What did they say? Did my mother help or anything?"

"They made me undress," said Mai Lee quietly.

Yuan knowing what happened behind the big door was embarrassed and tried to explain, "They have to… to see… to see if you are suitable… for…"

"I know."

"What did they say to you?"

"I am to be offered to a woman for her slave and maybe be adopted."

Yuan grinned and could not keep the joy from his voice, "I'm so glad. My mother listened to me. She listened!" he exclaimed and punched his fist in the air.

"You did this?"

"I didn't want you to be sold for men's pleasure. I wanted something better for you."

"But you don't know me."

"That's just it… I know enough. When I saw you… I don't know. How do I explain it? I felt as if I knew you. It's never happened before. I have seen many girls arrive on our shores and leave and never thought twice about them, I'm ashamed to say. But you… you are different and I wanted something kinder, something better for you and I thought that this would be a more pleasing way for you to go."

Mai Lee contemplated what Yuan had said and shook her head in confusion, "You better get back to the other girls or you will be in trouble."

She turned to go but Yuan pulled her back and made her face him. "I meant what I said. You are beautiful. I can't get you out of my mind. I hope… I hope…."

"You hope what?" asked Mai Lee, her eyes searching his.

"I hope that if this woman buys you that… that somehow… some way, you'll earn your freedom and that we'll see each other again, but see each other as equals…" He stopped and gently stroked Mai Lee's cheek. "I must go."

Mai Lee took her hand back. Her eyes filled with tears that threatened to tumble down her cheeks. She was so choked with emotion she couldn't speak and she retreated quickly into the hut.

Yuan turned away and walked back to the big house where the inspection and preparation for the viewing sale continued. Mai Lee returned to the door and watched him go. She gently caressed the pendant with her hands. She knew something had changed inside her. First with Lily, who had given her the power to hope and dream, and given her an identity, a name. And now with Yuan, who had somehow broken through her numb defensive barrier that had deflected all others and had made her keep her feelings to herself, which had stopped her from hurting. Her protective wall was down. Mai Lee found it difficult to understand these new feelings.

She felt the vulnerability of her situation. She didn't understand why Yuan and Su Li had helped her but she was grateful. A small voice inside her warned her to be careful and not to let down her guard. The unmistakeable scent of jasmine pervaded the room and although she couldn't see Lily she knew that Lily was trying to tell her something. She vocalised, "Speak to me, Lily. Tell me what to do and advise me. You know I will always listen."

The sound of light laughter that was caught on the breeze drifted to her ears. There was a voice like whispering grass that murmured inside her head, "Follow your heart, Mai Lee and be proud. Stand tall among the others and be brave."

There was a rush of wind and the scent was gone. Mai Lee heard the words and should have understood their intention, but instead, they filled her with a sadness and longing for her old friend, "Oh, Lily. Why did you have to die?"

Mai Lee sniffed hard and steeled herself to prevent the

tears from cascading down her cheeks but the moment was broken by the arrival of another girl who announced happily, "Now I have a name, too. I am to be Dandan."

Mai Lee embraced the surprised child, "Be proud. Take your name and use it. No more a number, no more a lesser being. You are a person." The two girls held onto each other drawing some comfort from the warmth of human contact in these very uncertain times.

That night the girls slept peacefully on the floor in their beds, tired after the day's excitement. Neither the thrum of the cicadas nor the whine of the female mosquitoes as they searched for more victims on which to feed disturbed them. Their sleep was tranquil and deep. None of them were sure of where they were going and although the uncertainty of their final destinations were somewhat alarming at least they had enjoyed some days' respite in a kind of paradise where they had been fed well and treated with due care and consideration, and the humiliation of suffering being naked before the Inspection team of women was diminishing.

The door crashed open and the girls awoke from their slumber as Su Li entered with an oil lamp. She set it on a table and clapped her hands, rousing the girls. "Girls! Quickly now, please get dressed. Hurry, all of you, except you," she pointed at Mai Lee. "You stay."

Mai Lee rubbed the sleep from her eyes and looked at the activity around her, "But, why…? Why not me?"

"Ask no questions. It's for your own good."

The girls murmured as they dressed themselves. They looked puzzled. Dandan looked at Mai Lee with worried eyes, "Will you be all right, Mai Lee?"

"Worry about yourselves, not this one," reprimanded Su Li. "The rest of you are to move on. Your transport awaits. Hurry now." Su Li took the lamp and waited by the door.

The girls bleary eyed, but becoming more alert, busied dressing themselves. One by one they murmured their subdued but emotional goodbyes to Mai Lee who sat there dazed. She watched as the girls and her companions for a lifetime were ushered from the hut. The door banged closed.

It sounded hollow in the deepening dark. The only light infiltrating the room was that of the ghostly silver moon and the fireflies that danced together outside the open window. Mai Lee was now truly alone something she had never been in her entire life. Whatever the circumstances, whatever had happened to her she had never been on her own. Mai Lee was frightened.

She drew her knees up to her chin and sat there, now wide-awake. There was a soft knock on the door and Yuan entered. He looked warily about him and tiptoed across to her. He sat by her on her cot and said gently, "Don't be afraid. I am not here to hurt you."

Mai Lee turned her huge haunted eyes on Yuan and asked in a tiny voice, "Where have all the others gone?"

"I won't lie. They have been sold."

"I know we were to go to those who paid the highest price but where have they gone? Will I ever see them again?"

"I hope not."

"Why?"

"Because you are not like them. I have told you that you are different. The others have been sold to brothels. That is where they are being taken now. For the use of soldiers."

"Soldiers?"

"A new brothel of comfort women is being set up and the girls will work there for the good of those men stationed away from home."

"They are to be used? Their bodies made as play things for the military?"

"If they are lucky they may meet kind men who will look after them if their needs are satisfied."

"That's horrible. I know this world and men can be cruel."

Yuan sighed. He had no answer for that as he knew Mai Lee's words to be true. For every good kind soldier there would be one who could be cruel. "Pray for them, Mai Lee and pray for yourself. Pray that they are not forsaken by God."

"I can pray. I can do that but what about me? What is really going to happen to me?" asked Mai Lee anxiously.

"You are to be introduced to Madame Aaryn Jong."

"Who is that?"

"It is important that you try and impress her. Your life will be so much better. Make her like you. You do not want to be resold as a comfort woman." Yuan rose and put his fingers to his lips. "Do not say I was here, promise me."

Mai Lee nodded, "I won't tell."

"Good," he turned to go and stopped, "Mai Lee, may I ask you something?"

Mai Lee nodded shyly, "Yes. Go on."

"May I kiss you goodbye?"

"But, I have never been kissed, by anyone."

Yuan kneeled down and tenderly brushed his lips against hers. He stroked her face gently, his eyes shone with pent up longing. "I will find you. We will see each other again. I promise."

Yuan stood up and left quickly. Mai Lee was sure she could see the glint of tears in his eyes. She gently touched her lips where Yuan had kissed her. The rippling feelings in her stomach were like none she had ever experienced. She felt a pleasurable shiver tingle down her spine. Her heart fluttered. A small explosion of melting sensation had travelled around her lower stomach. All these strange feelings were enjoyable and disturbed her. Her knees had trembled with some sort of surging fizz that had waved through her body. She was confused, as she had never felt like this.

Suddenly an inexplicable feeling of calm flooded through her and she settled down to sleep. There was a hint of jasmine in the air but Mai Lee didn't seem to notice it. Her eyes closed and she floated away on a magical rainbow ride of visions and dreams.

All too soon after she had drifted off in slumber she was awoken by a sudden rushing of wind. Her eyes blinked open and she saw the face of her friend, Lily, bathed in a golden light smiling at her. The aroma of jasmine was all around her. Mai Lee sat up, "Lily!"

"Yuan is a good person. He means what he says. This woman you go to and you **will** go to her will be better for you than the fate that awaits the others. But be careful. I am here to warn you."

"Of what? Of who?"

"Manchu. He is to be feared. Don't let yourself be alone with him."

Lily's face slowly began to disintegrate and vanished before her eyes. She cried out in anguish, "No! Lily. Don't go."

But Lily's angelic face had faded from view leaving Mai Lee to stare into the dark. She watched as the fireflies danced and she studied the stars shining from the black night sky and wondered what was going to be in store for her. Madame Aaryn Jong? Who was this woman? And more importantly, what was she like? And who was this Manchu? She shivered involuntarily with uneasiness as she settled back down to sleep but was comforted by the knowledge that her friend Lily had not forgotten her and was looking out for her as a mother would for her child and that was something Mai Lee had never known.

The next morning, Su Li came into the hut and brought Mai Lee some breakfast. "Here. A special treat. You will need your strength. For your last morning with us I have made you some crullers. It will make a change from your congee. We call it Yu za kuie."

"Deep fried devils?" exclaimed Mai Lee. "What am I eating?"

"Taste it, you will like it I'm sure."

Mai Lee picked up a strip of the deep fried dough and tasted it. She closed her eyes in delight as the light sweetened dough strips of batter melted in her mouth, "Mmm!" she exclaimed. "It is delicious." Mai Lee polished off the rest of them and licked her fingers.

Su Li smiled warmly, "I am glad you are to go to this lady. If you are lucky you should have a very good life just as Yuan wants for you. And I must agree with him. There is something different about you." Mai Lee smiled back and when she did she radiated a charm that Su Li had never noticed in any of her sale girls before. "What is it with you? What sets you apart from the others?"

"Maybe because I have hope," whispered Mai Lee shyly. "I have something to believe in. Something other than drudgery and danger; I believe in goodness."

"Heavens you'll have me in tears in a minute with your fancy ideas and beliefs. You are what you are. Make the best of it and you may be lucky. Now, come here and let me tidy your hair and dress you."

Su Li took a brush and restyled Mai Lee's tousled bedroom hair. She brushed it to one side and decorated it with a fresh scented flower that contrasted with her shining locks. She retouched her eyes with colour and stepped back approvingly. "Good. You look lovely. Now, what can we clothe you in? The dress we gave you is somewhat provocative but I don't possess anything modest in your size. We will have to make do."

Su Li picked up a variety of Cheongsams and examined them closely. Some were in vibrant colours but all had the same revealing thigh split. "I have no time to sew these up and even if I did they would be so tight you would be unable to walk. Let me see."

Su Li held up the various silk fabrics and picked one that was a serene buttercup yellow. She compared it with a coral flowered one and then decided. "This one, definitely this one. Put it on." She gave her the creamy lemon silk and Mai Lee, less shy now, slipped her body into the cool silk fabric.

Su Li looked over her critically, "This is a much more modest colour. You'll do. Come." Mai Lee scurried out after her benefactor and they walked up the track from the main hut at the beach to a waiting cart and oxen. Yuan watched from the door of the big house but Mai Lee didn't see him. He hung his head and retreated inside sadly.

Mai Lee mounted the cart and sat sedately inside careful not to snag the silk on the rough wood or mark her new clothes. Su Li clambered up to the front and waited while an old artisan in a straw hat made his way to the wagon. Sprightly for his eighty years he hopped up into the driving seat and took the reins.

"You know where we're going?" asked Su Li.

The old man whistled through the gap in his teeth stained brown with nicotine from a lifetime of smoking an old clay pipe and he nodded.

"You don't say much do you?" said Su Li.

The old man just shook his head in response and jerked the reins. The oxen began to plod out of the small waterside village.

"Well, Mai Lee, you're on our way," said Su Li. "On your way to a new life."

CHAPTER TEN

Aaryn Jong

Mai Lee waited patiently with Su Li. The ox and cart had stopped its relentless plod and the old man gave the oxen some hay to munch. They were standing outside a high walled garden with a stout wooden door. Fragrant bougainvillea draped the top of the wall its brightly coloured blooms a dazzling display against the grey masonry. Hibiscus trumpeted out alongside it and the perfume of orchids crept over the wall and titillated their senses.

The huge door opened and a gardener admitted them into a courtyard surrounded by a lush and verdant garden. Across the quadrangle was a house such as Mai Lee had never seen. She gazed in awe at the magnificent spreading building in three sections with its red tiled roof that was shaped and curved like a ship's sail when filled with wind.

The aromas of the exotic flowers tickled her nose and her eyes grew bright with wonder. "Lily would have loved to see this," she whispered.

"Hush, child!" reprimanded Su Li. But Mai Lee couldn't fully take in he magnificence of the place. Small sounds escaped her lips as she looked about her in awe. She saw an ornate house made of glass with a ribbed domed roof housing orchids of all colours and heights. The gardener retreated back to this place and Mai Lee could see him pulling out small shoots of weeds and feeding the plants with a thick liquid. She was mesmerised.

Another strange unidentifiable noise arrested her attention, as an internal door clunked and the ornate door to the courtyard on the outside of the house opened. Mai Lee focused her eyes as two people emerged from the building. A tall thin Chinese woman glided out. Mai Lee could see that her face was heavily made up and painted. It was difficult to assess her age but Mai Lee assumed she must have been in her early forties. At the side of her was a much more homely looking woman with a round cherubic face that bore little make-up. Mai Lee instantly warmed to this womanly figure who looked welcoming and kind. She took small shuffling steps to keep up with the elegant but harsh looking Chinese woman.

The two ladies approached Mai Lee and Su Li hissed at her under her breath, "Bow. Show your respect."

Mai Lee lowered her eyes and bobbed down in front of the painted lady. She held the pose, as Aaryn Jong walked around Mai Lee who dared to peer at her through her hair, which covered her eyes. She saw the woman frown as she noticed the revealing thigh split in Mai Lee's cheongsam, which displayed her lithe limbs. She circled Mai Lee again eyeing her up and down and Mai Lee attempted to close the split with her hands.

"You may rise," ordered Aaryn Jong. Mai Lee stood up but kept her eyes lowered.

The woman spoke again. She had thin reedy tones, which matched her appearance that was brittle and stern, "What do you think?" She addressed her female companion.

The motherly looking woman put her head on one side and whistled slightly through her teeth. "She is pretty enough." She turned to Su Li, "Is she a good worker?"

"That she is. She can clean and scrub."

"Is she bright? Respectful?"

"Very bright and a quick learner. You can see that she's deferential, well mannered."

Aaryn sniffed disdainfully and grunted. She whispered something in her companion's ear and began to walk away. Mai Lee was fascinated to see how the lady moved. No steps were discernible she appeared to glide smoothly and Mai Lee determined that she would learn how to walk like that, like a lady.

The homely woman addressed Su Li, "How much?"

"She'll fetch a good price..."

"I asked, how much?" the woman said insistently.

Su Li took the woman by the elbow and led her to one side and they began to haggle quietly. Mai Lee kept her eyes fixed firmly on the ground and she fingered her pendant nervously as the bartering went on.

They eventually settled on a price and the woman took two hundred and fifty Malay dollars from her purse and gave it to Su Li. Mai Lee dared to peek and could not believe the amount of money being exchanged.

Su Li commenced counting the notes and spoke to Mai Lee in hushed tones, "Go, Mai Lee. You belong to Madame Aaryn Jong now. They'll take you to your new home. You're lucky. She's adopted you as her daughter and slave."

"Will I not live here?"

"This is the town house. You are going to their country residence. Go now." Su Li could hardly look at Mai Lee and she didn't know if it was because she regretted her leaving or if she was ashamed of the sale. It was hard to tell.

Su Li scuttled out from the garden and back to the busy street where the ox and wagon waited. The woman took Mai Lee by the shoulders and looked directly into her eyes. "You may look at me. I am to be called Auntie Ko and I am the first person you should come and speak with if there is a problem. Now, follow me."

Mai Lee obediently followed Auntie Ko through the courtyard, into the big house, along a polished corridor to a strong front door and out into the street where another cart stood waiting.

"In the back, quickly now," ordered Auntie Ko in clipped tones. She took the reins and urged the animals on and the cart began to trundle through the streets. Before long they reached the country roads lined with bamboo stems and groves of mixed vegetation. They plodded along and Auntie Ko began to sing a wistful song as Mai Lee studied her surroundings.

The sticky heat was reminiscent of the climate she had left in China when she had worked in the rice fields. She wondered where they were headed. She finally plucked up the courage to speak, "Where are we going?"

"Ah! So you can talk. I was beginning to think we had a mute on our hands. We are going first to Chinatown and then onto the Orchid Gardens. Madame Jong has a big house there. But first I have to buy you new clothes and make sure that you are very clean."

"What's wrong with what I'm wearing?"

"Let's say it's a little provocative. In fact, it's more suited to a whorehouse. And we need to be sure you are clean. So I have to bath you in disinfectant before you meet your foster mother again."

Mai Lee looked concerned and bit her lip as she remembered the horrendous treatment at the orphanage where she was plastered with foul smelling sulphur paste.

"Don't look so worried. You'll have a better life than many."

Mai Lee said nothing and continued to gaze about her. They were entering the outskirts of a bustling city. It was a far cry from the fishing village where Mai Lee had stayed or even the small town where she had been sold to Aaryn Jong.

Mai Lee stared in wonder at all the many people busying themselves along the roadside; the numerous and varied nationalities, the rickshaws and market stalls, which graced the side of the road, the dust and noise of people trading and bartering their goods. The sights and sounds on the roadside, the hustle and bustle of market traders enthralled Mai Lee and she sniffed the air filled with a variety of aromas, from food stalls bubbling with freshly fried sweetmeats and assorted seafood to the fragrance of freshly cut flowers. Mai Lee was enraptured as she watched the activities around her.

"Fascinating, yes?" asked Auntie Ko.

"Yes, I have never seen anything like it."

"You'll get used to it," laughed Auntie Ko.

"Please, Auntie Ko," the name came with difficulty. Mai Lee was not used to such familiarity or niceties and Auntie Ko certainly seemed pleasant, very pleasant indeed. "What is expected of me?"

"Remember to speak when spoken to and do as you are bidden. Learn to flatter Madame. Pay attention to her. Compliment her and you will find great favour in her eyes. Your life will be unrecognisable, as you knew it. You have been blessed by the Gods, my friend. Grasp this opportunity with both hands."

Mai Lee fingered her pendant and wondered at its efficacy. It certainly had brought her amazing luck, which she hoped would continue.

The cart carried on its way on the journey and before long it entered the lively hubbub of Chinatown. Mai Lee sighed in astonishment at the rampant blaze of colours, which greeted them, and the huge ceramic red and green dragon that beckoned them in at the elaborate entrance.

Auntie Ko turned off down a side street and stopped outside a fashionable store. She signalled for Mai Lee to follow her and Mai Lee obediently traipsed after her.

Mai Lee stared in wonder that the many and varied items on display. Auntie Ko seemed to know exactly what she wanted and the shopkeeper smiled ingratiatingly at them as he packed up and wrapped the selected goods.

Auntie Ko pointed to an array of hair ornaments and made a selection. Mai Lee was quite overwhelmed by everything she could see. She was delighted like a small child and clapped her hands happily.

While Auntie Ko shopped and Mai Lee walked around the store, the shopkeeper's son came in and eyed Mai Lee lasciviously. Auntie Ko spotted him ogling her charge and her eyes narrowed, "Mai Lee return to the cart," she ordered.

Mai Lee sighed in disappointment but did as she was asked and made her way back to the wagon. The young man followed Mai Lee, who turned back to see Auntie Ko watching the youth suspiciously as she hurried to pay for the goods.

Mai Lee stepped to the cart and the shopkeeper's son, Peng, made a pretence of helping Mai Lee into the cart but allowed his hands to roam over her body. Mai Lee bit her tongue. She disliked him touching her so intimately but she did not know what to do or say. Mai Lee stroked her pendant, her fingertips running over the magical symbols on her talisman.

Suddenly, there was a whoosh of sound and a loud clatter as a pile of wicker baskets and containers toppled over and hit Peng forcefully in the back as he attempted to fondle Mai Lee's leg. Peng fell forward and sprawled in the gutter. Mai

Lee looked up in surprise and saw the face of Lily by the beaded curtained entrance to the store. She gasped, rubbed her eyes and looked again but Lily had gone. The image was so fleeting that Mai Lee wondered if she had imagined it. It was then that Auntie Ko emerged with the parcels and loaded them into the cart as Peng hurriedly rose and began to re-stack the fallen baskets and boxes.

Auntie Ko rubbed her back and grimaced in discomfort as she stretched to pack the goods safely. Peng sidled up, "Which brothel is she going to?"

"None," retorted Auntie Ko. "You keep your eyes and hands to yourself. This is the adopted daughter of Madame Aaryn Jong."

Peng grunted in annoyance and skulked back inside the shop as Auntie Ko climbed up to drive the wagon. "Be modest and lower your eyes in male company and once we have you dressed respectably it should prevent advances like those of the shopkeeper's son. You are a pretty girl and must be careful. Madame would not like it! We have one more stop to make before I take you to your new home."

Auntie Ko drove onto another store that sold both fabrics and a variety of clothes, sarongs, dresses and cheongsams that were less revealing and more in keeping with Mai Lee's new status as an adopted daughter.

Mai Lee was treated to a succession of outfits being held against her and she had to try on a number of items and model them for Auntie Ko, who either shook her head and frowned, or nodded appreciatively. An hour later Mai Lee had six modest dresses befitting her position. She felt charmed, like royalty and couldn't stop smiling as the clothes were parcelled up, Auntie Ko paid and they left the shop.

Auntie Ko straightened her spine and winced before clambering up to the cart. She reached behind her and rubbed her lower back. Mai Lee noticed the older woman's discomfort and went to speak but then thought better of it and sat quietly for the rest of the journey.

Mai Lee watched as they left the main thoroughfare and shops. The terrain changed and they approached a smart but quiet suburb. Palatial buildings, high walled gardens, parks and temples graced this fashionable and expensive part of this countryside hamlet.

They soon arrived at a traditional colonial style house, which was opposite a Buddhist temple. Mai Lee had never seen a temple before and like a child on a first outing she looked about her and noted the brightly coloured hanging garlands, the number of priests and people coming to worship. "Auntie Ko. What is that place?" she asked as she admired the construction.

"Why that is our Buddhist Temple where devotees go to worship and give offerings."

"Why?"

"Because they believe the Gods will bless them and be kind to them."

Mai Lee marvelled at the lavish gold decorative figures. She looked at the letters above the entrance, "What does that say?"

"My, my so many questions. You are clearly keen to learn. That is good. It just says that it is a Burmese Buddhist Temple and carries the traditions from that country, as each place and its religion can take many forms."

"I don't understand."

"Mai Lee I will tell you and answer what I can in time but first you must settle into your new home. I must make you clean for Madame."

Mai Lee nodded and they entered the country house. She gazed in jaw dropping wonder at the many spacious rooms and the glass doors leading to a veranda, which led to the large garden. She followed Auntie Ko to the east wing of the house and was introduced to her room. Like a small child she squealed in excitement at her bedroom and the ante room where her new clothes were hung up and her variety of combs and hair ornaments were laid out on a fancy dressing type table. Her footwear, too, was laid out in a neat and tidy fashion so that each pair of sandals could be clearly seen and matched with the cheongsams.

Auntie Ko ordered. "Take off your things and put this on." She passed Mai Lee a kimono type robe. "When you are ready come to the room at the end of this corridor where I will be waiting.

Mai Lee waited until Auntie Ko had left and slipped out of her dress. She ran her hands over the silks and fabrics of her new clothes. They felt soft and cool to the touch and she fingered them in delight. She donned the kimono and wondered what she would choose to wear. She had never enjoyed a choice before.

Mai Lee hurried excitedly to the room at the end of the corridor and Auntie Ko was there with her sleeves rolled up and a bath filled with warm sudsy water, which smelled of apple blossom. She sat Mai Lee down on a chair and examined her scalp using a fine toothcomb, which she raked purposefully through Mai Lee's hair. "Ow!"

"Hold still," ordered Auntie Ko. "How can I get you clean if you squirm and wriggle like this?"

"I don't have fleas or nits," protested Mai Lee with a pout.

"Hm! It seems to be clean. Certainly, I cannot find any lice, parasites or eggs."

Mai Lee explained how on the journey to Singapore all the girls had had their heads shaved and plastered with a sulphur paraffin type paste. Auntie Ko nodded and helped Mai Lee out of her kimono, "In you get and let's get you clean. It's not too hot, see." Auntie Ko put her hand and arm in the water.

Mai Lee stepped into the bath, luxuriating in the scented bubbles and ducked down under the water. She played like a small child in the tub and when the bubbles tickled her nose she sneezed loudly and Auntie Ko laughed.

Auntie Ko made sure Mai Lee was scrubbed clean and tingling fresh. She bathed her as a mother would her child. Mai Lee had never felt so good. Her hair was washed in heavenly scented perfumed liquid and rinsed carefully before Auntie Ko took a large towel and held it up for Mai Lee to step out of the water and then she wrapped it around her. She took another towel and wound it around Mai Lee's hair and rubbed it vigorously so that it was almost dry and it fell damp and loose onto her shoulders. Mai Lee giggled. "I am cleaner than when I had the salt sea scrub back at the village."

"And you must remain so. You must bathe regularly, now that you know what to do." Auntie Ko took a pot of aromatic oil. "When you are dry you can massage this into your skin it will leave you sweet smelling and fresh."

Mai Lee took a deep breath and closed her eyes. The aroma was all encompassing and she felt wonderful as the oil moisturised her skin. "I must be dreaming. Nothing can be as good as this. I never want to wake up."

Auntie Ko smiled. She enjoyed Mai Lee's child like enthusiasm for simple pleasures and warmed to her. "You are a sweet child. If you listen and learn you could do very well here. Very well indeed."

Mai Lee beamed. She knew she had been luckier than the others and in her heart she thanked the Gods and blessed Yuan. She thought of his smile and his last contact with her and wondered if, indeed, she would ever see him again.

CHAPTER ELEVEN

Three weeks later

Mai Lee was slowly getting used to her new life and she was feeling more relaxed now. Auntie Ko had been extremely kind to her and showed her how to keep clean, and how to dress herself and her hair, and to walk like a lady. She had explained something of the Buddhist religion and Hinduism, and their shared deities. They sounded desirable ethics; good and kind, and she liked the thought of reincarnation and the fact that her friend Lily could be born again and maybe into a better life. Mai Lee nodded in approval. If this was happiness, she was happy.

Mai Lee strolled through the spacious rooms and out through the glass doors to the veranda. She looked over the elegant gardens where a middle-aged gardener worked, trimming the shrubs and plants. Another worker carried potted orchids into a greenhouse and potting shed. The lawns were graced with ornamental fountains. Mai Lee breathed in the perfumed air and smiled happily.

Auntie Ko emerged to join her. She leaned forward and then straightened up and groaned before she rubbed her aching back.

"Auntie Ko? Excuse me for asking but do you have a problem with your back?" asked Mai Lee.

"Ah! It's my legacy. You see, when I was young I spent far too many days in the damp. I have trouble with my bones, now. Sometimes the pain, it's crippling." She sighed, "There's nothing that can be done. I just have to live with it."

"Maybe not," volunteered Mai Lee.

"What do you mean?"

"I am sure I can help. Please let me help you."

"Why? What can you do? I have tried everything, herbal remedies, Chinese medicine. Nothing works."

"At the orphanage we learned massage. How to use points

on the body to ease aches and pains. It works. Truly it does."

Mai Lee's tones were convincing and Auntie Ko considered what she had said. "You can really help?"

"I can. Yes."

Auntie Ko made a decision, "Then you had better come to my quarters."

Mai Lee followed Auntie Ko back into the house and along the polished corridor to her private rooms. Mai Lee looked around curiously as she had not been in this part of the house before. She studied the paintings on the wall. One was by an artist called Xu Beihong. Mai Lee studied closely the ink and wash painting of a horse in motion. She liked the line and flow of movement in the drawing. There were others of birds as well as a lion, and animals that she had never seen before. She was full of curiosity and questions, which bubbled out of her. "Excuse me, please. What is this? And this? Ooh and that?"

Auntie Ko raised her hands and laughed, "Enough! I do not know all the answers but I promise you, we will endeavour to find out together. I promise. Now come. These are my quarters." Auntie Ko opened a door and Mai Lee followed her into a spacious suite of rooms. "What would you have me do?"

"If you lie on your bed and bare your back then I can work on it. We can begin. Do you have fresh towels and some lotion or oil?"

Auntie Ko nodded and went into her bathroom and came out with some body cream. She removed her tunic top and wrapped herself in a towel and settled face down on the bed and Mai Lee got to work.

Mai Lee pressed and kneaded the old woman's tired back paying special attention to the areas, which needed firm massage to relieve knotted muscles and tension, and where crystals had gathered. Then she began to use the aromatic skin cream that Auntie Ko had provided and worked it into her back.

"Oh, that feels good. You have hands like little pads of velvet, but they are firm and strong," purred Auntie Ko.

Mai Lee laughed, "Thank you. You're so kind to me. I am

very lucky to be here and I wanted to show you my thanks. I can do this for you, whenever you wish."

"Ah, it is I who should be thanking you. This is wonderful."

"May I ask you something?"

"Go ahead."

"When will I see my foster mother?"

"Soon," answered Auntie Ko and then groaned in pleasure as Mai Lee found a particularly tough knot and worked on it.

"Please, tell me about her, my foster mother."

"Where do I start?"

Mai Lee giggled, "You could try the beginning."

Auntie Ko began to answer but her words were interspersed with grunts and groans of delight. "It's a sad story, really, very sad. She was from an excellent family and then she married the master. They were both very wealthy. Their union would bring two rich and powerful families together. Oooh, there! Ah… that's lovely… All was well between them until he found out that Madame could not bear him a child. That is a big disgrace for their kind, and then everything changed. Just like that… Ah yes, mmm," Auntie Ko sighed in ecstasy.

"Will I meet him?" asked Mai Lee.

"Who?"

"The master?"

"Manchu?"

Mai Lee stopped the massage abruptly as the name registered with her.

"Oh, don't stop," pleaded Auntie Ko. Mai Lee came to and began the treatment again and Auntie Ko continued to ooh and ah in pleasure. "The thing is, Madame withdrew from society and family such was her shame. The master, well, he moved out. He requires an heir. Clearly he intends to get one elsewhere, somehow. Then, Madame in her sorrow began to drink. She often drinks herself into a stupor to numb the pain and this has made her… how shall I say? Well…. She can become almost psychotic in her behaviour, unreasonable and violent. It is very sad."

"Psychotic? What is that?"

"Crazy, mad. Her behaviour can be strange sometimes, to say the least, and she can have outbursts, violent outbursts. You do not want to be around her then."

"Then I will do my best to keep her happy and sweet. How may I best serve her?"

"Be kind to her. Praise her. Tell her she is beautiful. Be convincing. Tell her all the things you like about her. If you do that, you'll go far and keep her happy."

"I will do my best," said Mai Lee and began a cupping technique on Auntie Ko's back. She cupped her hands and lightly struck Auntie Ko's sides and all over her exposed skin and finally, she finished with strong sweeping movements that ended with a light stroking. She stopped, "There. You should feel much better now, looser and less achy." Auntie Ko rolled over. "Take your time, relax. Don't get up immediately. Let the feeling of well being settle through you."

"That was truly wonderful. How right we were to pick you." Auntie Ko smiled and sat up. "I feel so much better now. You have done wonders to my old bones. Wait now until I dress and I will take you to meet Madame. Are you ready for this?"

"Oh, yes," sighed Mai Lee.

"Then I will take you to her." Auntie Ko sat up and Mai Lee helped her off the bed. Auntie Ko put on her tunic and adjusted her attire. "Come. Follow me."

Auntie Ko left her rooms and marched back along the polished corridor to the centre of the house then off to another wing. The walls of the corridors housed embroidered pictures and family portraits. Mai Lee took them all in and stored them in her memory such was their beauty.

Auntie Ko paused by one picture of a fresh faced young woman with glowing skin and shining eyes filled with hope. "There. That was Madame when she was young before the master deserted her. Now she paints her face like a mask to hide her deepest feelings but once she was a beautiful woman."

"And she could be again, I'm sure. She just needs some joy in her life. Joy and hope."

“My aren’t you the wise one?” laughed Auntie Ko.

They progressed to the end of the passageway and Auntie Ko stopped outside an ornate wooden door, carved with pictures of elephants, tigers and coconut palms. Mai Lee ran her hands over the texture of the wood. The touch of the soft wood felt silky smooth and the fragrant aroma of the hand carved door pervaded her nostrils and she sighed.

Auntie Ko knocked lightly on the door and opened it slowly revealing the room inside. She nodded encouragingly at Mai Lee and whispered, “Go. Go on. Take a deep breath and enter Madame’s chamber.”

Mai Lee looked back at her, excited but apprehensive. “I’m afraid, nervous.”

“Courage, Mai Lee. You will be fine,” she said reassuringly. “Just remember to give her lots of praise. Tell her she’s beautiful; that you admire her and she should like you. Go. Quickly now, go.”

Auntie Ko pushed her gently through the open door and closed it until it was just slightly ajar. Mai Lee tentatively moved forward into the sumptuous room with its opulent silk screens and wall hangings. She ventured further toward a standing screen and peered around it at an enormous bed with drapes, such as she had never before seen. A woman lay stiffly and still on the bed apparently asleep.

Mai Lee looked back at the partially open door where Auntie Ko still stood. She silently urged Mai Lee on, waving her arms and gesturing her forward before she retreated and finally closed the door behind her.

Mai Lee fingered her pendant and approached the bed where the female form stirred slightly. She spoke, her words were slightly slurred, “Mai Lee? Is that you?”

Mai Lee’s tone was quiet and deferential, “Yes, it is, Foster Mother.”

Madame Jong sat up and rubbed her eyes wearily. Mai Lee noticed the opium pipe at the side of the bed next to a glass and a bottle. She frowned and then smiled quickly as Madame turned to her. Her face was very heavily made up and some of the cosmetics had run underneath her eyes. The pupils in her eyes were dark and enormous.

Madame Jong grabbed the glass and bottle and poured herself a large drink and gulped it down. She turned again to Mai Lee and patted the bed, "Come and sit next to me. We must get to know each other. I am looking forward to it."

Mai Lee sat gingerly on the edge of the bed. Madame Jong gestured wildly to a book gracing the bedside table. "Read to me. Come, I am in the mood to hear you read."

"Oh but…"

"No buts…" insisted Madame Jong. She picked up the book and opened it. "There." She pointed at a page. "Read this."

Mai Lee bit her lip and hesitated, "… I am sorry, Madame. I… I don't know how."

"You can't read?"

"No…"

"Hmm. Then I will have to teach you. No matter, it will be fun. Now you listen… I will read to you. And you will call me mother." Madame Jong cleared her throat, poured another drink draining the bottle and took a sip. Then, she began to read, "The serving girl's name was Lotus Blossom and she was as beautiful as the sunset on a hot summer night…"

Madame Jong's eyes glazed over and she put down the book and turned to Mai Lee, "What do you think, Mai Lee? Am I beautiful?" Mai Lee hesitated. "Come, come, don't be shy. Tell me what you think."

Mai Lee remembered Auntie Ko's advice and spoke clearly, "You are indeed, beautiful Madame… er Mother."

"How? Tell me how. Explain to me how you see me, please. Don't be afraid."

Mai Lee took a deep breath and tried to keep her voice even. She studied her foster mother's face. "You have such fine skin like alabaster, and as smooth as porcelain. Your hair is of the raven and would make the night envious. Its lustrous sheen would rival that of the moon. I have never seen anyone so lovely."

Madame Jong sniffed, "Do you truly think I am lovely or have you been told to say that? Tell me."

"Truly, Mother, I have never seen anyone as lovely as

you. The clothes you wear are to me the clothes of a queen." Mai Lee indicated the rich silk brocade that Madame wore in her fashionable kimono. It was truly a work of art.

Madame Jong perked up and smiled. She picked up her hairbrush, "And you, too will wear the clothes of a princess. Come, brush my hair and tell me about yourself, but nothing horrid. I only want to know the pleasant things about your life."

Mai Lee faltered. She had little to say about her life that was good. So she spoke of her friend Lily who had taught her to dream and of her time at the seaside village with Su Li, where she had been allowed to play in the surf and had been fed and looked after well. All in all there was very little she could say, but she spoke with enthusiasm about the Rainbow Valley, the sights and sounds, the games she had played on the sands, her shopping trips with Auntie Ko and the hustle and bustle of the market place and of her wonder at her new home and how she was being treated in Madame's house. "It is wonderful here. I do not want for clothes or food and I can bathe every day. This house is heavenly. There is so much I want to learn," finished Mai Lee.

"And I will teach you," answered Madame Jong.

Mai Lee continued to brush her mistresses' hair with long fine strokes. She enjoyed doing this and was careful not to tangle Madame's hair. She teased and played with it adjusting it into a loose style and decorated it with a silk flower.

Madame Jong picked up an ebony backed hand mirror and gazed at her reflection looking first one side and then the other, studying her profile and looking deeply into the glass, "Why am I so ugly?" she murmured.

"You are not ugly. You are young and very beautiful," replied Mai Lee.

Aaryn rose and turned to Mai Lee. She stroked her adopted daughter's cheek with her long manicured nails, "Do you really think so?" she simpered.

"Why, yes. And I have never been happier in my life."

"Your happiness gives you a radiance and beauty that I envy..." Aaryn's voice cracked. She stopped abruptly. "Leave me now. I am tired and need to rest."

"Yes, Mother." Mai Lee dutifully replaced the brush, bowed to Madame and left quietly as Madame laid down on the bed once more.

She called out, "I will tell you again when I want you to visit."

Mai Lee closed the door softly after her and tiptoed away. She felt a strange surge of excitement and prayed that her life would continue in this way. Never before had she felt so calm. This new life was good and she didn't want it to end. She retraced her steps and knocked on the door to Auntie Ko's rooms and waited to be admitted.

Auntie Ko welcomed her in and questioned her, "How did it go? Was Madame kind? Did she talk to you?"

Mai Lee blushed with excitement, "She says she's going to teach me to read."

"Then you must have made a good impression. Excellent. I am well pleased, Come, we will take tea together."

Mai Lee sat with Auntie Ko who began to teach her the art of making good tea and Mai Lee watched eager to learn. She was like a sponge wanting to soak up every experience, to remember it, and be able to recreate it in reality or inside her head. Auntie Ko grinned in delight for Mai Lee was a good pupil.

"I shall be conversing with Madame later. She will tell me what she really thinks of your first encounter. But now, I believe you had questions about the Temple. Yes?"

"Oh, yes," enthused Mai Lee.

"Then I will teach you and we will begin with the Buddhist deities."

"Deities?"

"Gods." Auntie Ko went to a cupboard and removed a book. She opened it up revealing a splendid array of pictures of Gods and Goddesses. "You see we can ask help from any God. They will consider your request and bring the answer to you in a dream or with some sign."

"Like my friend, Lily… Are you Buddhist, Auntie Ko?"

"I am. And I will teach you what I know and what I believe to be true."

Mai Lee settled down and prepared to listen and learn.

CHAPTER TWELVE

Life goes on

Mai Lee sat with Auntie Ko in her rooms sharing some tea. This was now a regular occurrence and this time, Mai Lee had made it and laid out the tea tray in the proper fashion and presented it to her mentor and friend.

"Good. You have learned well. I have also had an excellent report from Madame. You surpassed yourself yesterday. She is keen to progress with you, but..." Auntie Ko stopped and put down her cup. A serious tone had entered her voice and her eyes took on a steely glint, "I have been instructed to tell you that in your household duties you must stay away from the main gate."

"Why, I hardly ever go there."

"Good. You must avoid it for the moment."

"Why?"

"It seems a young man has been here asking for you. It's much too soon for such visits, however innocent. He must be discouraged."

Mai Lee's heart leapt, "Of course. I cannot think who it can be." But in her mind she hoped it was Yuan.

"Maybe it's that crude shopkeeper's son, Peng, or whatever his name was. I don't remember but I know he took an unhealthy interest in you," said Auntie Ko.

"Yes, I remember him. He gave me a bad feeling, putting his hands all over me. I hated it." Mai Lee shuddered in distaste.

"Well, if it is him the servants will send him packing. Is there anyone else?"

"I have not met any young men on my journey..." Mai Lee hesitated as Yuan's face once more popped into her mind.

"You have thought of someone?"

"Yes... No... It can't be... The son of the woman who

sold me was very kind to me. If it wasn't for him I wouldn't be here."

"Hmm," considered Auntie Ko. We must be careful. Kind or not, it is not right, nor is it your place to receive male guests."

"No, Auntie Ko."

"So, put him from your mind."

"Yes, at once."

"And come to my bedroom. I would love another treat of one of your wonderful massages."

"It did you good?" asked Mai Lee pleased at the request.

"Oh, yes. I feel so much better. I am sure you will be able to keep all my old aches and pains away. Thank you, Mai Lee. Finish your tea and come with me."

Mai Lee dutifully obeyed and followed Auntie Ko to her room, where the old lady undressed and lay as before on the bed. Mai Lee began her healing, kneading massage drawing satisfied grunts and groans from Auntie Ko.

One day ran quickly into another and Mai Lee was happy with her duties, she was beginning to get to know her foster mother and enjoyed being with her. Madame Jong had begun in earnest in teaching Mai Lee to read.

Books had been selected for her with simple words and pictures. Mai Lee was going right back to basics. She was learning how to hold a brush and form the characters for these words on a plain piece of parchment. She had an endearing way of letting her tongue escape her mouth as she focused on these tasks, which Madame pointed out and they laughed together. "You're doing it again! How funny. Your tongue, it is like you would lick any crumbs from off your mouth to stop them from escaping to the floor. Are you that hungry?"

"No, Mother."

"Then try and keep it inside your mouth. It is not polite to expose it so. We are not savages."

"No, Mother." But Mai Lee would see the twinkle in Madame's eyes and a giggle would escape her and they would laugh again together.

"It seems you will have the cleanest chin in all Singapore," mused Madame Jong with a wry smile.

Mai Lee was an able student and could not get enough learning. She was eager and quick to understand her lessons. Her foster mother clapped delightedly at each step of progress that she made. Mai Lee was being educated, something she would never have believed possible from her years in the orphanage. Her vocabulary was increasing she was now using words that she had heard her friend Lily say, which she had never understood. She did now.

"Yes, yes, Mai Lee. Say the sound again!"

Mai Lee pursed her lips and pushed them forward to produce an 'ooh' sound.

"Good. That is good. Again, you see you are almost perfect. Now, with the sounds must come the letters, listen, look and learn." Madame took the brush and dipped it in the ink and swept it onto the page. She placed the brush in Mai Lee's hand and guided it to make the same sweeps on the page. "That's right. Well done! Well done!"

Praise came easily to Madame's lips and Mai Lee flourished in the encouragement and lavishly kind words. She was becoming more confident and more self-assured. Madame was pleased. "If you continue like this Mai Lee I will adopt you for real with all the correct paperwork. You will be my daughter and not a slave. Oh what fun we will have," and she clapped her hands again in that childlike way that she had, which belied her true age.

Of course the upsides were countered with downsides and every now and then Madame Jong would fall into a downward spiral of depression and drink herself into a stupor. She was then unrecognisable as Mai Lee's mentor and teacher. Mai Lee had become used to these changes and her heart filled with compassion and love for her foster mother. And she rued the master who had so cruelly used her and treated her so shamefully.

Many times Madame had collapsed dead drunk on the bed, knocking over her glass and empty bottle of liquor. Sometimes it was a surfeit of opium that was responsible. Each time this happened Mai Lee tidied up the debris. She tenderly put her foster mother into her bed. She tucked her in as one would a small child. Mai Lee kissed Aaryn Jong's forehead gently and she studied her painted face and wiped away the smudges that traced a line though her white caked on make-up and sat with her until her breathing was deep and easy. Only then, when she was satisfied Madame was fine, and in no danger, would she leave her. She returned to her rooms and sat purposefully studying her workbooks. She intended to continue to please her mother. Mai Lee ensured she would be ready for her next lesson.

Weeks passed and Mai Lee really felt she was being treated like a little princess as Madame had promised. One afternoon in her rooms she wandered to her window and looked out when a movement caught her attention. She saw a young man who approached the main heavy ornate gates. Mai Lee screwed up her face and stared. She gasped in surprise. It was Yuan.

Mai Lee's hand flew to her pendant that she still wore with pride and she traced the symbols on the talisman. She watched as she saw Yuan trying to attract the attention of the gardener. The bronzed old man hobbled across to Yuan, who pointed up at Mai Lee's window. Mai Lee tentatively raised her hand as if to wave but thought better of it and withdrew. However, she was irresistibly drawn back like a magnet and saw the old man sending Yuan on his way. She turned away wistfully.

Now it was clear to her that the young man who had come calling was not the shopkeeper's lewd son, but Yuan, who had only ever treated her with kindness and whom she had to thank for her current position. Mai Lee decided that she would wait a respectful amount of time and if Yuan ever came again, and she was aware of his visit, she would try to speak to him.

Another two weeks went by, but sadly, Yuan didn't return although Mai Lee had kept an eye out for him and had spoken to the gardener quietly, when he was on his own. She explained Yuan was an old friend and just wanted to say hello but she promised that she would not admit him to the property. The old man seemingly agreed and Mai Lee continued to keep an eye out for him when she was in her own quarters as her bedroom overlooked the garden and main gate. Mai Lee determined that she would try and watch at the same time each day, just in case he came calling again.

Mai Lee looked out, as usual, but seeing no one she made her way to Madame's chambers; where she was to dress her foster mother's hair before their next lesson. She knocked tentatively, uncertain of how she would find Madame. Would she be in good humour or would she be drunk?

Her 'mother' called for her to enter and Mai Lee swept in. Madame Jong was sitting at her dressing table. She passed her hairbrush to Mai Lee who began to brush Madame's hair vigorously, just as she liked.

"Ah! That is good. It stimulates the cells on my scalp refreshing it and helping my hair to grow. Just lovely."

Mai Lee continued to fashion and style Madame's hair brushing it this way and that. Mai Lee twisted Madame's long hair into a loose chignon, and decorated it with a freshly cut flower, which she was just positioning when Auntie Ko burst into the room. She spoke nearly hysterically and with urgency in her voice, "Madame, Madame! The master. He's here!"

Madame took the brush from the bewildered Mai Lee and rose. She clapped her hands, "Quickly now, you must hide."

Mai Lee stared about her and looked alarmed, "But why?"

"Ask no questions. Please do as I say. It is in your interest. Go now. Hide and stay silent until we tell you it's safe to come out." She turned to Auntie Ko, "Take her, hide her in the Orchid House. Quickly now."

"Is that wise?" questioned Auntie Ko.

Aaryn continued, "Under the Orchid House is a cellar storeroom. Take her there. If need be there's a secret tunnel, which leads to a crypt in the Temple across the street. She can escape through that if he finds her. Mai Lee, you must stay as quiet as a mouse. You understand?"

Mai Lee nodded; her eyes were wide with fright.

"Auntie Ko will fetch you when it's safe. Go now.

Hurry!" Madame Jong embraced Mai Lee and then nodded at Auntie Ko, "Take her. Quickly, now."

Auntie Ko bundled Mai Lee out from Madame's chamber and rushed her down the corridor and outside to the garden. They hastened down the garden path toward the Orchid House and entered quickly.

Yuan was peering through the gate and he spotted Mai Lee scurrying inside the glass building and cried out her name. Mai Lee stopped momentarily, but Auntie Ko pushed her on. They fled down the steps to the cellar. She opened the storeroom door, shoved Mai Lee inside and locked the door.

It was dark and dusty in the storeroom. Mai Lee settled down to wait quietly, her heart thumping wildly with unknown fear. She hoped her eyes would soon adjust to the dim shadows.

***

Auntie Ko crept back up the steps and looked furtively about her. She saw Yuan at the gate, staring into the garden but spotted Manchu as he approached the gate from the inside and he, too, saw the young man. Auntie Ko dashed away. She disappeared behind a bush and watched.

She nibbled her nail in anxiety as she saw Manchu stride to the boy. Yuan appeared to be explaining something to Manchu. He pointed at the Orchid House. Auntie Ko frowned as Manchu looked around with a quizzical expression on his face. He turned back to Yuan and then gestured him away.

Yuan moved off sadly with his head down.

Auntie Ko dithered. Uncertain as to what to do she stayed and continued to watch.

***

The cellar storeroom in the Orchid House was filled with packing cases. Ropes and netting hung from the ceiling and held little bits of sailcloth and other items, buoys, glass stars, wicker baskets and ceramic pots. A mouldy drape partly obscured a secret panel at the back of the room.

Mai Lee sat disconsolately on a wooden crate. She was frightened and didn't know what to do. Her eyes were slowly becoming adjusted to the gloom when a bright shining light filled the air on front of her. Mai Lee shaded her eyes and saw Lily bathed in gold before her.

"Lily!"

Lily put her fingers to her lips in a gesture to make Mai Lee quiet. "Hush now. Manchu is here. You must hide or he will hurt you. Don't let him find you."

"But, he's my foster father. He's never met me. Why would he want to hurt me?"

"You're young and beautiful. He will steal away your innocence. Please be careful. Trust in what I say..." Lily began to fade.

"No, Lily! Come back... Please." Mai Lee stopped as she heard a noise outside the storeroom door and she froze.

Lily's voice reverberated inside her mind, "Hide, Mai Lee. Hide!"

Mai Lee was prompted into action. She knew Lily had never let her down before. She stared around the storeroom and dashed to the very back of the gloomy underground room and ducked down behind more packing cases and boxes and pulled a piece of cloth over herself.

The storeroom door handle began to move and pressure was exerted against it but the door did not open. The handle moved up and down again and there was an exclamation of annoyance from outside.

Mai Lee peeped over the crate and her eyes grew wide as she heard the sound of someone fumbling with jangling keys. She ducked down again and kept very still. Her eyes moved rapidly from side to side as she thought what to do and what Lily had said. She was more frightened than she had been in a long while.

She heard a key being inserted into the lock. There was a metallic click as the key turned and the door began to squeak open. Out of nowhere came a sudden rush of wind as Manchu tried to open the door, but it blew shut in his face and stayed closed. Mai Lee heard the man swear. He grumbled again as he tried to force open the door. It wouldn't budge.

Mai Lee could feel what was happening. How she didn't know, but thought it must have had something to do with Lily. Manchu levelled his shoulder at the door and barged against it. It gave way. The man tumbled inside.

Mai Lee shivered miserably behind the crate trying not to let her panicked breathing become too loud. She heard Manchu enter further into the room.

He scanned the place with his eyes and edged slowly toward the packing crates. He moved into the corner and peered over the top of the boxes. He tugged at the piece of cloth and saw Mai Lee who cowered underneath it. "Don't be afraid, Mai Lee. It is Mai Lee, isn't it?"

Mai Lee nodded timidly and uttered a breathless, "Yes."

"Come, take my hand. Come out from behind there and meet your foster father."

With trembling hands Mai Lee obeyed Manchu and rose. He drew her to him as his eyes ranged over her. "Why? You're beautiful. Why would they try to keep you from me?" His voice was scratchy with a raspy quality and Mai Lee didn't like it. She lowered her eyes fearfully and remained silent. "Come, let me show you the Orchid House and my private quarters. Next time I come you can meet me there, yes?"

Manchu took her hand and began to lead the frightened girl toward the doorway. Suddenly, a rope swung loose and a rolled up canvas sailcloth tumbled out and struck Manchu, who fell to his knees. There was a sound like static electricity, a snicking and snacking and a flash of blue light as it happened. Mai Lee looked up and briefly saw Lily's face, which was now fading.

Mai Lee tentatively offered her hand to Manchu and helped him back onto his feet. Up close she could see the man's age, his lines and wrinkles in the crisp, parchment skin, the grey in his hair and beard and she detected a distinct waxy aroma around the man, which she didn't like.

They walked to the door, which had so stubbornly refused

to admit him, which now opened with ease. Outside stood a breathless Auntie Ko. "Sir, Madame wishes to speak to you, urgently."

His response was cold and unfeeling, "Does she now? Well, I have no wish to see her or speak to her …" Aware of Mai Lee's eyes on him he tempered his tone, "Not today…" He then ordered Auntie Ko, "Take Mai Lee to my quarters. I will be along shortly."

Auntie Ko bowed obediently, took a subdued Mai Lee by the hand and led her away. For some reason she felt compelled to look back at the ornate gates and saw Yuan climbing up them. He was hanging precariously like a monkey on a bough about to break, then with one hefty swing of his body he was over the top. Auntie Ko smiled to herself and said nothing. She slowly led Mai Lee toward Manchu's quarters as she had been bid.

***

Yuan silently dropped down into the grounds and skulked into the bushes unseen. He watched carefully to see where Mai Lee was being taken before turning his attention to Manchu and gauging what to do. Stealthily, he scuttled closer to the Chinaman to watch him.

Manchu climbed the steps to the Orchid House and stood on the balcony. He removed an opium pipe from his pocket and filled it with a mixture from a pouch left on a bamboo table and lit it. Yuan drew closer to observe him.

Manchu tossed down his matches and settled in a wicker chair. He inhaled deeply and puffed on the drug filled pipe. He leaned back in his seat and surveyed the gardens and grounds, a look of contentment seemingly swept over him.

Still, Yuan hovered below Manchu unseen.

As Manchu smoked his eyes filmed over, his pupils grew bigger and darker almost eclipsing the coloured irises of his eyes. Yuan could see the man was now clearly in the grip of the opium's power.

Manchu rose languidly and leant on the wooden balustrade. He was clearly in no hurry to move, enjoying the waves of dreamlike visions, which washed over him and he sighed. Yuan remained still, uncertain what to do.

***

Auntie Ko reluctantly deposited Mai Lee in the Master's quarters. "I am sorry, Mai Lee. I had hoped that this wouldn't happen. Neither Madame nor I wanted this for you."

"Why am I here? Why can't I go to my room or to Madame?"

"Because you can't. I am sorry."

Auntie Ko slipped out shaking her head sorrowfully. She retraced her steps and hastened back to her mistresses' rooms and knocked on the door. She knew by the instruction to enter that Madame was now the worse for wear.

Auntie Ko tried to explain what had happened and that Manchu had refused to see her. Madame Jong threw up her arms in a flurry of anger. She grabbed a long stemmed bottle and poured herself another large glass draining the bottle.

Madame Jong's eyes were bright. She hugged the large glass of red liquor, and sipped from it intermittently. Auntie Ko couldn't believe that in the short space of time since Mai Lee had left her Aaryn Jong had drunk so much that she was now well and truly inebriated. She cursed loudly and shouted indignantly, "He refuses to see me…?"

"This time. But, Madame it may be different another time."

"Where is he?"

"The Orchid House, but…" Auntie Ko hesitated before she blurted out, "He asked me to take Mai Lee to his quarters."

"You haven't done so?" Madame Jong asked sorrowfully.

"I had no choice. I'm sorry."

"The poor child. You know what will happen…?" Suddenly, her face twisted in pain and anger and she stumbled to the dresser with a sob and slammed down her glass, "Leave me."

Auntie Ko needed no further words. She bowed deferentially and backed out of the room quickly. Madame

Jong hardly noticed. She reeled toward the seat in front of her mirror and stared at her complexion, at her heavily painted face, and her coiffured hair.

She picked up a lipstick and with shaking hands applied it to her already crimson lips. Then she stopped and scribbled furiously on the silvered surface masking her reflection. She snatched another gulp of air, rose unsteadily to her feet and grabbed her drink. She began to walk away but turned back and glanced at her image in the glass. She gave an anguish filled cry and hurled the glass at her reflection smashing it. The drink stained the cracked mirror and her dresser like blood.

The vision seemed to propel Madame into a frenzy of hate. She searched through a drawer, throwing things out, which scattered on the floor as she searched. All the while she made small mewling sounds like the whimpering of a tortured animal.

Abruptly she stopped, her face suffused with colour in mad pleasure and she seized something in the drawer.

***

Mai Lee sat and waited nervously in Manchu's quarters. She gazed around the very masculine room with its boldly coloured rich drapes and paintings. All the while she played with the talisman around her neck, rubbing her fingertips over the charmed signs and letters.

A rushing wind swirled around her like the sound of beating wings. Mai Lee stood up and looked about her, "Lily?"

Lily's words of warning floated and echoed on the breeze, which now filled the chamber. "Run, Mai Lee! Leave, hide, get aw-a-a-ay." The last word was drawn out until it became just a whisper, which dissipated into the air.

Mai Lee looked about her fruitlessly. There was nowhere to hide. Her skin turned white with fear and a slick sheen of sweat appeared on her downy upper lip as her heart beat wildly and erratically, battering against her rib cage, as if trying to escape from her chest. She knew Lily had protected her in the past and had warned her of Manchu. Lily had never been wrong but Mai Lee's dilemma tore her reason to shreds, should she listen to Lily's warning or obey her master? But this man, she owed him nothing. She didn't know him. It was Madame who had adopted her and taught her, and been kind to her; Madame and Auntie Ko, not this Manchu whom they had tried to protect her from.

Mai Lee made up her mind. Lily had never been wrong and she told herself again that she didn't know this man. She knew she didn't like the look of him, his waxy elderly smell or his voice and she rose from her seat and bolted to the door, which opened with a flourish.

Mai Lee stepped back as she came face to face with Manchu who had now lost complete control of his sensibilities in a drug induced haze. His face was flushed red, and ugly thread veins and broken capillaries crisscrossed his cheeks and a pulse in his temple throbbed threateningly. He ogled her youthful, adolescent body and leered at her terrifyingly, "Not thinking of leaving are you?" he rasped.

Mai Lee had no voice; she could produce no sound, no speech. She just stared blankly at this drug-crazed creature in front of her.

Manchu closed the door firmly behind him and slid across a small metal bolt, which scraped loudly in that room, where the air was suffocating and cloying like syrup. She felt as if her mouth was stuffed with cotton wool and no sound came.

He turned and moved toward Mai Lee who backed away from him fearfully.

"There's nothing to be frightened of. I am going to lead you into womanhood. You can thank me later."

Manchu continued to bear down on Mai Lee until she had nowhere left to go. She stumbled backward and fell onto the bed. The master covered her body with his as he tried to force himself on her while Mai Lee squirmed and wriggled as she struggled to fight him off. She could feel his hot smoky breath on her cheek as she turned her face to one side to escape his searching mouth. He tore at her clothes, which ripped like tissue paper, and he fumbled with his fastenings when Mai Lee suddenly found her voice and emitted a small pitiful cry, "No please, Master. Don't."

The door splintered open and Yuan rushed in. He grabbed Manchu from behind and hauled him off Mai Lee who hurriedly tried to cover her exposed legs and partial nakedness.

Manchu roared in anger and Yuan hit him hard and full in the face, knocking him to the floor. His eyes rolled in his head until they showed white, blood spurted from his nose and he passed out.

Yuan pulled Mai Lee to her feet and held her trembling body in his arms. She buried her face in his chest and sobbed quietly.

Yuan breathed in her fragrance and whispered, "You can't stay here. I won't let them treat you like this. Come."

"I can't. They'll find me."

"Mai Lee, you must trust me. Please. Now, come."

Mai Lee blinked back her tears and nodded reluctantly knowing that it made sense. How could she stay now? "All right. I will come."

Yuan hurried Mai Lee out of the room, which reeked of old men, sweat, drink and drugs and they raced to the top of the stairs where Aaryn Jong came flying out of the shadows with a large wicked looking knife raised aloft in readiness to strike.

She screamed like a demented demon, "Mai Lee! You thief of men; I will kill you." Madame lunged at Mai Lee but Yuan stepped between them as Madame Jong brought down the vicious blade and slashed his hand. Blood spouted out spattering her face but Yuan shoved her roughly, the knife slipped from her grasp and she tumbled to the floor.

Aaryn Jong squealed in anger then burst into a pitiful wailing. Mai Lee paused filled with compassion at her foster mother's plight. She stopped but Yuan urged her on and raced her down the stairs, out of the house and into the grounds where the gardener watched in amazement. Yuan hurried to the main gate where Auntie Ko waited. She opened the gate and shooed them out, "Go quickly. Hurry now."

"But Madame, she's hurt… and the master…"

"Don't worry. I will deal with it. Go. GO!"

Mai Lee and Yuan stepped out into the road and Auntie Ko shut the heavy gates. Aaryn's voice and her cries for help could be heard outside, "Auntie Ko…!" she cried pitifully, "Auntie Ko!"

Auntie Ko watched as Mai Lee and Yuan ran off down the leafy lane and past the temple making sure they were unhindered and then as another shout assailed her ears she called back, "Coming, Madame! Coming!"

Mai Lee stopped on the corner and looked back longingly at what had become her home and sanctuary. Auntie Ko gave a small wave before disappearing from sight. Mai Lee whispered, "Bye-bye, Auntie."

Yuan dragged Mai Lee away and his hand continued to drip blood. They ran on into a back street where a cart waited. Yuan sprang up and grimaced in pain as he took the reins, "Quick, Climb up!" he urged Mai Lee who was hesitating.

"What is to happen to me? Am I to be sold again? No. I won't go."

"Please, Mai Lee. Come quickly before the alarm is raised No one is going to sell you. I am trying to save you."

Mai Lee stood defiantly, "I am no one's possession. I am me!"

"Mai Lee! This is no time for heroics. Come!"

The sound of a police whistle reached them and this spurred Mai Lee into action. She jumped up onto the wagon and sat next to Yuan.

"Your hand. It's bleeding." Mai Lee tore off a strip from her dress and wrapped around Yuan's injured palm.

He nodded indicating the back of the cart, "There. Behind you, there's a hat and an old tunic. Put it on."

Mai Lee leaned behind her and threw on the old garment over her silk dress. She thrust her hair under the hat and pulled it down over her head.

Yuan picked up a floppy rustic hat from the step of the wagon and put it on. He shook the reins and the oxen plodded on. They turned a corner as several policemen ran past in the direction of the big house. Mai Lee kept her eyes fixed firmly on her sandaled feet.

They travelled in silence until they reached the open road passing only a few other carts and farmers herding animals. "Where are you taking me?"

"Home. Back home."

"That was my home. The only home I have known."

"But we were kind to you, too, weren't we?"

"Yes," replied Mai Lee grudgingly. "But I don't want to go back and be forced into a death house or whore house. I won't do it. I am better than that. No one is going to steal my life. I would rather die."

"Hold on. No one is going to do that. You must know I wouldn't let that happen. You need to know that your Auntie Ko helped me. She wants the best for you, as I do."

Mai Lee sat silently. This fire that had spread into her belly and into her voice was a new feeling for her and she suddenly realised all that Lily had taught her was helping her become the person she was meant to be. She turned to Yuan, "Thank you. But you must understand I am not the same girl who landed on your shore."

"Your heart is still the same and that's what counts."

Mai Lee sat quietly ruminating over the day's events and she wondered what was going to happen next.

CHAPTER THIRTEEN

The plan

Yuan and Mai Lee sat quietly as they faced Su Li in their hut at the seaside village. Yuan nursed his wounded hand as Su Li treated and dressed it. Mai Lee was silent but thoughtful as she fingered her pendant.

"What were you thinking of? They're bound to come here. They'll demand their money back and I'll be forced to sell her again," reprimanded Su Li.

Mai Lee looked up sharply and stared at Yuan, who responded, "No. Auntie Ko, she promised. She's on our side."

"You trusting fools. She'll have no choice. What am I going to do with you?"

Mai Lee shivered silently not in misery but in the growing defiance that was now filling her soul. She continued to listen to the developing argument between Yuan and his mother.

Yuan remained quiet as he contemplated his mother's words. Su Li finished bandaging Yuan's hand and came to a decision. "Right! Yuan. Go and get some clothes."

"What?"

"Clothes, *your* clothes."

"Why?"

"Just do it."

Yuan hurried out and Su Li pulled Mai Lee to her feet and studied her. Mai Lee stared back sullenly. She went to speak but Su Li stopped her, "Enough of that." She turned Mai Lee around, "You know; it may just work."

"What?"

"You'll see. Wait here. Do not answer the door or speak out if anyone calls. Understand?"

Mai Lee nodded, but she was bewildered.

***

At the big house Auntie Ko helped a sobbing Aaryn Jong into her bed, "It's not your fault. It's the master. He's to blame."

"Where is he?"

"His manservant collected him. He remembers nothing. He thinks he fell when he was looking for something and struck his face on a packing crate."

"And Mai Lee?"

"I don't know. She was terrified…"

"I thought… I have been so stupid, so very foolish… I thought…" Aaryn dissolved into sobs again.

"Madame, she was so scared, she ran off. I tried but I couldn't stop her."

"Who was she with?"

"No one that I saw," lied Auntie Ko.

"But, I thought…"

"You had, had more than a little to drink," murmured Auntie Ko kindly.

"I know. I know. Curse me for being such a fool. I'm stupid and ugly and now I've lost my daughter."

"No, Madame, no. Not Mai Lee… She may come back, when it's safe…"

"Mai Lee gave me a reason to live. She brought me joy where there was none. I learned things about myself. She taught me to love and laugh again. I have been such a fool…"

Auntie Ko wrapped her arms around Madame Jong who cried into her shoulder like a small child. Eventually she came up for air and Auntie Ko gave her some water to sip.

"My head feels like it's been beaten with a sledgehammer."

"Well, you did have rather a lot to drink."

"Yes, you said. Tell me the truth, what exactly did I do? What part did I play in this disaster?" Auntie Ko hestitated to reply. "Tell me," ordered Madame Jong.

Auntie Ko sighed and reluctantly admitted, "You… you tried to kill Mai Lee… with a knife…"

"What?" Aaryn groaned and buried her face in her hands.

"Don't punish yourself. Nothing happened."

"Oh, Mai Lee… where are you? Do you think she will forgive me?" asked Aaryn pleadingly.

"Madame, you must face up to it. Mai Lee is gone."

"But where?"

"I don't know."

"We must find her."

***

Mai Lee looked questioningly at Su Li who approached her with a pair of scissors. "No! Not my hair!"

"Hush! If this is to work, we have to cut it."

Mai Lee reluctantly dropped her hands and sat in the small rustic chair in the centre of the floor and Su Li began to hack at the lustrous long locks as Yuan marched in carrying an armful of clothes, which he dropped on the floor as his jaw dropped in amazement.

"Close your mouth and sort out an outfit to fit her," ordered Su Li. "In fact, pick a couple."

Yuan rummaged through the garments and pulled out a flowered print shirt and a pair of plain harem styled pants. He also took a tunic jacket with a mandarin collar and loose cotton trousers.

Su Li looked them over. "Put them on the table and leave us. I'll call you when I'm ready." Yuan bowed and left. She ordered Mai Lee, "Put one of them on, quickly now."

Mai Lee removed her torn silk cheongsam and donned the tunic jacket and loose pants. Su Li removed Mai Lee's clothes and stuffed them in a bag. She finished cropping her hair and then made her stand as she eyed her critically. Mai Lee stood; her lovely hair, now cropped short, littered the floor and she wore Yuan's clothes. Su Li walked around her.

Su Li pointed at Mai Lee's breasts, "We'll have to do something about those." She went to the cupboard took out a wad of bandages. She lifted Mai Lee's tunic and began to bandage her chest, and flattened her bosom. She completed her task, pulled down her tunic and nodded, "Just one more thing."

Su Li took a cloth cap from off a peg and placed it on her head. She shouted for her son, "Yuan, come here."

Yuan ran in and stopped short in amazement and his jaw dropped again.

"I really will have to tie up your mouth if you continue to wear that stupid expression," warned Su Li then she beamed. "Meet your young cousin, Xin. He's come to stay with us for a few days."

Yuan stared in surprised delight at Mai Lee; then he picked up his mother and swung her around. "You're wonderful!"

"It'll only work if we make everyone believe it." Su Li paused and rubbed her hands together. "Now. Are you ready? We must get your story right. We all must learn the facts!"

The three sat around the table and began to talk, weaving an imaginary tale of Xin's birth and history until they had developed an agreed story. Then Su Li questioned both Mai Lee and Yuan until they were word perfect on everything, including birthdates, relatives and why 'he' was here. "Why am I here?" asked Mai Lee.

"Because my Auntie, mother's sister, is unwell. You have come to work with us and learn the family business until your mother is better and you can return home."

"Good. Good," nodded Su Li. "When is your birthday? What year were you born?"

"June 5th 1926 the year of the tiger."

"Which means?"

"I am intelligent, faithful and virtuous."

"Hmm! Now, who is your mother? What is her name?"

And so the questions continued until, they all knew every fact, and every conceivable thing about the manufactured life of Xin.

"Now, you can both come and help me. I have to prepare the main hut as I have another consignment of girls arriving tomorrow. Mai Lee? Oops! I mean Xin…"

"I'll help. What do you want me to do?"

"You can help me make up the beds, come."

Mai Lee followed Su Li to the storeroom where bedding was kept and she gathered armfuls of sheets, while Yuan carried a number of straw mats. Su Li brought a small cart in which she loaded pillows and bulkier coverlets. They processed to the main hut, which Mai Lee remembered only too well.

Yuan lay out the straw mats and left to get some more. Su Li placed the thin mattresses on top while Mai Lee added sheets. Su Li grabbed an armful of pillows and spoke to Mai Lee. "When they arrive, don't speak. Your voice will give you away."

Mai Lee looked up from the bed she was making and faced Su Li, who was placing a pillow down, "Why are you doing this?"

"Why? It's how I earn my living. I am a widow with a son? I need money. I can't fish."

"No. I mean, why are you helping me?" persisted Mai Lee.

Su Li straightened up to think and paused, "I must be getting soft in my old age... I don't know... But, I have never seen Yuan act like this, in this way before. There's something different about you, Mai Lee. Even I noticed it."

Their heads snapped around as a great hullabaloo was heard outside. Villagers were shouting and terrified screams followed. They stopped what they were doing and scrambled up to the door to see what was going on. Su Li flung it open. She gasped in horror and Mai Lee's hand flew to her mouth in alarm.

A platoon of Japanese soldiers was marching through the village. They kept in regimented rows and stamped their booted feet. Two young girls of about sixteen and seventeen were being hustled away from their family homes and being herded onto a cart filled with other young women, in their teens, who all looked terrified. One girl was being dragged by her hair. Her face was a mask of pain and she was shrieking in agony trying to prevent her hair being tugged out by the roots.

The girl's mother was screeching in fury at the Japanese soldier who had hold of her daughter and tried to stop him. He turned on her viciously and threw her to the ground. Undeterred she got up and tried to get her daughter back again and once more she was shoved away and fell sprawling on the stony path. This time the Japanese man towered over her and as she began to get to her feet once more he ruthlessly swiped her hard across the face, splitting her lip and loosening her teeth. This time the mother stopped and sobbed. The soldier turned, a triumphant look on his face and he barked something in Japanese to the other men who guffawed in derision.

Yuan came running and joined his mother and Mai Lee.

"What's happening?" asked Mai Lee, hardly daring to believe her eyes.

"Japanese soldiers. They are stealing women to become sex slaves, comfort women for their soldiers," replied Su Li with distaste.

"But why?"

"It's what they do. There were many rapes and massacres in the war. Some say as many as thirty thousand were butchered at Nan King," said Su Li bitterly.

"I don't understand," said Mai Lee. "Nanking?"

"That's another story," said Su Li.

"They often steal young village girls, virgins, ones they know they are healthy and clean," said Yuan.

"But that's not right. How can you let them do this?" questioned Mai Lee.

"How can we stand up to them? We are but a small village. They are armed men and there are too many. They are ruthless and just take what they want. Hush now," warned Su Li as a Japanese soldier emerged from searching the adjacent hut.

The soldier, Rin strode toward Su Li and looked her over. "Too old," he muttered. He pushed past them into the hut and saw the freshly made sleeping quarters. "What are these beds for?"

"Relatives. I have guests arriving for my son's betrothal celebrations."

Rin studied Su Li's face and grunted. He scrutinized Mai Lee who looked down and said nothing. The soldier snorted and marched back to his commander, Takagi. And reported back to him. Su Li and Yuan watched anxiously and Mai Lee continued to stand with her eyes cast down, afraid to look up and see what was happening.

Commandant Takagi issued an order before turning and eyeing Su Li. The oxen and cart trundled toward the harbour as the Commandant swaggered arrogantly toward Su Li. “You!” He pointed his baton at her.

“Me?”

“You are the one we seek,” he said officiously.

“I don’t understand.”

“You’re expecting a consignment of women to work in the Death Houses and brothels of Singapore. We are appropriating them and will ship them to Borneo for the use of our men.”

“But…”

“No arguments or it will be the worse for you,” interrupted Takagi, “I’ll take your sons.”

Su Li looked horrified and Yuan glanced at his mother in shock before lowering his eyes.

“Prepare the women as you would for sale. We shall be back in four days,” ordered Takagi who turned on his heel and left, barking an instruction to his waiting men who marched after the cart.

Yuan turned to his mother, “Now what do we do?”

“I don’t know. We must be very careful. There are many here that would betray us. We have few friends in the village.” Mai Lee looked questioningly.

“It’s the nature of the job,” explained Yuan.

“But why are they coming now?”

“The war in Europe is spreading,” said Yuan.

“I don’t understand,” said Mai Lee. “Europe?”

“I’ll show you.” Yuan took a stick and drew in the sand to try and show the world and position of countries. He explained as he drew and pointed at places with the stick, “Here is China.”

“Where I came from?”

“Yes, it is here. And here is Japan. This is us, Singapore.”

“We are quite small. China is so big,” murmured Mai Lee.

“Yes. Now over here,” he scratched again. “We have Europe made up of a number of countries, East and West, with Russia in the East; Germany, France and Britain in the West and many other places."

"I don't know any of this. It seems we are a very long way away…."

"We are looking at another World War…" He stopped and looked solemn. "The last one was disastrous. That's how we lost father."

Mai Lee and Yuan stood silently. Su Li hadn't spoken she was lost in her own thoughts, suddenly when she spoke the others jumped at the sound of her voice and Yuan hurriedly erased the drawing in the sand from Mai Lee's first geography lesson.

"It's iniquitous I must lose money and pay out to get the girls ready and for them to be stolen away for those brutes of soldiers. It will not do. Nor will it help your case, Mai Lee. Think, Su Li, think… We must have a plan."

"What do you have in mind?" asked Yuan.

"Come, back to our hut. We will discuss what we are to do."

CHAPTER FOURTEEN

More girls arrive

The following day Su Li stood with Yuan on the beach next to the harbour of the currently peaceful fishing village and waited. She watched as three sampans drew close to the shoreline. Mai Lee tucked herself away by a coconut palm afraid of being recognised.

The Captain of the slave vessel and with whom Su Li conducted business before arrived first. He jumped out of the craft and waded toward Su Li. "Ah, Su Li. We have twenty-two girls for you."

"I was told to expect twenty-five."

"Three died. Why? What's the problem?"

Su Li took the Captain by the arm and walked up to the hut as the other boats with their cargo of girls began to arrive. They were all aged from between fourteen to sixteen years old.

Five girls scrambled out from the boat as it landed on shore. They staggered about as they got used to being on dry land. They were filthy and dressed in rags. A gasp escaped Mai Lee as she watched Yuan help them ashore and one girl looked familiar. Mai Lee recognised her as one of the younger girls from the Wing Fong Orphanage. She murmured to herself, "Oh, no! What now?" She scurried back behind the palm tree.

Yuan looked up at the noise and movement and saw her hide herself. He turned to the girls, "Wait here. If you wish to wash in the water please do. We will bring you special soap to ease your itching skin. You may find the water will refresh you. I won't be long."

The girls hesitated, he urged them again, "Go. Go rinse yourselves in the water. It will make you feel better. I guarantee it." Yuan walked up the beach and called out, "Xin, come and help me with the girls."

Mai Lee didn't move. Yuan looked puzzled and hastened toward her as he noticed her reticence. "What is it?"

"That girl there; the little one with the spiky hair. Number Seventeen, she knows me. She had my friend, Lily's cage for a while. She's bound to recognise me."

"No. She won't know you like this. You are Xin. Act like it. Come on, be brave."

"Bravery has nothing to do with it. I don't want our plans ruined, I'll help but don't say I didn't warn you."

They walked back up the beach to the main hut where the tin baths were stacked outside. "You'll be fine. I promise. You look so different even your friend Lily would be hard pressed to know it's you. Be confident. Just remember not to speak."

Mai Lee bit her lip but nevertheless she helped Yuan line up the baths on the beach and fill them with warm water. None of the girls took any notice. They were so timid and cowed they kept their eyes cast down. One or two were violently ill as they struggled with being on solid ground, which had affected their balance.

Yuan instructed them, "Immerse yourselves in the water while we fetch carbolic soap and towels. Don't worry about your clothes as you are to have new ones."

The girls stepped into the baths of warm water and relaxed enjoying the feel of it, rinsing off the salt and sweat from their bodies. Yuan soon returned handing out the soap, which to the girls was a luxury and Mai Lee placed or handed a towel to each girl in turn. She didn't speak.

She approached Number Seventeen who received the towel gratefully without looking at Mai Lee.

Yuan watched the interchange. He crossed to her as she moved back up the beach toward the hut, "You see. Your fears are ungrounded. She didn't even look at you. It will all be okay."

She shook her head uncertainly, "I'm not so sure. She hasn't seen me yet, when she does. She will know it's me. We were friends, once."

"All right. But, we will see. Go back to our hut and I will finish up here. I will still need your help tonight at supper."

Mai Lee nodded, "That will be another test. They will be feeling somewhat better and more likely to try and engage us with their eyes."

Yuan shook his head and more for his benefit than Mai Lee's he reiterated, "It will be all right."

Evening was soon upon them and Mai Lee and Yuan took in bowls of chicken and rice to the young women. The response was the same as when Mai Lee had been a recipient and the girls fell upon the meals devouring them with relish. Yuan waited by the door and watched with Mai Lee.

The girls placed their empty bowls before them on the floor as they had been taught at the Orphanage and Mai Lee went up and down the lines collecting them. As she approached Number Seventeen, she was slightly nervous and tripped over the straw matting and her cap fell off. Number Seventeen looked up at her curiously and a glimmer of recognition flooded her eyes. "You remind me of someone…"

Mai Lee shrugged and continued picking up the bowls. She could feel Number Seventeen's eyes on her following every movement. The girl was clearly struggling to remember, so Mai Lee hurriedly finished her task and escaped from the hut.

She fled up the beach carrying the bowls and deposited them in the long washbasin to clean them. Mai Lee was worried. She didn't want her newly found freedom to be stolen away from her. She washed the pots and bowls until they were sparkling clean, buffed them with a clean tea towel, and stacked them up ready for collection in the morning. She mopped her brow now glistening with nervous sweat and left the kitchen to run to their hut. Yuan was just leaving the girls. He saw her and came after her. She heard his footfalls, turned to him and whispered, "You see? That was close. I better not have anymore contact with those girls or she will remember."

Yuan nodded, "You're right and I agree. Let's get back to mother."

The two made their way to Su Li's hut where she was

talking in hushed tones with someone. Yuan put his hand up to quiet Mai Lee and they listened at the edge of the hut.

Mai Lee instantly recognised her friend, Auntie Ko who was earnestly trying to persuade Su Li of something. "Don't you see? It'll be better for Mai Lee to return to us."

"But Madame tried to kill her!"

"It won't happen again."

"And the Master… he wanted to rape her."

"He believes she's gone. Mai Lee will remain in Madame's quarters. He won't come there."

"I don't know; it will be like she's a prisoner."

"Not really…"

"But… You said the Japanese Commandant is returning," said Auntie Ko. Yuan and Mai Lee moved further into the room to hear what was being said. "And what if someone gives Mai Lee away? She'll be doomed," finished Auntie Ko.

"Why will I be doomed?"

Auntie Ko turned, "Mai Lee!" Her face wreathed in smiles of pleasure, "Come back with me. Your foster mother is sorry, really sorry. She has sent me to find you. You will be safe with us."

Mai Lee looked from Su Li to Auntie Ko. She was undecided.

Yuan stepped forward, "She can no longer serve these girls. One of them knows her."

"You see," pleaded Auntie Ko. "She must come back with me. She knows she has a good home with us." She turned to Yuan, "And you… You can visit her. When the time is right she can be with you." She looked pleadingly and searchingly at each of them in turn. "By rights she does belong to us. We paid for her."

"I belong to no one," said Mai Lee firmly.

"Do you think Madame Jong would let her go? Really?" asked Yuan.

Auntie Ko remained silent.

"I didn't think so. No, let her take her chances with us. We can get you another slave, another daughter to adopt. Madame doesn't know your part in her escape, does she?"

Auntie Ko shook her head and muttered quietly, "No."

They were all focusing so intently on the subject in hand they didn't hear the rumble of an engine drawing closer.

Mai Lee looked sadly from one to the other, "I'll never be truly free, will I? It's just my wild imagining. I'll always be someone's property."

No one said anything and Mai Lee ran from the hut in tears. She raced around the corner and collided head on into the arms of the Japanese Commandant, Takagi.

"Not so fast young man. I need to speak with your mother. Is she there?"

Mai Lee was too terrified to speak. She stood there silently her fear stopping her tears.

"What are you? Dumb?" sneered the Commandant as Yuan emerged from the hut and caught what Takagi had said.

Yuan spoke quickly, "His hearing is not so good. I'll call my mother." He was about to shout out when Su Li and Aunti Ko came out from the hut. They both stopped short when they saw Takagi.

"Commandant! I wasn't expecting you, yet."

"Obviously. There's been a change of plan."

Su Li spoke evenly and coolly, "Xin. Go and prepare the evening meal.

Mai Lee squirmed out of Takagi's grip and scurried away toward the kitchen adjacent to the dormitory just as Number Seventeen exited the hut. "Number Twenty-Six! Mai Lee!"

Mai Lee froze as the girl ran up to her and threw her arms around her. The others looked on in horror.

Mai Lee lowered her tones, "You must be mistaken. I am Xin, Yuan's cousin."

"Why? Why do you pretend…?"

"Please…" whispered Mai Lee. "Stop!"

"Why? Why do you pretend?" protested Number Seventeen. She halted abruptly, as she saw Takagi striding toward them. "Oh, no…"

Takagi grabbed Mai Lee and pulled her round to face him. He wrenched off her cap, tilted up her face and studied it. Then turned back to Su Li, "So! Keeping the best for yourself. That's not very friendly, is it?"

"But…" protested Su Li.

Takagi roared at Rin who was standing at ease close by, “Seize her.”

Rin acknowledged, “Hai!” He marched toward the girls, handcuffed Mai Lee and roughly pushed her forward to a waiting vehicle.

“No, what have I done? I didn’t mean… I’m sorry…” whispered Number Seventeen.

As Mai Lee was pushed away she turned her head and looked back at them in abject sorrow before she was loaded into the back of a military jeep.

Auntie Ko stepped forward boldly, “You have just taken the adopted daughter of Madame Jong. You have no right…”

“I have every right. Maybe I’ll take this Madame Jong, too, or maybe yourself. My soldiers could do with a bit of fun.”

Auntie Ko fell silent and looked down. Takagi studied Number Seventeen. He shouted back at the foot soldier, “Take this one, too. I have plans for them both.”

Rin returned for Number Seventeen who was also cruelly hurried away. Takagi followed them to the jeep. He called back, “Until Thursday, Su Li.”

Takagi bowed and walked back to the jeep, which now had its engine running. He climbed in and hit the dash with his baton as a signal to proceed and the jeep moved off.

Yuan shrieked and tried to run after the vehicle, “No! Mai Lee! NO!”

His mother pulled him back, “Hush! There’s nothing you can do.” They watched defeated as the jeep gathered speed and raced up the rough track.

They stood silently in hopeless despair. No one quite knew what to say. Yuan eventually broke the silence, “What now?”

“I’ll alert Madame. She may be able to help,” said Auntie Ko.

“I won’t give up until I get her back,” stressed Yuan.

“I should never have allowed myself to be so stupid over a young girl. Forget her, Yuan. There’ll be another.”

“No, mother. There’s no other. Even you felt Mai Lee was different. She is special.”

"You are right, young man. She is different. Mai Lee has spirit and harbours hope in her heart. All we can do now is pray," sighed Auntie Ko.

***

The ride in the back of the jeep was bumpy as it climbed the hilly track from the village to the uneven road. Number Seventeen clung to Mai Lee and sobbed her apologies. "I am so sorry. I never meant for anything to happen to you. I didn't know. You were always kind to me. Forgive me, please."

"It cannot be helped. Stop crying. You never know. It may not be as bad as we think."

"They are Japanese. I have heard of their cruelty. It is worse than at the Orphanage. What will they do to us?"

"I don't know… I just don't know, but I tell you one thing. They will not win. They may steal my body. They will try to steal my mind, but they will not steal my soul."

The jeep hurtled round a bend throwing the girls in the back around like sacks of grain. "We won't have any bodies to steal if they keep driving like this," squealed Number Seventeen.

"Somehow I think we'll have enough of a body left to serve their needs," muttered Mai Lee.

The jeep travelled a further five miles and pulled up at a sentry box, where a guard stood on watch. He stopped the jeep and looked in at the Commandant and his officer. They exchanged words and the sentry peered in the back and saw the two girls. He barked a question at the Commandant who growled an answer and they all chortled together.

The sentry waved the truck through and it travelled inside the compound and stopped outside a row of huts. Mai Lee and Number Seventeen fell silent and huddled together, uncertain of their fate. Their future was now in the hands of the Gods.

CHAPTER FIFTEEN

The Japanese

Takagi studied the two very still and silent teens in front of him. He walked around them menacingly. He stopped by Mai Lee and tilted her head up with his baton and examined her face. "You have the look, one I like. You must grow your hair again. You will be far more attractive with long hair. Other than that, you are fresh faced," he prodded her breast, "And nubile. We must free you from this bandaged constraint." He considered her further, "Yes, you will suit me very well." Mai Lee shuddered in revulsion. "What is your problem, child? Are you afraid? Oh, I do hope so. It makes it much more rewarding if you are in fear of me. Much more exciting."

The Commandant turned his attention to Number Seventeen and ordered her, "You, turn around. Let me look at you."

Reluctantly, the young girl turned around slowly.

"Yes," he said appreciatively. "You are younger. I like them younger. Firm and tight." He laughed, "I don't like your number, I want you to have a name. There. That's civilised of me isn't it? I will call you Miko. That is Japanese for crimson truth. And if you are not obedient or truthful then you will have to be punished. Then you will see the crimson of your blood."

Takagi looked from one to the other and rubbed his chin thoughtfully. His voice took on an oily quality, "Nothing to say?" The girls didn't move. "Good. I don't want complaints. A guard will see you to your quarters."

Takagi strode to the door and threw it open as the newly named Miko shivered miserably. Mai Lee paced her arm around the younger girl and drew her into her. She raised her face defiantly; her expression was stony and her chin jutted out proudly. She whispered to Miko, "Do not fear. I will *not* be abused by this man. I will die first."

Miko raised her head, “Oh, Mai Lee, I fear for you. That attitude could cause your death… if we submit at least we have a chance,” she murmured back.

Takagi shouted down the corridor, “Guard!”

Footsteps were heard and a young soldier, Hiroto Sato, appeared at the door. He stood to attention and saluted Takagi.

Takagi looked suspiciously at the twenty-two year old in front of him, “Gocho Sato, I thought you were piloting freight to Borneo today?”

“There’s some problem with the supplies, Sir.”

“Hmm. I see.” He pointed to the two girls, “Take them to their cell.”

Hiroto clicked his heels and bowed in acknowledgement.

“On your feet,” barked Takagi.

The girls scrambled to their feet and Hiroto marched them away. They reached the back of the building where there were cells in rows facing each other with a corridor in between. Some were occupied, some were empty but the girls could not see inside at the occupants. Most of them were lying still on their prison beds or on the stone floor. It was impossible to see if they were men or women.

Hiroto removed a bunch of keys from the wall, which jangled alarmingly and he opened one of the vacant cells. He gently urged the girls inside and Mai Lee glanced at him in surprise. The young corporal’s tone was not harsh and he was not abrasive or rude in locking them up. Once they were inside, he locked the cell, replaced the keys and marched back up the corridor.

Mai Lee stared around the sparse space. “It’s better than the orphanage,” she said trying to cheer up Miko. “At least we have room to stand.” There was a wooden plank covered with a thin blanket, which served as a bed. It folded out on chains from the wall. Mai Lee sat on it. “You wouldn’t want to be fat and sleep here,” she smiled trying to make light of the situation. “It would break.”

In the corner was a filthy and foul smelling bucket, and although empty it was clear that it served its purpose as a lavatory. There was also a small rickety wooden upright chair, which Miko sat upon. On the wall, someone had scratched grooves. Clearly a previous inmate had been counting the days. The same wall was decorated with blood spatters and initials. The girls fell silent as they surveyed the uncomfortable scene.

Mai Lee poked her head out through the bars as far as she could and peered up and down the corridor. There was a clock on the wall by the hook, which held the keys to the gaol. The place smelled unsavoury and wreaked of despair and fear.

Mai Lee tried to squeeze herself through the bars but although she was petite there was not the room to get her head and shoulders through. She studied Miko, "You may be able to get out."

"Why would I want to do that?"

"You could get the keys and open all the cells and we could escape."

"And go where? How would we leave this place? It's too heavily guarded. Then, if we were caught we would be beaten to death. I have heard the Japanese are capable of great cruelty. We would be killed, beaten to a pulp."

"Maybe not," said Mai Lee. "There may be a way. If we have enough time…" she looked down and fingered her pendant when female shrieks and screams of agony, from the top of the corridor, interrupted their conversation. They both looked up and exchanged a worried glance.

"What's that?" asked Miko, with trepidation.

"I don't know," whispered Mai Lee. "But, I don't like it."

There was another blood curdling scream, then silence.

"What do you think will happen to us?" asked Miko.

"I don't know," sighed Mai Lee. "I honestly don't know."

The door at the top of the corridor was flung open. Rin, the soldier who had put the two of them into the jeep that had brought them to camp appeared. He dragged a young woman who was barely conscious along the floor. Hiroto followed behind. His face registered extreme distaste, which did not go unnoticed by Mai Lee although Rin had a cruel curve to his lips revealing his enjoyment of the young woman's appalling condition.

Rin ordered Hiroto to fetch the keys and the corporal unlocked the cell next to the girls who ensured now that they were silent and their eyes cast down. Hiroto opened the door and Rin threw in the young woman and snorted derisively. He ordered Hiroto to lock her up before he turned and marched back up the corridor.

Hiroto lingered and moved to the girls' cell. He looked in at them and spoke softly, "You are in grave danger here. Both of you. Please, don't annoy the Commandant." Hiroto gazed sorrowfully at them and shook his head before he turned and walked away.

He stopped as Mai Lee called, "Wait!"

The young corporal walked back slowly. He put his fingers to his lips as a warning, "Keep your heads down and say nothing." He strode back up the passageway and out through the door, which clanged shut and bolted behind him.

"What do you make of that? asked Mai Lee in a whisper.

Miko managed a tentative smile and said hopefully, "It seems we may have found a friend."

The woman in the next cell groaned painfully and rolled over on her cot. She drew her knees up to her chest in a protective foetal position. Mai Lee rose and tried to see in at her through the adjoining bars. The female coughed a little and blood dribbled from her mouth. She put her hand up to her face and Mai Lee gasped. The woman's hands were thick with blood and still dribbled blood spots onto her soiled tunic. Some of it had congealed down her arm. Her hands had obviously bled profusely. Mai Lee took a closer look she could see that the woman's fingernails had been ripped out. Mai Lee stifled a rise of bile in her throat. She jumped off her bed and regurgitated the little in her stomach into the bucket, which sat in the corner.

"What is it?" asked Miko, her voice quavering with emotion.

Mai Lee just gestured with her hand before another choking mouthful of stomach acid hit her mouth. She vomited again.

Miko pressed her face through the bars and saw what had upset Mai Lee. "Oh no, how terrible," she murmured as she saw the atrocious injuries that had been inflicted onto the prisoner. It was clear the woman had been tortured horribly. Cigarette burns adorned other visible parts of her skin on her legs. It was a sickening sight.

Miko took Mai Lee's hand and they sat together on the cot and tried to speak to the unknown woman in the next cell. They kept their voices low and hoped not to attract any attention from the guards they knew were situated behind the door.

"Hello… lady…"

The woman coughed and replied hoarsely, "My name is Peizhi…"

"Peizhi. I am Mai Lee and this is Miko. What has happened to you?"

"What has happened to me every day since I was put in here."

"They've tortured you," said Miko in a tiny voice, "The beasts." A tear rolled down Miko's cheek. She looked at Mai Lee, "Oh, my sweet friend, What have I done to you? You were free and now you're… you're … and it's all my fault." She choked back a small cry.

"Enough," commanded Mai Lee. "What's done is done. You were not to know." She turned back to Peizhi who tried to sit up. Her face contorted with pain and they could see her bruised puffed up eyes and broken nose. There were cuts and lesions on her cheeks, which looked as if they had been made by the edge of a blade, other marks were clearly made by a fist. Mai Lee was sure the woman had a splintered cheekbone. "Why? Why have they done this to you?"

"Why? Because they enjoy torture. They like to inflict pain. To them it is just sport. We are nothing more than animals, meat to them to do with as they wish."

"There must be a reason?" questioned Mai Lee.

"To begin with, yes… I know the next time they take me away they will kill me. But, I will tell them nothing… ever."

"But, *why* are they doing this?"

Peizhi coughed and some more blood frothed from her mouth, "They believe there is a traitor among their men. That I am involved with political activists."

"And are you?"

Peizhi paused she looked at Mai Lee through the one eye that wasn't completely closed and bruised black. "It's best you don't know any more," she sighed. "Then you can't tell. You can't be hurt... Listen, if you get a chance, get out and get away. Anyway you can. It would be better for you to be shot while escaping than to endure this living death, this hell."

"How? How can we get away?"

"Hiroto. He'll help you if he can." Peizhi stopped as she heard the door at the top of the corridor unbolt. She lay down weakly on her bed and drew her knees up once more like a child. She attempted to suppress her yelps of pain and discomfort.

Mai Lee and Miko cuddled together and fell silent. They turned away from the next cell and feigned sleep as the door opened and Rin marched down the corridor to the cells. Mai Lee could hear the aggression in the soldier's stomp of his feet.

Miko and Mai Lee scarcely dared to breathe as they heard the jangle of keys and clang of the adjacent cell door, where Peizhi pretended she was still unconscious.

Rin opened Peizhi's cell. He kicked her battered body and dragged her up by her hair. She whimpered pitifully, clearly in great pain. He yanked her out and savagely pulled her up the corridor. Mai Lee and Miko didn't dare move. They waited until they heard the door shut and bolt securely. Only then did they open their eyes. They looked sorrowfully at each other. Their expressions were filled with helpless despair. It was then that Mai Lee began to wonder if she would ever get out from this situation. Would she ever see the light of day and feel the sunlight on her face again? She filled with a profound feeling of helplessness and frustration but in her heart she told herself not to give up. She determined she would find a way to leave this place, somehow.

CHAPTER SIXTEEN

Getting her back

Outside the big house Auntie Ko left the ox and cart. She was running along the dusty road to the big gates. She puffed and panted with the exertion, fumbled with the stout key to the heavily ornate wrought iron gates and struggled to open them. She entered the garden and relocked the entrance to the mansion and hurried up the terracotta slabbed path, through the ornamental gardens, past the Orchid House and in through the glass doors.

Once inside Auntie Ko leaned forward and put her hand on her knees. She blew loudly and sighed as she straightened up, "Oh Mai Lee, how I could do with your help to ease my aching back," she said to herself.

She hurried down the corridor and hastened to Madame's rooms and knocked loudly, praying that Madame Jong wasn't drunk or high on Opium. But, Auntie Ko had to admit that since Mai Lee had gone Madame had been sober, remorseful and had not touched any drugs.

"Enter," called Madame and her words were not slurred. Auntie Ko went in and rushed to her mistress who was serving tea, "Would you like some?" smiled Madame.

Auntie Ko nodded appreciatively, "Just what I need after that run. Thank you."

Aaryn poured a cup of Jasmine tea and the two sipped their drinks ceremoniously, "Now tell me what has happened?"

Auntie Ko launched into an explanation of what had transpired at the village and the taking of Mai Lee. "It was awful. The Japanese Commandant threatened me, threatened us. He said if we interfered he would take us for comfort women or slaves in Death Houses."

"He was bluffing. He wouldn't dare. The scandal it would cause would make the Japanese even more unwelcome on this island … We have to get her back. At least now we know where she is."

"I fear for her. That man had a cruel twist to his mouth I fear he may beat her."

"Then there is nothing for it. We must go to the Japanese camp and demand that they give her back. After all she is mine by law. We have the papers to prove it."

"But, Madame after they threatened me and you…. If you dare question them…"

"There must be a way around this. Think…" Aaryn sipped her tea and screwed her face up as she thought. She stood up and spun around, "I've got it. What if we inform Manchu?"

"Oh, Madame, I don't think that's wise. He did try to rape the girl, after all."

"Men are beasts and Manchu is no exception. Believe me, I am under no illusion. But there has to be something we can do. Think, Auntie Ko, think…"

***

Yuan sat miserably in the hut while Su Li made a pot of stewed chicken and rice. She placed the bowl in front of him, "I've told you. Forget her."

Yuan picked at his food. He shook his head and raised his eyes to his mother, "Please, Mother. I can't. We have to do something. Please." He looked pleadingly at her.

"And what of the other girls? No one will be paid. They're coming for them Thursday. We have two days. There'll be other girls for you."

"There's only one Mai Lee."

"Oh, Yuan. You know I find it hard to resist your pleas. Let me think."

"Mother, you are not going to be paid for these girls. We will all be out of pocket. These girls are being abducted, stolen. Do not spend as much time on them… We can get them ready before they come, ahead of time, and we can try and help Mai Lee. She has been taken from us and belongs to Madame Jong. That must mean something."

Yuan pushed his bowl away and Su Li studied the sadness in her son's face. "All right. We will see what we can do."

Yuan leapt up and threw his arms around his mother's waist and swung her around, "Oh, thank you, thank you."

"Don't thank me yet. We have to employ cunning and I don't even have a plan yet."

"But you will. I know you will."

***

Mai Lee and Miko cuddled together in a fitful sleep. Outside it was still dark but the hour was early. It was before dawn and the air was still. It was hard to relax and Mai Lee tossed and turned.

A rushing of wind reverberated around the cell. It was the sound of many wings flapping and the metal bars of the girls' prison seemed to shake. Mai Lee came to full wakefulness and leaned up on one elbow. She knew what to expect and that this was a sign and she was not afraid. Miko remained asleep, seemingly undisturbed.

Mai Lee watched carefully as specks of light floated like dust motes but swirled and organised themselves into a recognisable face. Mai Lee gazed in fascination as Lily's features manifested before her.

"Lily! Am I going to die? Is that why you're here?"

"No, Mai Lee." Lily's voice was like a song on the wind uplifting and magical. The light she emanated caressed Mai Lee's face and made the girl feel warm and loved. "I am here to tell you to trust your instincts. All is not lost. You do have friends, friends who are working to help you and even a Japanese friend."

"And Miko?"

"Don't worry about Miko, what will be, will be."

Mai Lee frowned, "I don't like the sound of that," she protested.

Miko is not your concern. Trust me."

Further conversation was interrupted by a bloodcurdling scream, which rang out from the top of the corridor that was so chilling that it could turn blood to ice and was followed by the sound of a woman sobbing. There was another agonised shriek that was abruptly cut off followed by silence.

The painful cry from the woman sounded as if it had been dragged from the pits of hell itself. Mai Lee had never heard such a tortured utterance, not since the death of the fat guard, Lien. The brittle noise like a splintering note on the scale that could explode glass had blasted Lily's image into a thousand pieces and her face vanished from view. Miko awoke.

"What was that?" she whispered fearfully.

"I don't know. But, I believe it could be our neighbour."

"Peizhi?"

Mai Lee nodded and the two girls peered in the gloom at the neighbouring cell, their eyes slowly getting used to the dark.

Miko gazed at Mai Lee with sad eyes. "Is that to happen to us?"

Mai Lee put a protective arm around the girl and drew her closer as the door to the corridor opened quietly and Hiroto with the stealth of a cat padded toward their cell. He put his hand on the bars and placed his fingers of his other hand on his lips to warn them to keep quiet, "Hush now. No one must hear or see me speak with you. Peizhi is dead."

Miko shuddered and sobbed inwardly. Mai Lee looked questioningly at the young soldier, "But why?"

"I told you, she was accused of being involved with activists. But you… you should not be here. It's wrong."

"What can we do?" asked Mai Lee.

"And why are you telling us, this?" questioned Miko.

"I don't know… to both questions… not yet. But, I will…"

"Why should we trust you?" said Miko sullenly.

Mai Lee turned to Miko and whispered, "Because Lily said so, and she's never been wrong before."

Miko's breathing juddered and she nodded, "I believe you. I trust Lily."

Hiroto looked from one to the other, "Who is Lily?"

"It's best you don't know. You wouldn't believe me anyway."

***

The dusky pink hues of dawn broke and bled in the sky looking down on the seaside village where the fishermen went out to sea with their fishing nets and boats. The sun began to rise and sent its golden shafts to dance on the gentle swell of the water. The crafts bobbed past the Chinese Slaver moored up in the warm silky water and travelled out from the safe bay to the fishing grounds beyond the breaking surf to set up their nets.

A few women of the village sat on the harbour wall, their feet stroking the sand as they repaired the nets. Their hands were hard with calluses from manual work. They looked across suspiciously at the recently landed orphaned girls who played on the beach enjoying their newly found but limited freedom unsuspecting of what was to befall them.

Yuan stood and watched them. His face was immobile almost dead without his usual animated expression. He appeared lost in thought. It seemed his mind was someplace else and not focused on his job. Suddenly he snapped his fingers and grinned. He lurched forward and began to stomp up the beach a purpose in his step. He hastened up the track toward his mother's dwelling, where he stopped and listened.

Raised voices came from inside Su Li's hut where the Captain, Kaci and Barra argued. The Captain, a tall man with imposing features, rubbed his bristly beard and threw his hands up in fury and glared at the women. "I have not come all this way and spent all those days at sea to just give my cargo away. I have a big stake in those girls."

Su Li raised her hands, "We must all calm down," she said trying to reason with them and quiet the retorts that sprang from the other women's lips. "None of us like what is happening. We all need paying. It is just as much our livelihood as yours. But, that Japanese Commandant will just steal them from us. Worse still he expects us to spend time and money preparing them as we would for sale. It's iniquitous."

"It certainly is. I have customers waiting. They have

placed orders and paid a deposit, we need this consignment," said Kaci.

"Me, too," added Barra. "And we don't have enough of them, the girls need replacing as a number from the previous sale are already dead."

"What do you suggest we do?" said Kaci sarcastically, "Abduct some from our own villages?"

"No, no... but what do we do?" said the Captain in despair. "Arrgh!"

Yuan burst into the hut and they all turned to stare at him. He waved his arms excitedly, "I've got an idea! It could just work."

"I'm listening," said the Captain. The other women turned expectantly, a glimmer of hope in their jaded eyes.

"We need to enlist the help of Madame Jong and you, Captain need to play a role. Can you act?"

***

At the big town house another argument was in progress. Auntie Ko was pleading with Aaryn as they sat in her room, "You remember what it was like to be in love? You must do, I'm sure you do. Think Madame. Be sympathetic and understanding."

"That girl is rightfully mine, bought and paid for, my slave, my daughter."

"And she has been stolen by the Japanese. Come, Madame you have always been very persuasive. You have a way with words. Maybe you *can* get her back, or maybe get another to take her place."

"Yes, well... maybe Mai Lee is a little too pretty, but I do like her. Where would I get anyone to make me laugh like she does? Where would I find anyone so good at massage?"

"Another girl could be taken and trained. Another girl wouldn't be so attractive to the master. And you, you would be playing cupid to Mai Lee, she would love you forever."

"Yes," Madame Jong preened herself and picked up her fan and began to flutter it. "Maybe she would visit. Ah, but this is all make believe. I am a woman. What can I do?"

“If we go to the camp what is the worst they can do?”

“As you have pointed out… Throw us in a cell and leave us to rot….”

Auntie Ko paused and a gleam entered her eye, “But not if we are accompanied by a man.”

“What? I don’t understand….”

At last, Auntie Ko had Madame’s attention and she lowered her voice. Madame leaned forward to listen and a smile began to play on her lips. “I have spoken with the young man, Yuan.”

“The one in love with Mai Lee?”

“Yes. That he is prepared to risk his own life to save her tells of his love for her. You are a woman with a big heart. You understand young love and the pain it can bring.”

Auntie Ko played on Aaryn Jong’s vanity and Madame bowed her head in understanding. “Of course I know the anguish of love and being slighted. What is this plan?”

“Downstairs there are those who wish to meet with you. They will explain further.”

“Then let us go.”

Auntie Ko smiled and fawned over Madame as she followed her from her suite. “Oh, Madame your kindness is well known. News of your great goodness will spread far and wide….”

CHAPTER SEVENTEEN

Hopeless and helpless

The door at the top of the corridor loomed large like a sentinel blocking goodness and truth. Mai Lee felt as she stared at it that it was the gateway to doom and she shivered. She hugged Miko to her. There was comfort in human contact.

Mai Lee could smell death and feel the terror of souls passed who had been incarcerated in these cold prison cells. She felt a flutter of fear as she heard the bolt grind back and the door unlock. The noise echoed uneasily in that gravely insensitive space.

Mai Lee closed her eyes as the door clanged open and soldier booted feet marched along the wooden passageway between the cells. Her heart beat faster as they stopped outside her cell door. She heard the jangling of keys and finally opened her eyes. Rin in all his cruel glory stood there a sneering smirk on his face. He unlocked the cell door, which ground open, iron on iron, of the base scraping the frame. He moved quickly and grabbed Miko wrenching her from Mai Lee's arms. In vain, she tried to stop him but he smacked her hard across the face with the back of his hand and sent her sprawling. Blood trickled from the corner of her mouth. She flew at him again and he kicked her hard then flung her to the stone floor. He dragged the whimpering Miko out and fastened the cell door once more.

Still Mai Lee dared to speak, "Stop! Where are you taking her?"

Rin stopped abruptly and snorted, "You dare to question me?"

Mai Lee stifled the pain of the kick and pressed again, "Where? What is going to happen to her?"

Rin laughed unpleasantly revealing his brown nicotine stained teeth, "Why not? Why not tell you? It will give you much to think about while you sit and wait for *your* turn."

“What do you mean?”

“She’s for the Commandant. He will have her first… then the rest of us will have our turn.”

“But, you can’t…” protested Mai Lee.

“Oh, but we can. We can do anything we like. Don’t you fret now, you won’t be left out. Your time will come.” He snorted and began to march away, then stopped and turned calling back to her in icy tones, “He has something special planned for you… very special.” Rin laughed in glee and pushed Miko in front of him. “Move!” The young girl cried out in anguish and Mai Lee felt lost and forsaken, believing she had been totally abandoned and she did something she had never done before, she prayed. She prayed to the Buddhist gods that she had learned about with Auntie Ko and feverishly fingered her talisman as if it would save her. She looked up at the dirty ceiling and cried out, “I will not be taken. I will kill myself first, do you hear, God? Do you hear? If I am to be damned then I will be damned by own hand.” And she started to look around the barren cell for something, anything she could use. Her attention was taken by the stinking, latrine bucket filled with slops. Around the wooden pail were metal bands screwed into the wood. One of them was slightly loose. She studied the metal handle and how it was affixed. This she decided was a better proposition.

She wrinkled her nose in disgust at the smell and worked at the joins trying to winkle them free. It could make a good weapon and if she could sharpen the end on the stone floor and she would have something to cut into her veins and allow her life’s force to flow away and thus deny the Japanese their prize. They could do what they liked with her once she was dead. She would not give them the satisfaction of submitting to their cravings by being alive. She whispered, “Oh, Lily. I may be with you sooner than you expect and we can fly to Rainbow valley together.” Mai Lee worked at the bucket until her fingernails tore and her hands bled.

Mai Lee struggled on. Hours passed. Time was eaten away by her stubborn refusal to give up. In her mind, failure was not an option. Although weaker physically Mai Lee’s spirit was growing stronger and as each second fled her determination rose within her like an emerging warrior. Her exclamations were lonely in the hot silence. No other prisoners spoke or looked to see what she was doing. The few other inmates were so indoctrinated in fear and hopelessness that they had given up on life. Mai Lee finally managed to loosen one side of the handle but she let it fall when she heard the stout door that she perceived as the entrance to hell being unlocked and opened.

Mai Lee scampered back to the cot and lay there still. She tried to control the ague that beset her body by biting her lip to try and enforce an end to her miserable shivering and feelings of desolation.

Rin's boots clicked smartly on the wooden floor as he dragged a sobbing Miko back to the cell. Her battered, bruised body was raw with cuts and lesions. The inside of her thighs were crimson with congealed blood. The young girl was too weak to stand or walk and Rin hauled her along the floor as he would a sack of grain.

Rin opened the cell door and threw in the failing child. He tossed in what was left of her clothes, which Miko attempted to clutch to her violated body. Mai Lee rushed to her side and held the terrified girl whose plaintive cries tore at Mai Lee's heart. She shouted after the vicious soldier, "I hope you rot in hell!"

Rin stopped, threw back his head and roared in demented glee. He laughed and laughed as he retraced his steps to the door. Mai Lee could still hear him laughing as the door clanged shut and was bolted again.

***

Takagi sat in his office and looked at the odd collection of people before him. He studied the over painted face of Madame Jong, the plump woman, who had accosted him at the seaside village and the Slaving Captain who was now dressed as a very wealthy Chinaman. "So, why am I honoured with this delegation?" His sarcastic tone was not missed by the others but they glossed over it and proceeded with the pleasantries associated with Japanese culture and bowed deferentially.

Finally, when the Captain spoke, he altered his voice to sound more imposing and he looked imperiously at the Commandant. "I come here directly from Sir Shenton Thomas' residence."

"So, you have high connections?" said Takagi unimpressed.

The Captain cleared his throat, resisted the urge to spit on the ground and spoke again. "As I said, I am from Sir Shenton Thomas. I am required to inform you that you have violated our laws and grossly overstepped the mark."

Takagi rose from his seat and moved to the front of his desk. He eyed them up and down and leaned back to perch on the edge of his heavy officer's desk and he placed his baton to the side of him before responding, "The British Governor knows it is unwise to interfere in Japanese affairs."

The Captain pressed on in his pretended role, "You are but a small platoon, here, Sir and not officially welcome."

Takagi pursed his lips. He chose his words carefully, "What you fail to realise is that we intend to nurture the whole of the Malays. We will be the saviours and guardians to you all. It is our intention to eventually release you from British control. It is in your interest to look after us"

"That's as may be. But, if I may put it delicately, we all need friends on this island and upsetting important, influential people will damage your reputation severely," responded the Captain.

Takagi stood and eyeballed the Captain, "Are you threatening me?"

"No. But what you fail to understand is that this girl, Mai Lee, is our adopted daughter. We are one of the wealthiest families in Singapore. Our family could be very useful to you; especially with your future plans. Surely that will be of benefit? You can see the sense in that?"

"Hmm!" Takagi considered what was being said. The group knew the Commandant could not afford to alienate people of influence who could help his cause on the island. "What of the other girl?"

"She's of no consequence."

"And my consignment of comfort women?"

"The Assistant Financial Secretary, William Allmond Coddrington Goode implores you to relinquish your attempts to procure these women."

"But my men's needs are of paramount importance. Away from home they need to satisfy their physical needs. And we need clean girls. We don't want ones likely to infect our men."

"This is all understood. But in Singapore we have clean brothels."

"But the men are expected to pay," countered the Commandant..

"I understand these women were to be sent to Borneo for the use of troops there?"

"They are… they were…"

"Then I'm sure new arrangements or negotiations can be made again. The Governor is aware of your needs. He is also aware of the needs of the local community and financial implications to the local economy if the girls are effectively 'stolen'. You understand?" The Captain played his part beautifully, "My wife is singularly distressed. She has taken the girl under her wing and is teaching her to read. She has been lost since Mai Lee has gone."

"Then why was she hiding out at the village?" demanded the Commandant.

The Captain rolled his eyes, "There was an unfortunate incident at the house where some vagabond wastrel gained entry when the gate was unlocked. He attacked Mai Lee and no one heard her cries for help. She managed to escape and ran. She ran back to the village, as it was the only other place she remembered. The woman known as Su Li knew that the retribution that would fall on her, if Mai Lee was taken by your men, and in her wisdom she decided to disguise her to prevent such a thing happening until she could safely return the child. By that time, my wife's maid and companion," he indicated Auntie Ko, "had arrived to take her home but you refused to listen and took her away, abducted her."

The Commandant returned to his seat and the delegation waited.

***

Mai Lee tenderly covered Miko with the thin blanket and comforted her until Miko's whimpering sobs had finally subsided. Mai Lee was horrified at the assault on her friend and hot, stinging salt tears streamed down her cheeks. She brushed them away in defiance, "We must pray. Pray and hope for our rescue and redemption," urged Mai Lee.

Miko looked up at Mai Lee with sorrowful, soulful eyes and whispered weakly, "Pray? We're the forsaken and the damned. No one can help us. No one ever has or ever will..."

Mai Lee raised her eyes to the dank, damp ceiling with metal rafters and poor lighting. The faint semblance of a smile played on her lips. "No, Miko. No." she said stroking the little one's hair. "There are good people out there; ones who won't let us die."

Miko coughed and bright red frothy blood spewed from her lips, "Maybe for you. But for me... I fear it's too late." Her voice became weaker.

"Hush, don't say that. We have guardian angels who want to help."

"Not me."

"Yes!"

"No, I am one who's been forgotten... No one will remember me."

"No, no! See..." Mai Lee stopped.

The grim forbidding prison cell filled with a radiant light and Lily in shining clothing appeared before them. A sense of peace fell over the girls.

Miko rallied and gasped in awe, "The light... it's beautiful..."

Mai Lee was stunned, "You can see her? You can see Lily?"

"I see her, she is holding out her hands to me, and my mother... my mother is with her..."

The skin on Miko's face became almost translucent, the

lesions and marks seemed to heal and her expression changed to one of perfect serenity. Her eyes lit up with love as she stared past Mai Lee and into the distance as if there was a road or tunnel before her.

Mai Lee was aware of the subtle change in Miko and called out, "No, Miko, don't die! Please..."

"At last... No more suffering, no more bad things, only peace." Miko's last words faded like a whisper on the breeze as the ethereal golden light faded and Miko's last breath was drawn and she died in Mai Lee's arms.

An anguished cry ripped from the belly of Mai Lee as she held Miko's body tightly to her and rocked her back and fore. A disembodied male voice came from the cell opposite, "We're all going to die. She's in a better place. No more torture."

Mai Lee sobbed, "I don't care. She was my friend." She slumped forward on the floor and continued to cradle Miko's body. Her face became smeared by blood and she hugged her friend even closer. She remained like that for what seemed like hours. The numb reality of what had happened set in and Mai Lee lost all colour from her face apart from Miko's blood spatters and she became perfectly still. Her eyes wide and distracted, blankly staring ahead.

The door at the top of the passageway unbolted and Hiroto walked toward the cell. He quickened his step when he saw what appeared to be two still bodies locked in each other's arms and muttered sorrowfully under his breath, "No. Oh God, no!"

He unlocked the cell and seeing Mai Lee blink and the rise and fall of breath in her chest he tried to pull Mai Lee to her feet, "Come. We must go."

"No. I won't leave her."

Hiroto tried to untangle Mai Lee's hold on Miko. He urged, "Come. There's nothing you can do. She's dead. Leave her."

"To be thrown to the dogs or pigs to eat? No. I will not!" Mai Lee's body became stiff and leaden, and unresponsive. She refused to move.

"Please, you must come with me, to safety. Before Takagi changes his mind. You are to be freed. Please, hurry."

Reluctantly, Mai Lee relinquished her grip on Miko's body and released her. She stood up. Her legs were filled with pins and needles so long had she sat in one position. She struggled to make her legs work and stamped her feet on the ground. "Promise me," she begged. "Promise me her body will be respected."

"I can't promise that... You know I can't," implored Hiroto.

"Then I'm not going." Mai Lee stubbornly sat down on the cot.

"Then you, too, will die like Peizhi and Miko. Is that what you want?" Mai Lee looked at him in confusion. He stretched out his hand, "Come with me, now and live."

The disembodied voice called out, "Go. Take your chance and go, for here is only death."

Mai Lee took a deep intake of breath and as she did so she seemed to be filled with courage and fire in her belly. She boldly followed Hiroto but a mantle of sadness rested on her shoulders. As he locked the cell door, Mai Lee turned back and blew a kiss at Miko, "Rest in peace, sweet friend."

Hiroto helped her up the corridor, which seemed interminably long. His footsteps echoed in that foul space as he marched forward on the harsh wooden floor. They reached the heavy door and Hiroto whispered, "Now don't complain. Keep quiet and only speak when spoken to. We want nothing to go wrong. Understand?"

Mai Lee nodded reluctantly and Hiroto opened that forbidding gateway leading from hell and death. She stepped through and Mai Lee took a deep breath. They walked through the attending guard's office and outside into the warm evening air. Mai Lee stumbled down the wooden steps and again she could hear the cicadas hum and feel the gentle light of the moon on her face. It was then, more than anything she realised that she wanted to live and that she would live."

"Where are you taking me?" she finally managed to whisper.

"Your foster mother and father have come for you."

Mai Lee stopped in fear, "No..."

"Yes, and your aunt. Believe me you will be safe and you will get out of here. Do not argue and do not speak. Show your pleasure at seeing Madame. The Commandant must believe you want to go home or the same fate will befall you as Miko."

Mai Lee wrestled with her thoughts. She didn't understand. Was she being rescued to be the Master's plaything or to be punished by Madame? Mai Lee shuddered and faltered.

"Don't stop now. Walk proudly. You are someone from a family of great wealth. Act like it. We are almost there."

Mai Lee hesitated and then as if imbued with Lily's courage she thrust her shoulders back and lifted her head and kept pace with Hiroto. They arrived at the steps of another building. Outside stood an oxen and fancy cart.

"Take a deep breath," advised Hiroto. "We are here."

They walked up the steps and Hiroto knocked on the door politely. Mai Lee heard the Commandant's voice instruct them to enter and fractionally, just fractionally, Mai Lee had the thought that she had been betrayed that she was being taken to Takagi for him to use and abuse her. But, she had no time to say anything as Hiroto opened the door and she saw Auntie Ko, her foster mother and she blinked in surprise at the man recognising him as the Captain and not Manchu. The door closed behind her. There was no going back now, no opportunity to run.

Auntie Ko smiled, "Mai Lee. We are so relieved to see you."

Aaryn Jong opened her arms, "My daughter, Mai Lee. Come to me."

Mai Lee was bright enough to know she should not show fear and she allowed herself to be enveloped in her foster mother's arms. Auntie Ko joined in the embrace and kissed the top of her head.

The Captain questioned the Commandant, "What has happened to my daughter? Why is she covered in blood?"

"It is not her blood," said Hiroto but that of her cellmate who was punished for disobedience.

Takagi grinned humourlessly, "Prisoners have to be disciplined." He added, "Your daughter has not been hurt."

Mai Lee bit back the retort that readily sprang to her lips. She said nothing.

"Is this true, Mai Lee?" asked the Captain.

Mai Lee nodded dumbly, afraid to speak in case her words ran away with her and she would ruin this attempt to rescue her.

"You see, " said Takagi. "No harm has been done."

"We must get you home, " said Madame and hugged Mai Lee to her. She whispered in her ear, "I am so, so sorry."

Aaryn Jong and Auntie Ko moved to the door, which Hiroto opened. They walked toward the cart, which seemed a very long way away.

Takagi spoke again. He addressed the Captain, "You'll not forget your promise? To help us in our cause?"

"Of course," said the Captain glibly. "Am I not Manchu Jong? I am a man of my word." He bowed at the Commandant and followed the others to the cart and climbed aboard. Mai Lee sat between her foster mother, who put a protective arm around her, and Auntie Ko. Mai Lee snuggled into her as any daughter would.

The oxen plodded out of the camp past the sentry box and onto the open road. Aaryn Jong heaved a sigh of relief. The Captain warned, "We are not home and dry yet. Come Madame, we must get you home."

Mai Lee stuttered out her thanks, "Thank you, for rescuing me. I never thought I would feel the air on my face again."

"Oh, Mai Lee. I am so sorry. Can you ever forgive me? I did you so much wrong. It will never happen again."

Auntie Ko added, "Madame has not taken a drink since that fateful day. She has found it hard to live with herself."

"I have, Mai Lee. I have turned my life around. Please come home and stay with me. You can live in my quarters with me. Manchu need never know that you are here."

"You know that's not possible," interrupted the Captain. "We have to adhere to the plan."

Mai Lee said nothing. She was still in shock and the fact that she had left that miserable prison she could still not quite believe.

The oxen plodded on.

Before long they reached the neighbourhood of Madame Jong's house. Reluctantly Madame and Auntie Ko alighted and Mai Lee stepped down. She hugged them both. "Thank you," she whispered.

"Promise me you will come and see me," asked her foster mother. "I will never treat you badly again."

Auntie Ko added, "I'm sure if it is remotely possible that you will, won't you, Mai Lee?"

Mai Lee nodded, "You have been good to me. With you both has been my happiest time. I will not forget you."

The Captain urged, "We must hurry. Rest assured, Madame I will find an excellent replacement for Mai Lee. And you must be on your guard."

"Do not worry, Captain. My house can be made into a fortress. I will not be caught unawares again by Manchu or the Commandant."

"And the Japanese army?"

"That is another matter, but I always have a means of escape as Auntie Ko knows." Aaryn Jong hugged Mai Lee once again. "You are my little dove. You will always be my little dove." Madame Jong sniffed back the tears that threatened to fall. She turned away swiftly, "Come, Auntie," and proceeded into the house.

Auntie Ko stroked Mai Lee's face, "I will miss you, Mai Lee. You and your velvet hands."

Mai Lee hugged Auntie Ko fiercely but said nothing. She didn't trust herself to speak. She climbed back into the cart and the Captain turned the wagon in the street and they began the trek back to the seaside village.

Mai Lee allowed her thoughts to drift back to that place of horror and the death of her little friend. She retreated inside herself to a place of safety from which it would be difficult to emerge.

CHAPTER EIGHTEEN

Escape

Mai Lee shivered not with cold, for Singapore nights were far too hot and sticky for that, but with the trauma of all that had happened and the loss of her friend. She sat in silence, her eyes wide and staring. Still in her protective mind state she was only half listening to the conversation that was taking place around her.

Su Li was waving her arms in front of the Captain's face, "You're not listening to me. It won't be long before they realise that they've been duped and you're not Manchu, Madame Jong's husband. They will know you have no authority and will be back."

The Captain slapped his fist into his other palm, "The girls must be moved to another location. Somewhere much safer."

"They're almost ready. We have the place. I shall soon have them ready to move. Now, what of Mai Lee?" asked Su Li.

"She stays with me," said Yuan firmly.

"That could be tricky," said Hiroto. "The Commandant will be back, of that I have no doubt. He will demand that she accompany him to Borneo. He has singled her out as his."

Su Li studied the young Japanese Officer and shook her head in confusion, "Why are you doing this? Why are you helping us? To what end? What advantage?"

Hiroto hung his head in shame before he lifted it up and met Su Li's gaze, I have witnessed many things no man should ever see. I need to put right what I can. If I don't, I will not be able to live with myself."

Su Li continued to hold Hiroto's eyes. The silence between them continued until the others looked at each other uncertainly. Eventually she spoke, "You believe in Karma..." It was a statement not a question. She paused again before decisively announcing, "We move the girls tonight." She glanced at Mai Lee, and indicated her, "She can't stay here."

"She can't return to Madame Jong. That will be the first place they'll look," said Yuan.

"Ah, yes, Madame Jong. She demands another girl, and rightly so."

"That can be arranged," said the Captain. "See to it. I'd rather lose one than all twenty two."

"I'll stay with Mai Lee," confirmed Yuan.

"Yuan!" exclaimed his mother in horror.

They were at an impasse and each looked at the other. Mai Lee was slowly coming to awareness and she began to listen more carefully to what was being said.

Su Li snapped her fingers, "We move the girls tonight. Now. No matter what Yuan says," and she glared at her son, "Mai Lee cannot stay here. The Japanese will rip the village apart to find her. No one will be safe and no disguise will protect her."

"But she can't return to Madame Jong, either," protested Yuan again, squaring up to his mother.

"Find another girl," ordered Su Li.

They stood uncertainly all eyeing each other in their confusion. The young Japanese soldier spoke, "I can help."

"You? How?" asked Su Li, anxious for any crumb of aid.

"I have friends in the Cargo Airbase where the supplies come in," replied Hiroto.

"But how? How is that possible?" demanded Su Li.

The Captain raised his eyebrows as realisation dawned and he gasped, "You're an activist! You're one of those they seek."

"Information I know could be useful to you. I am admitting or denying nothing. You may or may not be aware that I am a fully qualified cargo pilot. It would have been my job to fly your consignment of women to Borneo."

"How does this help us?"

"I think I can smuggle Mai Lee out of Singapore to start life anew in America."

"America? How?"

"You will have to leave the details to me. I haven't worked it out yet, but I will."

"What about me?" asked Yuan.

"You are not in danger," Hiroto answered.

The Captain looked from one to the other. "Enough talk. We need to move now. We have wasted too much time already. If we don't hurry we will regret it and all of us might see the inside of that hell hole, which Mai Lee was imprisoned in."

"And what of Mai Lee?" pressed Su Li.

Hiroto turned to leave, "For now, let her go with the others to the safe house. I can stay no longer. I have to go before I'm missed."

"Wait! When will you come?" asked Su Li.

"I don't know, but I promise you I will come. I will not let you down. Do you know Wei Fong the herbalist in Chinatown?"

Su Li nodded, "Yes. I have seen the shop."

"I will leave word there. He's a friend and won't betray us. Now, you must move quickly." Hiroto left the hut rapidly. The others looked after him and then galvanised themselves into action.

"Captain you get changed and get the carts. I'll organise the girls. Yuan, you come and help. Mai Lee, stay here."

Mai Lee suddenly was shaken from her numb silence and became alert, "No, I'll help."

Su Li stopped, "All right, come with me. You can help me with the girls, too."

Mai Lee followed Su Li to the dormitory and stepped inside the door, where twenty-two girls quickly assembled as if on parade. They all looked attractive and clean with shining hair and makeup.

Su Li eyed them up and down. She nudged Mai Lee, "Select a girl for Madame. Go on while I speak to them."

Mai Lee walked down the line of teenagers and looked at each one. She selected three and murmured to Su Li. "It is between these three, may I talk to them?"

Su Li nodded agreement and Mai Lee took them to one side. One girl was surly in her responses and Mai Lee asked her to return to the line and spoke with the other two. A few minutes later she took one girl by the hand and made her stand out of the line whilst the other returned.

Su Li spoke, "There has been a change of plan. We have to get you girls out safely before the Japanese return. You do not want to be taken by them. They can be very cruel. I want you to change into your new clothes. Yuan will collect your cotton sarongs. As soon as you are ready wait outside the hut where we will take you to safety.

The girls needed no second bidding. They hurriedly changed and Yuan collected their sarongs and placed them in a big basket ready for washing and took them up to the main house whilst the other girls waited outside.

Su Li looked at the girl Mai Lee had selected, "Why her? Why this one?"

"She is versed in the art of massage and will help Auntie Ko and Madame. She is also keen to learn and Madame will teach her to read and write. She will educate her. She should stay in the cotton sarong it is more modest and she will get new clothes when she is collected."

"Hmm." Su Li nodded approvingly. "Very well. Tell the child what she is to do."

Mai Lee continued, "You will be going to a beautiful house and have pretty things. You will eat well and wear lovely clothes. You must be deferential and praise Madame. Tell her she is lovely, and that you want to be like her. Be nice to Madame. She is basically good and has a kind heart. Auntie Ko will help you. She suffers with bad bones and back. Massage does her good. You will help her. I envy you. My life was good when I was there. Do not anger Madame and stay out of sight of the Master. What is your name?"

"Liling," answered the girl and lowered her eyes.

"That is good," said Mai Lee. "It is a good sign. Your name means white jasmine tinkling. My best friend was Lily, her favourite fragrance was jasmine and when she laughed it was a sound like tinkling bells. Good luck. And give Madame my love and to Auntie Ko, also."

"Yes," said Su Li. "Outside you will see Pa-Ru, one of the

women who dressed you, and she will take you to Madame Jong. You do not know how lucky you are. Go quickly now."

They left the hut where Pa-Ru took Liling by the hand and hastened her to a cart that was laden with pottery. They climbed aboard. Liling clambered inside one of the large pots and hid. They set off quickly to a neighbouring village where Liling could be hidden until it was safe to travel. Pa-Ru had the perfect place with an underground chamber beneath her house where she hoped Liling could hide unobserved.

The rest of the girls changed and were now in their silk cheongsams. They all looked pretty and well cared for. They walked in a crocodile to the top of the village where another cart was waiting. They were ushered quietly toward it and ordered aboard and told to be as quiet as possible. The girls sensed the urgency and their excited whispering ceased and they sat on board in silence and the cart pulled by oxen took the trail that led from the beach.

The wagon rumbled up the stone track and out on the road. There was no sign of Pa-Ru and Liling. They had long gone. Mai Lee prayed that they had escaped safely. The night was dark and the moon obscured by clouds, which afforded the group cover from prying eyes but also lent an air of gloom to the fleeing party of young women.

The cart plodded on into the night and along the mountain trail when Su Li pulled the oxen up short and they stopped. "What? What is it?" asked Yuan.

"There. In the distance. See? There are lights and they are headed this way. I don't like this. I don't like it at all." She passed the reins to Yuan and whispered to the girls. "You must remain quiet and still unless you want us all to be appropriated by the Japanese. I swear it is them."

The girls remained quiet and concerned at Su Li's worried expression. Mai Lee sat silently in front between Yuan and Su Li biting her lip. Su Li turned back to her son. "Turn off the trail. Now."

The sound of Jeep engines could be heard approaching on the night air.

"But, Mother, the ground is treacherous. What if we lose a wheel?"

"Better than losing a life," she snapped back. "Move it. Now, come on."

Yuan turned the cart off the track. They proceeded slowly toward a wooded area. Su Li jumped down and took a branch from a tree and brushed at the track where they had turned off to hide the wheel marks. The wagon moved on into the wooded area and Su Li dashed back after the cart. "Okay, Girls get out and scatter into the woods and hide. Remain very, very quiet and as still as possible. Yuan try and hide the cart. Mai Lee, stay close to Yuan. Hush now everyone. Go!"

The girls climbed off the cart and scattered as instructed. They hid throughout the woods and undergrowth and waited fearfully. Su Li remained until Yuan had moved the wagon and oxen to some sort of cover and she stayed to ensure that it couldn't be seen from the track. Satisfied that no one and nothing could be seen she stepped back stealthily from the path. Minutes later a military jeep came hurtling past followed quickly by another and then, two more.

Su Li stepped from the shadows and watched as the jeeps sped toward the village and the beach. The jeeps converged and stopped with their lights blazing as the Japanese jumped out of their vehicles. Mai Lee crept out from cover and watched in horror as she saw the soldiers shouting and invading the homes of those in the beachside village.

***

Takagi screamed to his men who searched each hut before them. They lit paraffin torches, which blazed furiously against the night sky. The flames danced and jumped fiercely. The soldiers shouted viciously and rousted the occupants from each humble dwelling who tumbled in confusion into the night air.

A number of men swarmed to the dormitory. They turned over the beds, smashed the cooking pots and mirrors. The little bits of furniture were tossed and splintered. They were intent on wreaking havoc throughout the small beach settlement.

An elderly woman was beaten out in her nightgown and

stumbled in front of Takagi who swung his baton at her and savagely flailed her. She fell sprawling onto the stone track, her face bloodied and swelling with angry welts.

The woman's daughter emerged and shook her fist at Takagi as she rushed to her mother's side. Takagi slapped her across her face and she fell across her mother who was now unconscious. Other elderly residents were treated in the same manner and the villagers thronged together in fright as the Japanese surged through the village.

One of Takagi's men, the cruel Rin, grabbed a young girl who timidly came out after her mother and father. He wrenched her arm and twisted it behind her back. She squealed in pain and was rewarded with a sound slap. The soldier laughed, ripped at her nightclothes and stripped her naked. The girl cowered by a palm as Rin bore down on her and dragged her to the beach. Her screams were heard all the way up the track and carried to Mai Lee and the rest of the girls, who shivered miserably in fear together.

An old man attempted to square up and face the onslaught of the Japanese military. He was shoved roughly to one side and the soldier tossed his blazing torch onto the roof of the hut. The straw quickly caught alight and the flames greedily devoured the dry thatch and rapidly spread to the wooden struts supporting the porch and veranda. Soon the dwelling was engulfed in crackling, roaring flames.

The smoke drifted up and sparks from the blaze flew across to the next hut, which in turn set that one alight. This seemed to instil in the men a kind of firebug frenzy as they torched the rest of the beach houses and razed them to the ground. The villagers were left broken spirited and homeless.

Takagi's fury was more than visible as he fumed and barked orders at his men and abused the inhabitants of the small community. He screamed at his men, "Find them! They have to be here somewhere. They can't have got far."

The soldiers scrambled over the surrounding land and shouted obscenities in their anger and frustration. They examined every bush and shrub, and each cave in the cliff side, which was on the shoreline.

Rin left the ravaged girl cowering on the sand and began

scrambling back up the trail. He spotted something in the sand and looked more closely before he shouted to his Commandant, "Here! Cart tracks, I am sure of it. They are headed this way," and he pointed at the winding trail.

Takagi stamped his foot in anger and smashed his baton at an old woman hobbling by, "Quick! To the jeeps. We may catch them yet. They can't have got far."

The platoon raced back to their vehicles and they began to move up the steep trail.

***

Su Li retreated back into the woods with Mai Lee and they crouched down next to Yuan. She whispered to her son, "See. We were right to leave."

"But, what do we do now? We can't stay in the woods. They will be looking for us. If we set off now we are bound to be caught," replied Yuan.

"Hopefully, they will move on. Then we can get away."

"I agree with Yuan, it's too dangerous to stay here," murmured Mai Lee.

"We must remain quiet until they have passed," insisted Su Li.

"I don't like it," said Yuan. "I'm moving further in, come on."

"We have no choice but to stay. Hush now," ordered Su Li.

They moved further into the undergrowth and Yuan shinned up a tree to keep a lookout.

They waited.

Soon they heard the sound of the soldier, Rin, who grunted in difficulty as he struggled to negotiate his way up the rough shingle track. He stopped and examined the path at the side and noticed the place where the cart had turned off into the undergrowth. He pointed his rifle in front of him and pushed his way into the woods through the thick vegetation and stopped to listen.

The others hardly dared to breathe. All that could be heard were the distant shouts of soldiers and the rumble of Jeep engines as they started up and began to climb the hill. An ox suddenly snorted and Rin's head whipped round toward the sound. He crept further into the trees and could just discern the shape of the cart in the gloom. He approached tentatively a smirk creeping over his face.

Yuan braced himself as the soldier approached. He waited until Rin was directly beneath him and dropped down from the tree and took Rin by surprise. He floored Rin, and before the soldier had a chance to cry out he swiftly grabbed his head and snapped his neck. Rin fell forward his head twisted awkwardly to one side. Yuan's heart pounded and his hands trembled at what he had done.

Su Li scrambled across. She checked for the soldier's pulse, "You've killed him!"

Yuan picked up the soldier's rifle and nodded. "Yes, I had to. There was no other choice… I'm sorry." Su Li shook her head in despair.

Mai Lee stared at the soldier and even in the gloom she recognised him. She turned her haunted distraught eyes on Yuan. "Don't be sorry. He deserved it. He was the fiend who helped to destroy Miko. I'm glad he's dead."

"Oh my…." Su Li stopped in weary despair. She pulled Yuan down to crouch with her and Mai Lee, as the lights from the jeeps drew nearer and their engines rumbled louder. They waited hardly daring to move or breathe but fortunately the vehicles roared past without stopping. They raced back up the trail and disappeared into the night.

Su Li heaved a sigh of relief. "Thank goodness, they have gone on." She glanced down at the body at her feet, "What do we do about him?"

Mai Lee looked at Yuan who shrugged and said, "When they realise they're a man down, they'll be back. You can count on it."

Su Li shot her son a look, "And if they do and they find him. Then they will be looking for you. We have to get away and move on."

"What do we do with him?" asked Yuan looking at the dead soldier.

"I'm not sorry he's dead," said Mai Lee. "He was cruelty

personified. We have to hide him or place the body in such a way that it looks like an accident," said Mai Lee. "I'll help you."

"How do we do that?"

"I have an idea." Mai Lee glanced around her. This place is full of creepers and vines. What's over there?" She pointed through the gloom to the edge of the trees.

"A sheer drop, why?"

"If we can make it look as if he was searching through here and got caught up in the trailing vines and creepers, they may believe he lost his footing and hung himself."

Su Li nodded, "It may just work. It's worth a shot. Come on."

Yuan hoisted the soldier onto his back and carried Rin through the woods. They reached the edge by the cliff and Su Li twined an ivy vine around his neck and arm. Yuan ensured the creeper was twisted tightly around his throat He placed the rifle over his shoulder, which swung precariously. They secured him and dropped his body over the side, which dangled and his foot caught in a crevice. He had made it look as if the man had stumbled and lost his footing. "What do you think?" he asked.

His mother and Mai Lee nodded, "It looks possible. Now, let's thrash around and make it look as if he struggled in the undergrowth," suggested Mai Lee.

The trio flattened patches of brambles and bushes before retracing their steps. They urged the girls back aboard the cart and slowly trekked out from their hiding place and moved back up the trail.

"I only hope there is no one lying in wait up there," said Su Li.

"We must pray," said Mai Lee and fingered her lucky talisman.

The cart sauntered on and it was with great relief they arrived on the road to see the way was clear. Su Li took a loose branch from the roadside and as the oxen plodded on she swept the signs of the wheel tracks in the dusty ruts and evened them out. It appeared as if no one had passed this way.

They trundled on. The girls were hushed and quiet. They knew the danger they were in. They continued on and moved through a mountain pass away from the main towns and civilisation and out to a mountain village where Barra and Kaci lived and had set up a place to receive the girls.

They eventually reached a stone track that didn't need sweeping and Su Li clambered back onto the wagon. They turned off to another mountain trail, which led to the village. The place appeared deserted and no one came out to see.

Barra and Kaci were waiting for them and led them to a cave in the hillside. The girls dismounted and were given fresh water to drink and offered some fruit whilst Su Li talked with her partners.

Yuan and Mai Lee sat on a bench quietly and listened to the proceedings.

"First we must assemble them and look them over," said Kaci.

Su Li clapped her hands, "Girls. I want you all to line up and face this way. Come on, everyone."

The girls reluctantly rose up from the sand and shale floor and got into line. Kaci and Barra walked up the line and around the back of them studying each girl. Kaci took notes after asking each girl their name.

Barra grumbled, "I don't like this. I dislike rushing things. The girls were made ready too soon and my clients are not yet prepared to take them. There are too few rooms available."

"Then they will have to share," said Kaci sagely.

"Clients prefer privacy. They don't want observers," argued Barra.

"We have no choice. It's sell now or lose the deal," explained Su Li.

"And the girl for Madame Jong?" asked Barra.

"All done. We picked a fresh-faced fourteen-year-old, Liling. Pa-Ru has taken her to Madame."

"Liling?"

"That's what she wanted to call herself."

"Unless Madame changes it," said Kaci.

"No matter. That is none of our concern, now," answered Su Li.

"What about her?" asked Kaci pointing at Mai Lee.

"She's my responsibility now," affirmed Su Li. "Go!" She clapped her hands and the girls filed out of the cave obediently with Barra and Kaci leaving Su Li, Yuan and Mai Lee. Su Li sighed, "Well, my son. It seems you have your wish."

"Yes, Mother. But I promise you when we are safe I will find a way to bring you to us. I promise," he said again.

"For now, we must wait. Wait and pray that we won't be caught."

"Once that beast of a soldier is found. I fear they will try and hunt us down," said Mai Lee.

"Unless they believe it is an accident. We may be lucky," said Yuan hopefully.

Su Li raised an eyebrow. It was clear she thought that unlikely.

CHAPTER NINETEEN

Back at the camp.

The jeep convoy arrived back at their base camp and unloaded. Takagi strode into his office and alerted the guards. He was in a furious temper and needed someone to vent his anger on. He barked an order, "Bring me Miko. I have use for her now."

The two guards, Bing and Dao exchanged a look.

Takagi glared at them, "What? What is it? Why are you looking so stupid?"

"Sir," faltered one. "The girl, Miko, she's … she's…"

"She's what?" he roared.

"I'm sorry, Sir," said the other. "But… but Miko is…" he hesitated and he physically flinched as he said the next words, "She's dead."

"What? How?" he bellowed.

"Um… Rin… he used her and…"

"Yes?"

"She was nearly dead after he finished with her. She died in her cell."

Takagi was almost apoplectic. He shook with rage and the air between him and his men was frighteningly charged with fury and fear. Finally, he spoke and his voice was icy, "Get Rin in here, now!"

"Sir!" The two soldiers ran outside and hurried to the barracks where Rin slept. They hammered on the door and walked in on the platoon that had raided the village. The men were relaxing, playing cards and smoking.

The first guard, Bing, asked, "Rin? Where is he? The Commandant wants to see him now."

The soldiers shrugged their shoulders and looked around. After discussion it emerged that no one had seen Rin since the incident on the beach.

"No," said another. "He had his way with a village girl

and then went in search of the whores to serve the units in Borneo."

Then Dao asked, "How did he travel back? Which vehicle?"

The men looked blankly and finally agreed that he had not travelled in any of the convoy. "No, He started up the track to look for signs of where the girls had gone. He was the one who alerted us to the hill trail, I'm sure," said one.

"But he didn't get back in any of the jeeps?"

The soldiers shook their heads, "No." They turned away ending the conversation, resumed their game of cards and the guards left the hut.

The guards walked slowly back to Takagi's office. They argued amongst themselves as to who was to tell the Commandant what they had learned. Eventually, they stopped and Dao pulled out a coin and tossed it in the air. Bing called, "Tails." His face fell as the head side of the coin was revealed. Dao heaved a sigh of relief. They approached Takagi's office and entered reluctantly.

The Commandant turned as he heard the knock and the door open. He looked questioningly, "Well?"

"I'm sorry, Sir," muttered Bing. "Rin has not been seen since the beach raid."

"Who did he travel back with?" demanded Takagi.

"No one. No one has seen him, Sir."

"Do you mean the man has been left behind?"

The guards shifted their feet uneasily but said nothing to their commanding officer.

"Then you had better return. Go. Take one of the drivers and return. Take Hiroto Sato with you. He speaks the local dialect." Takagi opened the connecting door and bellowed, "Sato!"

Hiroto came running and saluted his Commandant. "Sir."

"Go with these men to the fishing village. Rin has been left behind. Stupid man. Bring him back to me. I have much to say to him." Takagi's voice was brittle and sour as if he had sucked on a lemon. "Let's hope he is on his way back."

Takagi dismissed the men by turning his back on them and they exited quietly from his presence.

***

The soldiers boarded a jeep and left the camp. They drove speedily through the country roads toward the village but passed no one on route. An hour later they had reached the mountain track. Bing paused the engine at the top of the hill and the men gazed down.

Hiroto could see the dying blaze from the village, "Did our men do this?" he asked quietly.

"I heard some boasting of it. Yes," replied Dao. "They seemed proud of it."

Hiroto frowned, "It is wrong. We are trying to make allies of these people not enemies."

Bing added, "I agree. Who knows what kind of a welcome we will get but we have to investigate."

The trio moved on cautiously down the hill to the harbour and beach. They saw distressed families huddling together and villagers valiantly trying to douse the blaze. Hiroto ordered the others, "Come let us help."

The soldiers got into line with the villagers and carried water to the huts that were still alight. They worked tirelessly to the amazement of the villagers. One old man ventured to speak, "It was your men who did this, why are you helping now?"

"To prove to you that we are not all the same."

"Why did you come back?"

"One of our men is missing. We were sent to find him."

The old man shook his head, "We have seen no one. After you left we have spent all this time trying to put out the fire."

Hiroto put a hand up to wipe the soot from his face now slicked with sweat. "Someone must have seen something?" he asked the assembled villagers.

"What did he look like?" asked the old man.

Bing began to describe the soldier, "He was tall and thin with a scar on one cheek."

"His skin was none too good," added Dao.

A woman stepped forward, "It sounds like the beast who raped my little girl."

Hiroto's heart sank. He hated this destructive and evil behaviour. "I am sorry," he said and he meant it. "Have you seen him?"

"I hope he's dead and he rots in hell," said the woman and spat on the floor.

The old man continued, "If that is the one you seek he went on foot up the mountain trail searching for tracks.

Hiroto bowed and clicked his heels, "I am sorry for these actions and the hurt caused to you. Come men."

The trio tried to help clear up as much of the debris as they could. They scavenged among the wreckage and salvaged what could be saved dragging it out onto the sandy paths.

The moon that had flirted with the clouds in the night sky showed its face and bathed the villagers in its gentle light. It shone so brightly that the cliffs could be seen and a shout went up from one of the villagers. "There! What is that?"

They could see something dangling from the cliff. Hiroto called to Bing and Dao and they returned to the jeep and travelled back up the mountain trail.

As they turned the bend in the track they saw where the brushwood had been disturbed and stopped the jeep. They ventured into the undergrowth and further into the woods calling Rin's name.

Hiroto struggled through the vines and creepers to the cliff edge and looked down. He saw clearly the body of a man in uniform with his rifle lodged in a crevice. The man had a length of vine twisted around his neck and was caught fast on the side of the cliff.

"My God!" exclaimed Bing. "He hung himself."

"I don't think so," said Dao. "It seems he was chasing something and got tangled up in this stuff, fell and broke his neck."

"And that's what we will tell the Commandant," said Hiroto. "Come help me haul him up."

The three men struggled to pull up the dead weight of Rin whose foot seemed to be caught. He came free with another wrenching tug and as they strained to heave him up, his body smacked against the cliff face causing further injury. They finally pulled him up over the edge and laid him out. Hiroto checked for a pulse whilst Dao untangled the creepers from around his neck and body.

"What about his rifle?" asked Bing.

Hiroto looked over the edge, "It's a bit risky to retrieve it. We don't want to lose another man."

"I can do it," said Bing. "I used to dig guano from hillside caves inaccessible by any other means. Trust me."

Hiroto looked doubtful but didn't stop him. Bing tied a stretch of a liana vine around his waist. He gave one end to Dao and disappeared over the side of the cliff. He shouted up, "When I tug on the creeper, pull me up."

Bing swung out from the rock face and abseiled to the rifle. He winkled it free from its prison and slung it over his shoulder. He tugged on the vine and Dao and Hiroto held fast to the creeper and pulled as Bing started to walk up the rock face. His cheerful face appeared at the edge and Hiroto stretched out his arms and helped the man back to safety.

"I've not done that in a long time," puffed Bing.

"And we better get back with him," said Dao. "Help me get him up."

Rigor mortis had not yet set in and Hiroto assisted Dao in lifting Rin until Dao could throw the dead man over his shoulder and they made their way back to the jeep. They tossed his body in back and climbed aboard.

A feeling of trust had built up between the men and they talked uneasily about what they had seen. "No wonder they hate us," said Bing. "Raping that girl. It could have been my sister. I am from a village just like that at home."

Dao agreed, "Those people had done nothing wrong. In my eyes Rin deserved to die."

"You better not let the Commandant hear that. He will court martial you. I'm sure," said Hiroto.

"Then our story will be the same," said Bing, "We searched the village and the woods for Rin until we found him. He must have had an accident. Agreed?"

"Agreed," said both Hiroto and Dao, as they sped back the way they had come and made for camp. Again they passed no one and when they rolled up at the sentry box they were waved through. They pulled up outside Takagi's office.

Hiroto looked at the others, "Thanks for your help. You go about your business. I'll see to this."

"Are you sure?" asked Bing secretly relieved not to have to face the Commandant.

"Quite sure. But if questioned I hope you'll back up our agreed account."

"Absolutely," affirmed Dao. "Good luck. I wouldn't want to face the Commandant's wrath."

They got out of the jeep. Dao and Bing walked off to their barrack. Hiroto dusted himself down and walked smartly up to the office door and knocked. He heard the surly call to enter and opened the door.

Takagi was seated at his desk on the phone. He waved Hiroto to stand and wait until he had completed his call.

"Of course, Sir. You will be the first to know… Yes, if this consignment escapes we will take the next. Meanwhile our men can go on a few raiding parties to the outlying villages… No, Sir… we won't make ourselves unwelcome. I shall see to that… Yes, Sir. Thank you, Sir." He replaced the receiver and rose from his seat striding toward Hiroto. He picked off some leaf detritus from his uniform and a piece of ivy. He eyed Hiroto critically, "Well? Have you found him?"

Hiroto nodded, "Yes, Sir."

"Where was he?"

"On the hillside."

"Where is he now? Why isn't he here?"

"His body's in the back of the jeep."

Takagi gasped incredulously, "He's dead? How?"

"It looks like an accident. He was tangled up in some vines. It seems like he broke his neck."

"Or someone broke it for him," said Takagi suspiciously. "What of the villagers?"

"No one had seen him. They were busy putting out fires…" The rest of the sentence was left hanging accusingly.

Takagi dismissed this with a snort, "The men were just having a little sport."

"At the expense of the villagers and their homes."

"Do you have a problem with that?"

Hiroto backed down not wanting to attract any undue attention to himself, "No, Sir. It's just they didn't see anything as they were otherwise occupied. One witness saw him leave the beach and walk up the trail where he entered the woods."

"And?"

"We searched the area thoroughly. It was dangerous with heavy undergrowth and pits covered in leaf mould. It appears in the darkness he stumbled over the precipice and was hung up with the vines. Death would have been instantaneous."

"Hmm." Takagi paused as he considered what he had been told. "A pity. The man was due for a severe reprimand. Get rid of the body. Thank you. That will be all."

Hiroto clicked his heels and bowed deferentially before turning and leaving the office. He sighed in relief as he emerged into the night air before he jumped into the jeep and circled around the camp to the back where he enlisted the help of two other men to help him with Rin's body and dig a grave.

The ground was like iron and he had to pound it with a pickaxe to loosen the soil. The other two dug at it creating a small trench into which they rolled Rin's body before covering it over. There was no ceremony, and no tears shed. Rin had not been a popular soldier in camp.

The other two walked away and Hiroto checked his watch. He wiped a hand across his dirt-streaked face. It was time he ventured into Chinatown. He had to alert Wei.

CHAPTER TWENTY

Chinatown

The sun was up and bright in the sky beating down on the colourful sights and sounds of Chinatown. Exotic aromas filled the air from various street vendors selling delicious smelling food from little carts and restaurants. The streets were bustling with market stalls selling everything from fruit and vegetables to trinkets and fabrics. Market traders plied their wares and rickshaws travelled the roads picking up passengers and ferrying them to bars and brothels that hid in the back streets. The place was vibrant and alive.

Painted ladies stood on corners and encouraged men into conversation. They slipped away to dark alleys passing the many imprisoned songbirds that hung in cages outside each establishment. Old men smoked clay pipes and sat drinking and playing cards. They talked and ruminated watching the world go by.

Su Li dressed in a simply patterned sarong, disguised as a flower seller, hurried along the dusty road with her basket of posies. She walked quickly down the bustling streets. Her eyes searched the names on the shop fronts as she explored Chinatown, as if for the first time. She pushed through the busy throng of street traders past the vegetable stalls and food carts, reluctant to stop for anyone who spoke. Ahead she saw a Chinese Herbalist Emporium. She studied the name, Wei Fong and she entered the premises, a bell clamoured in her wake as an elderly Chinaman with a thin, wispy beard stood up behind the counter.

She looked about her and ensured the shop was empty before she spoke, "Wei Fong?"

The old man asked, "Who wants to know?"

"I have to know, is it you?"

"You are in much of a hurry, I can see. I am Fong. How can I help?"

"I am Su Li."

There was a flicker of recognition in the old man's rheumy eyes, "Yes?"

She took a deep breath and looked around once more before she dropped her voice and whispered, "Hiroto sent me. Hiroto Sato."

"Well, why didn't you say so? Step this way." He opened the hatch in the counter and led her through to a back room filled with jars, miniature scales, pestle and mortars, phials of liquid, containers of dried herb and fresh plants and mixing pots. "Sit. Sit down," and he offered Su Li a chair. He glanced across at a young man who was busy preparing a potion. "Deshi, leave that and go through and watch the shop."

The young man bowed and slipped quietly through to the front of the shop. Fong called out. "The window displays need dusting."

"Yes, Grandfather."

Sue Li again looked around her. The old man noticed, "You have no need to be afraid. You are safe here. No one will betray you."

"I have left my son and his girlfriend in a café. Hiroto said you would help them to escape."

"And I will. I have a timetable of Hiroto's flight schedule. We are to pick a time when they can safely get to the airfield and he will smuggle them out. We need to work out how to do it, but first we need the date that will give you enough time. Here." He passed Su Li two sheets of paper. "One is the schedule, the other a map. On the back of the map is a message from Hiroto. It is written in your local dialect in case it gets into the wrong hands. If you get my meaning?" Su Li nodded her acknowledgement. "And another thing you read every third word for the interpretation, you understand? It will help you if the message gets into the wrong hands."

Su Li smiled and a rush of gratitude poured from her lips as she hid the papers in her basket of posies, "Thank you so much. If I need anything else I will come back."

"Please do. I am happy to help. Now go and be careful. Remember not all are whom they seem."

"Yes, thank you."

Su Li followed Fong out of the shop and went back into the bustling street.

***

Inside a street café in Chinatown Yuan and Mai Lee sat at a table, sipping tea, disguised as students. They wore shorts and shirts and carried canvas bags, which contained study books. More tomes were on the table together with notepads and pencils. They spoke in hushed tones and kept a wary eye out on the street.

Two Japanese soldiers, part of Takagi's platoon, strolled past the café and peered in. Mai Lee froze and knocked one of her books onto the floor. She stretched down to pick it up and Yuan flicked through the one in front of him and began to read avidly.

Mai Lee did the same and to an outsider it appeared that they were both studying and making notes. The soldiers took a cursory look around at the occupants and moved on. Mai Lee and Yuan heaved a sigh of relief. She whispered, "That was close."

"We have to be careful and on our guard."

"I know. No relaxing for us. Anything could happen."

"We have to pray that mother will be back soon. Only then will we know what we're going to do."

"We can't sit here forever. People will get suspicious," said Mai Lee.

"We'll be fine as long as we keep buying tea."

"How much cash have we got? Do we have enough?"

"Yes, mother gave me some money from our savings. It should last a couple of days. We will be all right for a little while, especially if we're careful."

"And when the money's gone?" asked Mai Lee.

"We will have to think again."

"I'm sure Auntie Ko would help us. And Madame."

"That must be a last resort. They may be watching for you there," said Yuan.

"I can always work. I can do massage."

“And have it lead into something less than wholesome? No. I will not risk you like that. Let’s hope it won’t come to that.”

“I will do what I have to do to survive. I have two good hands I can work, cook, scrub and clean,” said Mai Lee valiantly.

“I know… What’s the time?”

“About five minutes since you last asked.”

“Mai Lee, I’m getting worried.”

“Let’s have some more tea. Calm down.”

“And what? Pray.”

“If we have to.”

***

Su Li hurried back the way she had come. She spotted the two soldiers that had paused at the café and hesitated. Her nervous behaviour was such that they stopped and started to watch her.

Su Li began to stop people in the street and tried to sell her posies. She turned her back on the soldiers and approached anyone who passed, “Buy my flowers? Pretty flowers for sale, Missy? Sir?” The passers by ignored her and shook their heads as they went about their business.

Su Li wandered into a bar and again tried to interest customers in her flowers. She hardly dared to look at the soldiers but became aware of one of them pointing at her and saying something to each other. The two men crossed the road and began to walk toward her. Su Li panicked as she saw them come nearer. She pulled out the papers and thrust them into the top of her sarong, dropped her basket and ran. The soldiers shouted and chased after her.

Her breathing was heavy, she was not used to running so fast. In blind fear she raced down a side street and darted into a fabric and dress shop. She slipped behind a rail of clothes and waited. The shopkeeper eyed her curiously.

The soldiers ran past. Their boots echoed loudly on the concrete outside. Su Li waited and breathed a sigh of relief. She jumped when the shopkeeper spoke to her.

"The Japanese are no friends of mine. How can I help?"

Su Li turned her haunted eyes on the kindly Chinaman. "Those soldiers… they destroyed my village, ravaged young girls and put us all in fear of our lives. They stole my livelihood. They are after my son's young lady. They want to steal her."

The Chinaman nodded, "I have heard many similar stories. How can I help?"

Su Li looked at her attire. "They will recognise me now in this. I need somehow to change my appearance."

"Well, you've come to the right place. Let me see…" The old man appraised Su Li and selected some garments. "Here, try these. We must try to change your appearance from a market trader or artisan to a more up market personality."

Su Li took the clothes and went into the changing room. First, she removed the papers from her sarong and looked for somewhere to hide them. In the corner of the small cubicle was a container holding parasols. Su Li folded up the papers and hid them at the bottom of the stand out of sight. She felt she could retrieve them safely later as she didn't want to entrust them to a stranger. Satisfied that they were unlikely to be discovered she changed out of her clothes and put on a fine silk chemise and trousers. She hurriedly restyled her hair and successfully transformed herself.

She came out of the cubicle and the old man studied her appreciatively. "Yes, you look very different now. I doubt they will recognise you."

"How much is all this? I am afraid I will not have enough to pay for them."

The old man considered and said, "Give me your cotton sarong and what you can afford. We will forget the rest. I don't want to deplete you of your money, but I, too, have to make a living."

"I understand." Su Li handed over her simple dress and fished in her purse for some dollars and gave the Chinaman some cash.

The old man nodded and accepted her offering. There was no bartering or haggling. "Good luck to you. May you safely go on your way."

"Thank you, thank you."

The old man waved away her thanks and added, "If ever you need a friend. You know where I am."

Su Li bowed and left the shop looking very different in her upscale outfit. She looked warily about her and strolled elegantly down the road and back to the hustle and bustle of the main street populated with rickshaws and market stalls.

***

Back in the café Yuan and Mai Lee are getting worried. Yuan glanced at the clock on the wall and Mai Lee bit her lip anxiously.

"She should have been back by now. Something must have happened to her."

"Don't say that." Mai Lee looked about her and peered into the street, "We can't stay here all day."

"No. I know. I'll settle up."

"Then what? Where do we go?"

"We'll find the herbalist ourselves. Then we'll know for sure if mother has been there."

Yuan walked to the till at the counter and paid their bill. He collected his bag and took Mai Lee by the arm, "Come. Let's go."

They walked purposefully along the street hunting for the Herbalist Shop called Fong. There were many to choose from but none of that name. They pressed on their way.

Showing more confidence than they felt they presented an assured picture of two students engaged on some assignment or student task. They stopped on a corner and were about to turn into a side street when Mai Lee tugged at Yuan's sleeve. "There, opposite, look."

Yuan stared ahead and saw the Herbalist emporium with the name Wei Fong.

"How strange!"

"What?"

"The name. It is almost the same as the orphanage I grew up in. That was Wing Fong. It is a sign I am sure of it. Come."

They hurried across the road. "You wait here and keep

watch, in case you see mother or any of the soldiers. I'll go inside. If it is a trap you will have the chance to escape."

Mai Lee nodded and her eyes searched the road. There was no sign of Su Li or the Japanese. Yuan entered the shop. The bell rang loudly announcing his presence. Mai Lee stood and waited. She caught sight of a uniformed man on the corner of the next block and feigned interest in a market stall selling beads and trinkets. The trader pounced on her interest and began hassling her and pressing her to look at various oddments and offered her bargain prices.

Mai Lee tried to ignore him but he was very persistent. She turned her back on him to no avail. He merely marched around to the front of her and waved some gilt chains in front of her face. She had no recourse but to run up the steps to the shop. It was only then the stallholder gave up and began to tackle someone else.

Mai Lee entered the shop and again the shop bell rang out. Yuan was in deep discussion with the herbalist. He turned at the sound of the bell and looked surprised as he saw Mai Lee standing there. She moved quickly to his side.

"I thought I told you to wait," he remonstrated.

"I couldn't. A trader was bothering me and the Japanese soldiers were not far away. They would have noticed me. I didn't have the money to purchase anything so I had to come in."

"Ah, yes," said Fong. "They can be extremely annoying and don't give up easily. Is this the young lady?"

Yuan nodded, "Yes." He turned to Mai Lee. "Mother has been and gone. Either something's happened to her or she's at the café waiting. We must get back."

"But what about our instructions?"

Fong answered, "I gave Hiroto's schedule and plan to your mother. I do not have another copy. At least, I have the flight schedule but not the message and plan. Here." Fong went into the back and emerged with the timetable of planned flights. "That's all I can do. I will get word to Hiroto and if you can come back I may have the other papers for you. Oh, and one more thing… Hiroto said that he will take both of you."

Mai Lee beamed with joy and Yuan nodded delightedly, "We must get back. If you don't hear from us, you will know that we have the information and all is well."

Fong bowed deferentially and pressed his palms together, "I will pray for you both. Good luck."

Mai Lee and Yuan returned the respectful bow and left the shop.

***

Su Li had walked unscathed, unchallenged back to the café where she was to meet her son and Mai Lee. She took a deep breath, entered and looked around for them. They were nowhere to be seen. She seemed puzzled and moved to the back of the shop where she scrutinised the customers at each table and in each booth.

"Can I help you, Madame?"

"Ah, yes. Tea please."

"Certainly, where would you like to sit?"

Su Li indicated a table at the front of the shop, "This will suit me nicely," she smiled. She was afraid to ask if he had seen Yuan and Mai Lee and settled down to wait.

She glanced at the clock. Time passed slowly and as each second ticked by Su Li was unable to remove the worried look on her face. The restaurant owner came out with her tea. Su Li rubbed her furrowed brow. She was becoming increasingly more nervous and apprehensive.

Su Li sipped her tea and tapped her fingers annoyingly on the table. Another customer looked at her and frowned. The noise of the constant tip tap of her fingernails was clearly an irritation to him. He grunted in annoyance and stood up throwing some money on the table and stamped out.

He walked straight into the two soldiers that had entered earlier and apologised profusely, "Please forgive me, Sirs."

One soldier questioned him, "What is your problem?"

The man sighed, "It is nothing. I have a condition where certain sounds get under my skin and that..." he pointed into the café at Su Li who was still drumming her fingers on the wood, "Is one of them."

The soldiers glanced at Su Li and one of them stared, really stared at her. A flicker of recognition flashed across his face and he nudged his companion and muttered something.

The man shrugged his shoulders and walked away as the two soldiers strode into the café and stopped at Su Li's table. She glanced up and a look of horror manifested itself on her face and she suppressed a small cry.

***

Outside on the street Yuan and Mai Lee neared the café and stopped as they heard a hullabaloo erupt inside. There was much yelling and screaming in Japanese and a woman's voice. Yuan prevented Mai Lee from running to the café and entering. He took hold of her arm and pulled her to one side. They feigned interest in a stall selling made to measure sandals.

Another shout went up. The two soldiers emerged dragging Su Li out onto the pavement.

"Oh no! That's mother," gasped Yuan in horror.

"Why is she dressed like that?"

"I don't know. Clothes like that come from an elite store."

"What shall we do?"

"Watch and wait"

They observed quietly as Su Li was hustled away. Suddenly, she broke free and ran toward the elaborate Chinatown entrance. The soldiers raced after her and barged past anyone in their way knocking several people to the ground.

Mai Lee and Yuan tried to follow without attracting too much attention. They dodged between stalls and avoided the rickshaws as they attempted to keep up.

"Now what?" asked Mai Lee. "Where is she going?"

"It looks like she's headed for the great entrance."

"But why?"

"She can lose herself down a side street or get to a safe house."

The Chinese and Singaporean traders deliberately tried to impede the path of the Japanese soldiers who were drawing closer to Su Li. Frustrated they swore and shoved people out of the way knocking old and young alike sending them sprawling into the dirt road.

Suddenly, there was a squeal of brakes, a horrible thudding sound and crunching. People ran from all directions and shouts went up. Yuan and Mai Lee approached cautiously and joined the throng around the accident.

Su Li was lying on the ground, her body broken and twisted in front of a motorbus. Yuan gasped in horror. An old woman crouched down at the side of Su Li who managed to whisper something to her. Her eyes fluttered open and lit upon Yuan. She smiled briefly at him and a look of peace and serenity filled her face as she breathed her last.

People continued to crowd around. The soldiers reached her body and one of them delivered a savage kick to her side. The old woman looked up and cursed them, "You can do no more to her now, you yellow fiends," she yelled for which she, too, received a vicious blow and she fell forward. The soldiers laughed scornfully and walked on.

Yuan attempted to cross to his mother his face streamed with tears. Mai Lee restrained him, "There's nothing you can do, Yuan. She's dead."

"That's as maybe but I can still help her." He freed his arm and lifted the old woman up and helped her to the side of the road, where he sat her on a seat at a pavement café.

"Are you all right?" he asked kindly.

The old woman nodded, "Thank you, I'll live." She grunted, "I know what I'd like to do to those pigs."

"Tell me, what did she say before she died?"

"I don't know. It was muddled. It didn't make any sense."

"Try and remember, it could be important."

The old lady paused, "She said, the bottom of the parasol stand in the shop…"

"The parasol stand?"

"Yes. I told you it made no sense."

"Thank you. Is there anything I can do?"

"No. I'll be okay, just a bit winded and bruised. Bastards."

Yuan stepped away and Mai Lee stepped forward and crouched down, "Are you sure there was nothing else?"

"Oh yes, she said it was a fancy shop and then muttered something about cinders. I didn't catch the rest."

"Thanks." Mai Lee straightened up. She took Yuan's hand, "Come, we have to search Chinatown for a fancy shop. There can't be many of those and I bet it has something to do with the clothes she was wearing."

"Do you think?"

"What else can it be? Come on."

They walked back along the road and studied each shop front searching for a store, which sold more expensive items.

"This is hopeless," grumbled Yuan. "How are we supposed to find it? It could be anywhere."

Mai Lee could see that Yuan was distraught and struggling with his emotions. She tried to be encouraging, "We have to try."

They continued on but Yuan was blinded by his tears and his voice choked with strangled emotion, "Mai Lee. I can't do this."

"Yes, you can. Wait!" She pulled up short and pointed at a road sign, "Look, Yuan. Look!"

Yuan raised his eyes miserably; the life seemed to have dropped out of him, "What? What is it?"

"Cinder Street. See? That's what the old woman said, something about cinders. She thought it didn't make any sense. Maybe this is the road the she was in. Come on."

They speeded up and turned the corner with more of a spring in their step and searched the shop fronts. Yuan wiped his eyes and squeezed Mai Lee's hand, "I'm glad you're with me. I'm sorry… I…"

"Ssh! There is no need to apologise. I cannot imagine how you must be feeling… Really… Wait!" Mai Lee stopped and pointed at the clothing emporium in front of them. It was an expensive shop displaying garments similar to those they had seen Su Li wearing. They stepped forward and entered.

The shop was large and filled with all kinds of, tunics, cheongsams, Western styled suits, and accessories. Mai Lee nudged Yuan and alerted him to a simple flowered cotton sarong, which was laid on the counter. "That's Su Li's. Look!" she whispered.

Yuan's eyes fell on the plain dress and he blinked back tears, "Excuse me," he asked the old Chinaman behind the counter. "This sarong."

"What of it?"

"I believe it belonged to someone I knew."

"I doubt that young man."

"It's very pretty, may I try it on?" smiled Mai Lee.

"I am sure we can find something more fitting for you, let me look." The old man crossed to a rail of silk dresses with mandarin collars. Mai Lee whispered to Yuan. "Look for a parasol stand."

Yuan began to look around the shop as if browsing, while Mai Lee insisted, "Yes, by all means please do show me something else but I really like this one."

"Very well," said the old man. He passed her a couple of silk dresses and picked up the sarong from the counter. "The changing room is over there."

"Thank you." Mai Lee scuttled across to the cubicle and pulled back the curtain. Her eyes lit up when she saw the container of parasols. She went inside and closed the drapes. She knelt down and carefully lifted up the parasols and peered inside the pot. She could just see something in the bottom and stretched her hand inside and pulled out the papers hidden so carefully by Su Li. She stuffed them into her canvas bag with her pretend study books and stood up. She opened the cubicle and stepped out holding the sarong, "Sadly, it's not really my colour and the others, although beautiful are out of my price range." She handed the garments back to the old man and fled from the shop closely followed by Yuan.

"I got it," she said excitedly as they ran down the steps.

"What? What is it?"

"There was a bunch of papers hidden in the bottom of the pot holding the parasols."

"What are they?"

"I haven't looked. We must wait until we are safe."

"Then let's go!" urged Yuan and they warily made for the main gate of Chinatown keeping a sharp lookout as they walked for any Japanese soldiers.

CHAPTER TWENTY-ONE

Safe house or not?

Yuan and Mai Lee hurried from Chinatown. They walked toward the docks and ghettos that serviced the sailors and other seafaring men. They were careful and ensured that they weren't followed until they reached a seedy boarding house. Yuan knocked twice. Footsteps were heard and an ancient Malay crone opened the door. She looked both sides down the street and admitted them before securing the door securely.

"Quickly, upstairs now." Her voice was scratchy, "Room eight, same as before."

Yuan and Mai Lee dashed up the stairs and unlocked the door. The room was sparsely furnished with a rickety bed, two wooden chairs, a bench and a nightstand with a cracked mirror above it. Mai Lee flopped onto the bed while Yuan walked to the window and looked out into the street.

"Is it clear?"

"For now." His shoulders raised and he sighed heavily. Mai Lee studied his back. She was full of concern as she heard him trying to stifle a sob.

"It's all right to cry, you know." He turned and looked at her his lips trembled and his eyes glistened with tears. Mai Lee said softly, "Here, come and sit with me."

Yuan turned back to the window and closed the blind, "If we can't see out then they can't see in," he explained. He crossed back to her and sat on the bench. His eyes were puffed and red from crying and his voice choked with emotion, "She gave her life for us, so she wouldn't be tortured and give us away."

"I know… She loved you very much, you know? She did everything for you."

"What about you?" asked Yuan his voice little more than a whisper.

"What about me?" asked Mai Lee somewhat puzzled.

"Do you love me?"

Mai Lee took his face between her hands and stared deep into his eyes, "You have been kinder to me than anyone I've ever known."

"Yes. But do you love me?" he insisted.

Mai Lee bit her lip and stroked his cheek. She lowered her eyes and said shyly, "Yes, I do."

Yuan embraced her and held her close. He buried his face in her fragrant hair and whispered in her ear, "Then say it. Please. I need to hear the words."

Mai Lee pulled back and lifted her gaze to his face and said with precision and as a sincere declaration, "I love you, Yuan."

Their lips met and he kissed her tenderly, a kiss that led to something more passionate and burning. A knock at the door interrupted them and they broke apart.

"Yes?" called Yuan.

"It's us. Can we come in?" said a female voice.

"Of course."

The door opened. Barra and Kaci entered. They both looked flustered and anxious. Barra spoke with urgency, "You can't stay here any longer. I'm sorry."

"It's too dangerous," added Kaci.

"The soldiers are on the move and the British Special Forces are searching for you, too. They think that you murdered that soldier." Barra pointed at Mai Lee, "They believe you are with her."

"I'm so sorry, Yuan," said Kaci sympathetically.

"We won't put you in any danger. We'll leave," said Yuan.

Kaci stepped forward. She put her hand in her tunic pocket and pulled out a wad of notes. "Here. This is your mother's share of the sale. Take it." She offered it to Yuan who accepted it gratefully.

Barra nodded, "Sorry, Yuan. We wish you well, both of you. Good luck."

Yuan stuffed the cash into his tunic and took Mai Lee by the hand.

"Where will you go?" asked Kaci.

"I am not sure yet. Maybe back to Chinatown."

"They will be looking for you there," said Barra.

"Or Little India."

"That will be a better bet," affirmed Kaci.

They picked up their bags and left together trying to be as unobtrusive as possible.

The two women waited quietly until they heard that the footsteps had retreated down the stairs and the front door had slammed. Kaci turned to Barra, "Do you make the call or do I?"

Barra looked stunned, "You're not going to betray them, surely?"

"What else do we do?"

"I don't believe it. What if it was your son or mine?"

"Well, it's not. We have to think of our own safety. If we look as if we're neutral or helping the soldiers then they may leave us alone."

Barra pursed her lips in dissatisfaction. "I don't like it. It's wrong. What if it was you? Someone around here could easily betray us. Remember, we're not the most popular? Or suppose it was someone we cared about? Come on Kaci, think."

Kaci squirmed uneasily but was emphatic in her reply, "We have no choice."

"Well, at least give them some time to get away. And you don't have to tell them everything."

Kaci shrugged, "I'll give them an hour and then I'll make the call. Here." She passed Barra some cash.

"What's this?"

"Your share." Barra looked at her. "Well, you didn't think I'd give it him all, did you?"

***

Mai Lee and Yuan looked about them carefully before they proceeded down the street. Mai Lee asked, "What do we do? Where do we go?"

"We find a boarding house, hotel, anywhere and keep moving. That way we are less likely to be found."

"True. We need to get out of the docklands. The authorities know that those women live there."

"Yes, and I don't trust them. They'd trade us in as they would their own grandmother."

"Do you think so?"

"I know so."

"I suppose so. It's obvious really. They tell on us and the authorities leave them alone. What I don't understand is why they gave you the money?"

"They had no choice. They know I knew money was owed to my mother, but I bet this isn't the full amount.

"Yes, they would try to lull us into a false sense of security. I see what you mean. We must be careful."

"We'll head for Little India. There are some hostelries there. They'll search the docklands first. Come on."

Yuan grabbed Mai Lee's hand and they ran away from the harbour side and back toward the town. Yuan stopped a passing rickshaw and they jumped in, "Little India, please."

The runner, a wiry old man, nodded, "Where?"

"Take us to a good rooming house. Do you know somewhere?"

The man nodded, "I know the perfect place." He sped off down the road. Yuan and Mai Lee ducked back inside the cab as they saw a troop of six Japanese soldiers marching toward the direction of their previous safe house.

Mai Lee held her breath as the rickshaw raced past the men. But the soldiers didn't give them a second look. She turned to Yuan as they travelled on, "Looks like you were right."

"I know I'm right. You can't trust anyone in this game. Let's hope my mother is watching over us."

Mai Lee fingered her pendant, "And that Lily is looking after me."

The rickshaw runner had half an ear and listened to them as they talked. He ran on and turned a corner, tirelessly. The man had not even broken into a sweat in the sultry air. He hurried on, passed a Hindu temple, tawdry trinket stalls, food carts, and finally pulled up outside a lodging house in Little India.

"This do, Missy? Young, Sir?" He studied their features and their clothes.

"It looks fine. Thank you." They alighted onto the roadside. Mai Lee looked up at the four-storey block as Yuan paid the driver. He gave the old man a tip and the man grinned toothily at him.

"Thank you, kind man," he murmured as he raced off to find another fare.

Yuan and Mai Lee walked up the worn stone steps into a shabby foyer and reception desk. A young Asian girl dressed in a gold and scarlet sari sat behind the counter reading. She looked up. "Yes?"

"We need a room for the night maybe longer."

"You have money?"

"Yes. How much?" Yuan took some notes from his pocket and the girl picked some from his hand.

"I'll take a deposit and one night. That will give you two nights. You stay longer you pay more."

Yuan nodded and the girl took a key from the rack behind her. "Up the stairs, second floor, room nine." She turned away seemingly disinterested and returned to her book.

Yuan and Mai Lee mounted the stairs. The hotel stairs creaked with each step. Sounds came from rooms where prostitutes entertained men and shouts echoed on the air where couples argued and children cried. Mai Lee shivered, "This is a bad place. I can feel it."

"It may be unsavoury but here we'll be safe. I can't see anyone here reporting us to the police, can you?"

"Maybe not. But we must be on our guard. I expect some of the clients to these women are Japanese soldiers."

"We will have to lie low."

"No one followed us. I don't think."

"No…" They reached the second floor and walked along the dirty corridor with its filthy stained carpet and grubby dirt streaked walls. The smell was less than wholesome. Yuan fumbled with the key and opened the door to number nine. They walked in and closed the door behind them. Yuan locked it, leaned against it and sighed. "We are safe, for the moment. We should get some rest."

"We must look at those papers and see what we are supposed to do," said Mai Lee sensibly. "Come." She sat on the bed and emptied her canvas bag and picked up the papers.

Yuan sat next to her and they studied the schedule. "He has flights to Borneo every four days."

"And to the islands on every other week. What do the other papers say?"

Yuan picked up the handwritten sheet and tried to read it, "This doesn't make sense."

"Why? What does it say?"

Yuan screwed up his face and slowly began to read the words aloud, "The Gods get forgiving love to father all air and the field on or at any cloudless night. Each coming Thursday will be late for active evening. Sing up seven songs and thirty more please," he looked up, "And so it goes on…"

"What?"

"It's meaningless, nonsense…"

"Maybe not. There has to be a message in it for us."

"But what? How are we supposed to decipher it?"

"Think. It's a puzzle or a riddle. Are there any words that could be meant for us? It's supposed to guide us about when we go, isn't it?"

"Possibly… It mentions Thursday."

"What could go with that? Night? Evening?"

"Maybe seven?"

"We're not looking at this the right way. Is there a pattern with the words?"

"I don't know."

"Read it again, slowly. Stop and pause between each word."

Yuan did as she asked and took his time. Mai Lee listened and shook her head, "Again."

Yuan repeated the words and Mai Lee counted the words. She snapped her fingers "I've got it! Try reading every third word, miss the others out."

Yuan complied, "Get to airfield at night, Thursday late evening seven… I think you're onto something. "His face creased in a big grin. He went through the rest of the message employing the same method. He turned to Mai Lee and hugged her. You clever, clever girl! How did you do that?"

"I don't know. It's like a voice in my head said three… don't ask me why."

They looked at each other and chorused, "Lily," and laughed.

"So, we have to wait until Thursday night. And get to Raffles…"

"Seven thirty and we fly out…. I can't believe it. So near yet so far away."

"So what do we do until then?" asked Yuan.

"Stay out of sight and hope for the best," said Mai Lee philosophically.

"Still we have to eat. It will be best if I go out alone and bring something back for us. You need to stay hidden."

"Don't go yet." Mai Lee stood up and crossed to the bed. She lay down and patted the space beside her.

"What's wrong?" asked Yuan as he moved to her.

Mai Lee said nothing but took his hand and pulled him onto the bed beside her. Her eyes searched his, which were filled with longing. She nodded and said, "It's time."

Yuan eyed her questioningly, "What is? What do you mean?"

Mai Lee propped herself up on one elbow, "I want you to be my first."

Yuan went to speak but Mai Lee quieted him. She put her finger to his lips, "No, listen. I don't know what is going to happen to me. If I am caught I know I will be killed like Miko." She took a deep breath, "I want to know that my first time was with love and tenderness. It will give me something to hold onto if I am captured. Those Japanese brutes will not have the satisfaction of taking me first." She lowered her eyes shyly; "I give myself to you."

Yuan studied her face so earnest in her reasoning, "You don't have to do this, Mai Lee."

"I want to. But you will have to help me," she paused, "I don't know what is expected…"

"Nor I," admitted Yuan. "I am not experienced. I have only… but that is unimportant. We will learn together."

Yuan took her into his arms and caressed her face before

kissing her tenderly. He slowly began removing her clothes whilst showering her with kisses on her neck, her arms, her face and lips. He took her hands and gently kissed each fingertip. As he revealed her body bit by bit he sat back, drinking her in, and whispered, "You are so beautiful."

His lips brushed against her firm full breasts and teased her upturned pert nipples and Mai Lee gasped in pleasure. She arched her back, but he did not stop there. He moved on over her midriff and stomach before focusing on her thighs and most secret places.

Mai Lee sighed in ecstasy. Never before had she felt like this. Her body quivered in delight. Tentatively she tried to reciprocate. She lifted his shirt and helped him to take it off. Her soft velvet lips explored his chest and neck. She traced her finger down to his navel and beyond. Fascinated she watched his awakening manhood and following his lead she fondled and caressed him with her hands and mouth.

Their lovemaking was gentle, slow and satisfying. It went on long into the night when the moon had risen and the sounds from the other occupants in the hotel had subsided.

Mai Lee snuggled into Yuan's strong arms. An aura of peace and contentment enveloped them. She closed her eyes dreamily but Yuan's remained open. He murmured, "I never knew it could be so beautiful."

"You have made me a woman and I am glad. No one can take this away from us, whatever happens."

"And you still have my pendant."

"I will wear it always," said Mai Lee as she fingered the talisman, sleepily. They lay together quietly and continued to enjoy the moment.

Suddenly, Yuan sat up, "I'm starving," he announced. "In fact, I'm ravenous. Aren't you hungry?"

"No, not really. Although, if we had some food I wouldn't say no, I'm feeling more like I want to sleep than wanting to eat… But, Yuan, where will you find something to eat at this late hour?"

"There are some places I know of. Trust me."

Yuan was already on his feet and dressing, "Here. I will leave most of my money with you." He took the money from his tunic pocket, peeled off a couple of notes and placed the rest on the pillow. "I'll take enough for us to have a decent meal and I will be as quick as I can. Don't answer the door to anyone. Be careful." He leaned over her and kissed her gently on the cheek. "Lock the door after me."

Yuan slipped out quietly. Mai Lee stepped out of bed and closed the door quietly engaging the bolt and deadlock. She moved cautiously to the window and peeped out through the curtains and saw Yuan disappear down the shabby side street. She studied the street and noted the clock on the wall of an old shop opposite. She checked it with the one in the room. The time was the same. Her restless movement and her tumbling thoughts brought her to full wakefulness and she sat and waited in the gloom. Every now and again she would peer out of the window but she guarded her presence from the street as she fingered her pendant in the half-light.

The heat in the room was sultry and her body was slick with a fine sheen of sweat from her ardour and lovemaking. She utilised the jug of water and basin, and rinsed herself clean. She didn't know why but she was afraid to settle and decided to dress and she lay fully clothed on top of the bed. She listened hard for any strange sounds and kept an eye on the rustic clock, which hung on the wall. Possibly a necessity for a working girl, she thought.

Mai Lee sighed, she felt uneasy being alone without Yuan and prayed for his safe return. She found herself constantly watching the clock and she counted every minute that ticked by. She was becoming more awake and alert as time went on and sleep fled her thoughts.

She began to softly pace the room. Her steps were silent. Each one was measured, executed with the stealth of a cat. Some drunken ruffian sang bawdily outside her window. She stole a look. The disreputable looking man clutched a bottle and swigged from it. He stumbled on the pavement and cursed as he fell and rolled in the gutter. A light went on across the street and a window opened. A woman poked her head outside and shouted, "Clear off! Or I'll call the law."

The man staggered to his feet and made a lewd gesture at the woman who whistled shrilly. Mai Lee was alarmed to see a policeman turn the corner. The man fell again and the official yanked the man to his feet. He slapped handcuffs on him and started to haul the man away. She prayed Yuan would hurry back but not at this minute. She didn't want him to run into the police.

The woman opposite closed her window and the light went out. The street became relatively still and quiet again apart from a few scuttling rodents trying to scratch a living from the rubbish that was strewn in the road and littered the vacant door fronts. She waited for what seemed an interminable length of time. She heard footsteps approach and was relieved to see Yuan turn the corner. He carried a brown paper bag filled with goodies and he crossed to the boarding house.

Mai Lee waited by the door until she heard his soft knock and she unlocked the door and admitted him. He secured the bolt again and sat on the bed. "I'm so glad you're back. I'm no longer weary. But I was anxious for you to return."

"Well, I'm here now. I managed to get some fruit from a corner store and a few savouries from a street vendor packing up to go home. Here." He took out some vegetable pakoras and curried meat samosas. They shared the food without a word. Mai Lee was surprised to find that she, too, was now hungry.

"Mm. It tastes so good," she finally said.

"A veritable feast," he agreed. "And we have a juicy mango to share and a banana each for our dessert."

They ate their fill. Mai Lee wiped her mouth. "Now what?"

"We must get some sleep and leave before the hotelier rises."

"Why? I thought we were safe here. We have paid a deposit."

"They mustn't know we've left. Believe me our safety lies in them thinking we are still here and in us secretly moving on. If we sleep now we must be up and out by six."

"But where to? And how do we prevent ourselves from oversleeping?"

"I know an alley where the homeless live. We can hide

away there until mid morning when the streets will be bustling again and then we find somewhere new to stay."

"Then we'll take it in turns. You sleep first and I'll keep watch," said Mai Lee. "I'll keep an eye on the clock and wake you in two hours."

Yuan nodded, "Now my belly's full I will sleep. Are you sure you don't want to rest first?'

"I'm fine. I promise, now go to sleep."

Yuan flopped onto the bed in his clothes and drifted off to sleep as Mai Lee watched. She studied his face, the curve of his cheek, his long curling lashes and clear skin, his firm chin and silken dark hair and she smiled. She felt as if her heart would burst as she was filled with such an overwhelming feeling of love for him.

Time passed. The hands of the clock moved slowly forward and the time read four a.m. She started as she heard the distant sound of marching boots and momentarily she froze. She tiptoed to the window and peeked outside. To her horror she saw Takagi with six of his men turn the corner and stand to attention under the street clock, which hung over a shoe repair business. The man with the rickshaw who had carried them was with them. He pointed across to the house before running back into the lanes and back streets.

It was almost as if Takagi felt her eyes on him and he turned and peered up at her window. Mai Lee allowed the curtain to fall closed and stepped back into the shadows. Her heart began to race and she crossed to Yuan and shook him gently, "Yuan. They're here."

He was instantly awake. He arose and grabbed his rucksack of meagre possessions. Mai Lee rescued the money from under the pillow and picked up her canvas bag. She stuffed the cash inside and turned to Yuan, "What about the papers? If they get into the wrong hands…"

"It's too late to do anything now. We have to pray we don't get caught. We'll destroy them at our next stop."

He quietly unlocked the door. They crept out and tiptoed down the stairs flinching at each creak and squeak of the wood. They reached the foyer and hurried to the back of the rooming house and managed to slip out the back way.

They heard a thunderous knocking on the front door as they fled and raced off down the alley.

***

Takagi stood in the street and looked up at the windows. There was no movement. He hammered on the door again before he instructed his men, "Batter down the door. Now!"

The men gathered their strength and heaved their shoulders against the door. It didn't budge.

"Again!" he demanded in his brittle tones.

The men stepped back and ran at it again and this time the door gave way and splintered open. The men burst in.

"Search the rooms. Two to a floor."

Two marched down the corridor whilst the rest took the stairs. The proprietor came out looking dishevelled and half asleep. The soldiers pushed him out of the way and dismissed his protests as they broke into each room rousing the outraged occupants.

Indignant shouts were heard from other guests as their slumber was interrupted. The soldiers pulled them from their beds, turned the mattresses over and opened closets. They rooted through the clothes racks and opened cupboards in their search for Yuan and Mai Lee.

***

Mai Lee and Yuan cautiously made their way down a back alley. They could hear the hullabaloo and commotion at the boarding house as they made their escape. "What now? It's too dangerous to go to Hobos' Alley. They'll find us for sure."

"I know," exclaimed Mai Lee as she took charge. "We'll go to Madame Jong's."

"But surely, they'll be watching the place. It's one of the first places they'll look."

"May be, may be not. We can go to the temple opposite. There's an underground passage that leads from the crypt to the storeroom underneath the Orchid House in her garden."

"Why didn't you mention it before?"

"Because I've only just remembered. They'll never believe we'd return there. Quickly now. But, which way? Do you know how to get there from here?"

Yuan nodded, "Yes. Hurry. We can take the back roads and alleys and hopefully avoid Takagi's men. They will be a while searching the house."

"They'll only have to feel the bed. They'll know we haven't been gone long."

"Then run!"

CHAPTER TWENTY-TWO

On the run

Yuan and Mai Lee rushed through the lanes, behind houses and shops and out of the Little India district. Each time they heard a sound they scuttled into a doorway to hide or crouched down behind anything that could mask their presence. They ignored the street vendors setting up their wares with the coming of dawn and those up early to go to their places of work.

The sky was a deep dusky pink. The air shimmered in a foggy heat haze as the sun began to rise and chased away the remnants of the night and hid the moon from view. Birds chirruped in the trees as they awakened and ruffled their feathers. They began their morning ritual of welcoming in the first light of day and sang to herald in the morning.

Lazy lizards stretched and emerged from nooks and crannies to warm their bodies to get them moving and explore the different avenues in their hunt for their breakfast.

Long tailed macaques dropped from trees at the roadside to forage near the town's food stores and bins or to head for the shore to join their cousins the crab eating macaques on the beaches. They shrieked their presence noisily as they scampered along the dusty roads.

"Not far now," whispered Yuan.

"Yes, I recognise these streets," agreed Mai Lee.

They turned a corner and approached the back of the temple, which was opposite Madame Jong's residence. All was calm and peaceful. They slipped into a doorway. Devotees were starting to arrive for prayers and communal worship.

"You go first," advised Mai Lee. "They are looking for two people not one. Act as if you're a devotee and no one will take any notice of you."

"But..."

"Don't argue. Go now and wait in the main chamber at the top of the steps. I will see you in a little while. Go!"

Yuan didn't hang around or contradict Mai Lee. He nodded and stretched himself up to his full height. He brushed his lips across Mai Lee's cheek and stepped into the road. He crossed to the temple in full view of the Buddhist Monks who stood on the steps and inside the entrance as they waited to commence their early morning devotions.

Just as Mai Lee had said, no one gave Yuan a second glance. He mounted the stone steps that dipped in the middle from the many feet that had stepped that way before him and made his way into the temple.

Mai Lee remained in the shadows. She waited a respectable amount of time before she too stepped out and walked to the front of the temple and strolled nonchalantly up the temple steps. She looked like a typical student stopping off before class to attend to her religious devotions.

One of the soldiers who stood on guard at the gate glanced at Mai Lee cursorily. As she passed him she bowed her head deferentially. The officer turned away and continued to scan the street. She willed her beating heart to be still and to stop pounding erratically in her chest. Her blood rushed to her head and whooshed through her ears almost deafening her.

She sat in one of the chairs that was set out in front of the giant golden statue of Buddha, which in turn was in front of the opulent silkscreen hangings and she prayed. To the right of her was Ganesh the elephant headed God and to her left was a model of Hanuman the monkey God worshipped by Hindus and revered by Buddhist followers alike.

Devotees worked their prayer beads and murmured mantras, as Mai Lee repeated verses that she had learnt with Auntie Ko. She was relieved that her learning from her time at Madame Jong's would be put to good use. She kept her head bowed but peeped through her sweeping fringe until she spotted Yuan. He was in the centre of the temple kneeling on the floor close to the stairs. He had lit some incense sticks. He rose and placed them on the offering table.

As if aware of Mai Lee's presence he turned and saw her

approaching. She signalled with her eyes to the stairs and without saying a word. Yuan returned to the offering table and bowed. He moved off and quietly headed for the stairs. He didn't stop and he didn't turn until he reached the stairwell. He cast a look around him and ensuring he wasn't being observed he slipped quietly down them and out of sight.

Mai Lee bought a garland and placed the offering of flowers onto the altar. She said a prayer, placed her hands together and bowed in obeisance to Lord Buddha. She, too, was careful and glanced about her. The soldier was still watching the street; the monks and other devotees were intent on their own worship. Mai Lee walked unobtrusively toward the stairs and she, too, trotted down the steps and no one saw her leave.

She soon reached the temple corridor where Yuan waited. She ran up to him and took his hand. "Where now?" he asked.

"I don't know. I've never been here before. I just knew of its existence."

They walked silently along the passageway until they reached an antechamber. They hurried down some more steps into the ornate room, where there were four doors leading off.

Yuan looked around, "Which? Which one do we use?"

Mai Lee shrugged. "We'll try them all," she said cheerfully. "That's if I can't get my bearings. Better to be sure."

They opened the first and closest door. The chanting of prayers reached them. Mantras repeated over and over again in a collective tone. They closed the door.

They opened the second. It was a small cell like room with no other way out and a single chair with small offering table and nothing else. That door, too, they closed.

They crossed to the end of the chamber and opened the third door. A musty smell assailed their nostrils and Mai Lee wrinkled her nose. She nodded, "This is it. I think." They both entered and closed the door behind them.

Yuan and Mai Lee stumbled along the dark corridor.

Water dripped and roots from vegetation dangled through the rocky ceiling. There was very little light and the twisted roots resembled alien creatures in the gloom. Yuan hesitated, "I don't like this."

"It's just a little dirty. Nothing to be scared of," said Mai Lee.

"You don't understand. I dislike being in confined spaces, where I can't see the air or get out easily. I shall be happier once we get out of here."

"After my upbringing I have no such fears. I spent many years in a tiny bamboo cage. But, I suppose it was open to the night air."

"I don't know how you survived." He stopped and pointed forward into the murky dimly lit passage. "Look, what's that ahead?" They hurried to the end of the gloomy corridor and arrived at a flight of stairs.

They exchanged a glance. Mai Lee squeezed Yuan's hand. "This must be it!" She led the way and began to mount the steps, which wound around in a spiral. They eventually reached another door. Mai Lee took a deep breath, "Let's hope there's no one behind it," she whispered and crossed her fingers for luck a sign she had learned from her time at the orphanage. She turned the handle and pushed, but the door did not budge. Yuan put his shoulder to the wood and Mai Lee tried again. She put all her weight behind it and together they forcibly pushed together. The door finally creaked open and they pushed the worn drape back and stepped into the storeroom where Mai Lee had hidden from the master, Manchu. They closed the door quietly and sat on a packing crate.

"We should be safe here," affirmed Mai Lee.

"Unless someone comes in."

"That's unlikely. So, now you can tell me. What is the full plan?"

"We have to get to Raffles. There we will meet Hiroto. He will have with him the uniform of a Japanese officer that I will change into."

"What about me? Am I to be a boy again?"

"No, this time you will dress as a courtesan. It will attract least attention. You will look as if you are our plaything, our sex toy. No one will take any notice. Men often have women visiting them at the camp." Mai Lee nodded in understanding. "From there we travel to the airbase. Hiroto has a consignment of goods supposedly for Borneo but the consignment is you."

Yuan looked up, "Is that the only light?"

Mai Lee nodded, the sun just creeps through in the morning and the moonlight, too."

"I hope so. I find it suffocating here."

"Don't think about it. Keep occupied and think. Now... How do we get to Raffles from here?"

"We wait. We still have two days to sit out and avoid the authorities. Then on Thursday we wait until late afternoon. Then go."

"So until then we sleep here. What about food?"

"I have some, but not enough."

"I could make myself known to Auntie Ko."

"It's too dangerous."

"It may be our only option. I suggest we rest now."

Yuan nodded and they dragged an old canvas tarpaulin onto the packing cases and attempted to bolster up the surface with an ancient worn coverlet to make something reasonable to slumber on.

"We must try and get some sleep. We had little enough last night." Mai Lee stretched out on the makeshift bed and closed her eyes. Yuan took an old splintered chair and wedged it underneath the door handle from the passage. Mai Lee opened one eye, "The door to the garden is stiff it won't need much to jam it tight."

Yuan smiled. He placed a packing crate against the door and then clambered on the make shift bed next to Mai Lee. He put an arm around her and the two drifted off to sleep.

Mai Lee was awoken in the early hours by her tummy rumbling. The room was dark and for a moment she felt disorientated not knowing where she was. Then she remembered and sat upright waking Yuan. He was instantly alert.

"What? What is it?"

"Sorry, I didn't mean to wake you. I was just confused, lost my bearings for a moment. What's the time?"

"I'm not sure. I can't really see and we can't put a light on..."

"Even if there was one," laughed Mai Lee. "I'm hungry. Do we have any food left?"

"I think there's a pakora left." Yuan stumbled up and felt around for his rucksack. His eyes adjusted to the gloom and he opened his bag.

Mai Lee murmured, "One pakora isn't going to sustain us both for two days."

"No," said Yuan resignedly. "And it's not even one. This one is crushed... sorry."

Mai Lee picked it, "It has extra fluff protein..."

Yuan laughed, "You can't eat that. It's just in bits."

"Believe you me I've eaten worse."

"Can you remember where?"

Mai Lee grinned, "You wouldn't believe me if I told you."

"I'm wide awake now, too, and hungry," said Yuan. "I can always slip out and visit the market."

"And leave me here? Not likely. I would be worried to death that you'd been caught."

"But they are looking for two of us."

"More so you than me. They want you for that soldier's death," she paused for a moment, "I have a better idea."

"What's that?"

"I can raid the kitchen here. I know where it is. It'll be much safer."

"And if you get caught? No, I don't like it."

"At night or very early morning there won't be any servants or gardeners around. Trust me. I can do this." Yuan shook his head in dissent but Mai Lee would have none of it. "I can. I know I can do this and with a bit of luck I can get enough to keep us going until we have to leave."

Yuan sighed heavily, "And just supposing someone sees you? What then?"

"I am sure Auntie Ko would help us or even my young replacement, Liling."

"And what of Madame Jong? She tried to kill you, remember?"

"But she regretted it. No, I'm sure it will be fine."

"You are headstrong and foolish. I don't want to lose you."

"You won't. I promise." Mai Lee refused to listen and stepped to the door. She yanked hard on the handle and there was a rush of warm air. "Close the door. I'll be back as soon as I can."

Mai Lee crept up the stairs and out into the garden. The garden looked surreal in the silver moonlight. Mai Lee moved stealthily across to the veranda. She tiptoed up the wooden steps to the decking and to the garden doors, which led into the house and tried the handle. It was locked.

Mai Lee swore softly. She gingerly stepped along the boardwalk toward another door that led to Manchu's quarters. She fingered her pendant and prayed, "Lord Buddha deliver me from harm and let me find safe entry to the house." She reached the balcony with its chairs and table strewn with Manchu's opium pipes and she held her breath. Her heart was now pumping so vigorously it seemed to thud in her chest and head like an out of control imprisoned living animal, which was seeking to escape her body.

Her hand reached out for the door handle, which led to Manchu's room. She shivered as she remembered her last encounter with the master. Her hand flicked up to her pendant again and she told herself, "Courage, Mai Lee, Courage." She pushed against the door and found that it opened easily. Once more she found herself in Manchu's very masculine apartment. A swift look around showed it to be clear of Manchu and her heart pounded a little less erratically. She closed the door softly behind her.

Making as little noise as possible Mai Lee's soft footfalls dissipated into the silence as she traversed the room and headed for the door, which led to the corridor that would take her to the other wings of the house. She slipped out of the room and entered the highly polished corridor and walked quietly along its length passing many doors on the way.

She soon arrived at the centre of the building and glanced about her trying to remember the direction of the kitchen. The place looked so different at night. A noise behind her startled her and she spun around to see what it was. The light was such that it was difficult to see and she tentatively tried the handle of the nearest door, which led into a sitting area, which she recognised. She slipped inside keeping the door open a fraction to see whatever or whoever passed by. No one came. The sound of a door clicking softly further up the corridor was heard on the warm but gentle breeze, which blew along the passageway. Whoever it was had gone into another room.

Mai Lee secured the door and jumped as a voice behind her spoke, "Just what do you think you are you doing?"

Mai Lee turned and faced Liling. "Liling!"

The girl gasped in surprise and lowered her voice, "Mai Lee? What on earth are you doing here?"

"Ssh! Please. I had nowhere to go and I'm hungry…" said Mai Lee placing herself at Liling's mercy. "I have to lie low for a couple of days until I can leave the country. Will you help me?"

"It's dangerous here. We are visited frequently by soldiers who are looking for you and that young man. Madame keeps me in her apartment most of the time, so I won't get taken."

"Are you all right?"

"Apart from hiding from the Master when he's here and the soldiers, life is good."

"Why are you walking around, now?"

"I couldn't sleep, and then I heard a noise. I came in here and found you."

"I will only be here a short while. Will you keep my secret?"

Liling nodded, "Come. Let's get to the kitchen and get you some food."

Mai Lee followed Liling through the apartment that had once been hers and out toward the central kitchen where all the meals of the house were prepared. Liling took a stout paper carrier from the store cupboard and went into the larder. She gathered some fruit and dried fish together with some cooked chicken and rice that lay covered in the cool pantry.

"How will you explain this?" asked Mai Lee.

"Don't worry. No one will know. If anyone says anything I

shall tell them I was hungry one night, or blame the master. Honestly, it will be fine. I have had the odd midnight feast myself on occasion."

"How are you getting on?"

"Like I said Life is good. I help Madame and Auntie Ko with massage and Madame is teaching me all sorts of things. I am blessed that you chose me to replace you."

There was a crash outside the kitchen door. The two girls looked at each other. Liling grabbed the bag and pushed it at Mai Lee and shoved her into the larder. Mai Lee darted down behind a sack of rice and stayed very still. She heard the door open and a masculine voice addressed Liling, "So there you are. I heard that I had a new foster daughter. Come here and let me look at you."

Mai Lee shuddered as she recognised Manchu's tones. She wondered what would happen to Liling.

He spoke again, "I know Madame has been hiding you. It was just a matter of time before I found you. Why, I was even contemplating speaking with Madame again."

Liling said something, but Mai Lee couldn't quite catch the words. She strained hard to listen.

Manchu raised his voice, "You dare to defy me? You will have to be taught a lesson. I can see that I have been too lenient with Madame and her whims. Come here, now."

Mai Lee heard Liling plead, "Please, Master. I am only doing as I have been bid. I have been told not to speak with you. I do not want to enrage Madame."

"Stupid woman. Is she still drinking?'

"No, Sir. Madame has been good and kind. She has not partaken of any liquor since I came to the house."

He snorted, "That won't last long. Besides, she need never know. If you come with me to my quarters I will make it well worth your while. I have need of some comfort and you are just the person to provide it. It will be our secret. Come."

Mai Lee heard Liling squeal and stiffened in anger. There seemed to be a scuffle between Manchu and Liling.

"Feisty, are we? I like that. It makes the conquest all the more fun."

There was a further squeal from Liling and Mai Lee was

filled with anger that this man felt he had the right to abuse the young girl or anyone else in the house and she determined to do something about it. She heard the door open and the sound of Liling being dragged to Manchu's rooms. Mai Lee sneaked out of the pantry. She crawled on her hands and knees into the kitchen and placed her food bag on a shelf housing cooking implements at her level. She could detect the unmistakeable aroma of opium that clouded the air. Manchu was obviously in its control and that would help her cause as he would be in such a haze that he would remember nothing.

Mai Lee opened a cupboard and selected a heavy iron based wok. She tested it in the air and crept to the door making sure to keep low. She watched as Manchu pulled the unwilling girl along the passageway almost wrenching her arm from its socket. He flung open a door and shoved her inside. Mai Lee stood up and ran down the corridor after them. She paused at the door and gathered her strength before opening it and stepping inside. She crossed the floor to the next room and pushed open the door to Manchu's bedroom. The air was thick with choking smoke from an opium pipe. It hung in the air like a threat.

She watched as Manchu threw Liling onto his bed and he began to paw at her clothes as the young girl sobbed. Mai Lee moved further into the room and sneaked up behind Manchu. She saw Liling's eyes widen when she noticed Mai Lee as she appeared behind Manchu.

Mai Lee raised the heavy iron pan and brought it down hard on his head. Manchu faltered, his eyes rolled back in his head and he collapsed on top of Liling who tried to push him off. Mai Lee hauled the man back by the shoulders and he fell on his back facing upwards and Liling scrambled up.

"Thank you," she paused. "But what do we do now?"

"Don't worry. He was in such a fog of opium he will not remember. He didn't remember the attack on me when Yuan rescued me. Help me with him. We will stage it so it looks as if he slipped and fell, so hitting his head."

The two girls struggled with the weight of the old man and pulled him to the floor. Mai Lee toppled the bedside nightstand and made it looked as if he had pulled it over when he fell. She wrapped a swathe of cloth around his foot. It appeared then he had caught his foot and taken a tumble.

Mai Lee nodded, "This will work. Has the master seen you before?"

"No, this was the first time."

"Then you must obey Madame and take sanctuary in her rooms. Do not come out under any circumstances unless with Madame or in safe company. Do you understand?"

Liling nodded her head, "Yes, you are right. Thank you my friend."

They took a cursory look at Manchu who was still out cold and they hurriedly left his room. Mai Lee stuck her head back around the door. It definitely did look as if the man had just tripped and fallen.

Mai Lee sped after Liling back to the kitchen. She stopped her as she reached the door, "Liling, go back to your rooms now or to Madame and stay there. I will manage."

Liling was more than relieved. She nodded her agreement and retraced her steps anxious to get away to safety. Mai Lee scurried into the kitchen and bent down to retrieve her bag of goodies. It wasn't there. Mai Lee prostrated herself on the floor to look under the cupboards but could not see the food bag anywhere. She scrambled up confused when a voice spoke from behind her, "Are you looking for this?"

Mai Lee turned at the familiar voice and gasped in both surprise and pleasure, "Auntie Ko!" Mai Lee rushed to her and hugged her old friend. "Oh, Auntie Ko. How I have missed you."

Auntie Ko returned Mai Lee's hug before disentangling her arms from around her. "Mai Lee, what are you doing here?"

"Forgive me. I had no choice. It was the only thing I could think to do."

"But, it is not safe. There are those who hunt you."

"I know. Coming here was a last resort. I promise you. I have missed you."

"And we have missed you. Oh, I know Liling has learned how to massage but she has not got your velvet touch."

Mai Lee laughed, "You flatter me."

"Not at all. Ah, Mai Lee, you touched our hearts."

"As you did mine."

"We missed you."

"And I you." The two embraced again.

"What has happened? Where is Liling?"

"She is safe. She will not venture from her rooms or Madame's again."

"The master?"

Mai Lee nodded, "It was as before. He attacked her whilst filled in a drug haze."

"Opium?"

Again Mai Lee nodded, "You think he would learn his lesson."

"What happened?"

Mai Lee explained the details of the evening's events and Auntie Ko nodded sympathetically.

"It will be fine. We will ensure he believes your manufactured version of events."

"How long is the master to be here?"

"Who's to know? He must have arrived tonight. I was unaware he had come. It makes it awkward. How long do you have to stay?"

"Just tonight and tomorrow. Then we leave."

"Then I have something to ask of you."

"Anything."

"Come with me to see Madame Jong."

"But…"

"Please. Madame has never got over your loss. If she sees you she can at least have some closure over losing you."

"Is that wise? Is the hour not too late?"

Auntie Ko thought a moment, "Maybe you are right. But, come tomorrow. Tomorrow evening we will know if the master has gone or if he is still to linger here. Let us say, I will meet you here, in the kitchen. Can you do that?"

"At what time?"

"Be careful. Get here as close to ten as you can. I promise you it will be safe. If anything changes, I will bring word. I promise. You are in the storeroom?"

"Yes."

"Then I will leave the door from the main house onto the

veranda unlocked. You won't have to risk walking into Manchu's rooms."

Mai Lee nodded, "Until tomorrow." They hugged again and Auntie Ko passed her the bag of food. Mai Lee quietly returned to the storeroom underneath the Orchid House where Yuan waited anxiously.

CHAPTER TWENTY-THREE

Another night

Mai Lee and Yuan laid low throughout the next day. Every sound, every rustle put them on their guard. Yuan jiggled his knee in frustration, "I don't know how long I can stay in here," he muttered.

"It's too dangerous to go out," reasoned Mai Lee. "I know you are claustrophobic but we just cannot risk you being seen."

"I can go into the temple at least I can see outside. It will make me feel so much better. No one will notice me. They will believe I have come to worship just like everyone else."

Mai Lee sighed, "I really feel that you have to tough it out. What if Manchu sees you? Or the Japanese?"

Yuan pursed his lips, "And what if this confinement sends me mad? Please, Mai Lee. You have to understand. I promise I'll be careful."

Mai Lee nodded reluctantly. They had been arguing around the same points for most of the day and she could see that Yuan's condition and mental state had deteriorated. He was nervy and sweating. His phobia of being virtually trapped was taking its toll. "I understand, but please, can't you wait just a little while longer? I know that the temple will be busy around four and then you can lose yourself in the crowds."

"Thank you. I know I will go mad if I have to sit here for much longer."

Mai Lee put her arms around him and embraced him and they held each other close. "You make me feel so much better," he said. "I can't believe we will soon be out of here and on our way to a new life."

"That's if all goes well."

"And that's what we must believe. We must look forward and believe we have a bright and happy future together. Oh, Mai Lee, we will have such fun. Think of what we can achieve. We can be whatever we want to be, have an education and most importantly we can be free."

"It does sound wonderful," smiled Mai Lee.

They embraced again and Yuan kissed her gently, "I will go and I promise I will not be too long; I will just spend time enough to calm my beating heart although I am sure it is the closeness of you that puts me in such a panic."

Mai Lee giggled, "Go on with you. You flatter me. Hurry now, I will be waiting."

Yuan jumped up, he kissed Mai Lee once more. He pulled his cloth cap on his head and crossed to the door. "Secure the door. When I return I will knock softly three times so that you know it's me." He looked back at her as he delicately pulled back the old drape and removed the chair blocking the way to the underground passage. Mai Lee could see the relief was clearly evident in his face before he turned and left.

Without Yuan, Mai Lee was at a loss to know what to do. Chatting with him filled the time. She decided to rest but took herself into a corner, whereby if someone did enter the room, she wouldn't be seen and there she stayed.

Time passed. Mai Lee rested fitfully. Her sleep was plagued with dreams that made no sense and she awoke with a start as she relived her nightmare encounter with Manchu. She sat up, stretched and yawned. How long had Yuan been gone? Too long she felt, and she wondered at the time. As if to answer her query the clock near the temple chimed and Mai Lee counted. It was eight o' clock. She had slept for four hours.

Mai Lee negotiated her way through the dark to the passage door and listened. There was no sound. Yuan should have been back by now. In two hours she was to meet Auntie Ko. "What do I do?" she whispered aloud. "Oh, Lily. I wish you could help me now."

Mai Lee gingerly opened the door to the passageway and crept along it. She climbed the spiral staircase and entered the dank rocky corridor. She could see a faint strip of light at the far end and moved quietly toward it. She listened carefully for any extraneous noise before she gently opened the door and emerged in the underground chamber at the bottom of the stairs to the temple.

Her heart again thudded in her chest. It hammered against her ribcage and she took a deep breath and tried to steady herself as she slowly mounted the stairs. She peeped up into the inner temple there were very few people at worship. She scanned the area quickly. She noted the monks in their predominant orange robes, an elderly man, and a couple of women. There was no sign of Yuan. The single Japanese guard had been replaced by four soldiers. Two stood on the temple steps surveying the street and another two were laughing and joking together as they kept an eye out on the occupants within the temple.

Mai Lee quickly ducked down and hurriedly began to make her way back to the underground storeroom. She had no idea what had happened to Yuan but was certain that something bad had happened and now she didn't know what to do. She ran the last few steps of the rocky corridor and down the spiral staircase and with relief she closed the door of her sanctuary and leaned against it.

Now what should she do? If she blocked the door and Yuan returned he wouldn't be able to gain access and then again nor would anyone else. Mai Lee decided to collect her canvas bag with the money and plans. She cleared up the debris from the food she and Yuan had consumed. She examined the space and at first glance it looked as if no one had been in there, except for their footprints in the dust. There was nothing for it, Mai Lee took an old piece of cloth and dusted the floor cleaning away the footmarks and dust. She threw the tarpaulin over the crates where they had sat and it made look less likely that anyone had been hiding there.

Mai Lee, removed the chair securing the door to the Orchid House and garden. She opened it carefully and made her way up the steps. She knew she was early and prayed that the door to the centre of the house on the veranda had been left open as arranged.

She needn't have worried Auntie Ko had kept her word. Mai Lee slipped in through the double doors and along the polished wooden corridor. She crept like a cat stalking its prey, passed the numerous rooms and into the wing, which housed the kitchen. Once there she ducked down behind the table and crawled on all fours to the pantry door. She opened it and slipped inside to wait.

Mai Lee had not felt so nervous since her time in the Japanese cell. She prayed aloud, "Oh, Lily, if you are able please keep Yuan safe and bring him back to me." She sniffed back her tears that promised to tumble from her eyes.

Her ears pricked up sharply as she heard a small sound. She retreated to the very back of the cupboard and ducked down behind some heavy baskets and waited. The pantry door creaked open and a plump shape filled the doorway. In the partial light Mai Lee recognised the figure of Auntie Ko and she stood up.

Auntie Ko put her fingers to her lips and ushered Mai Lee from her hiding place. She warned her not to speak. They scurried quickly to Madame's wing along the corridor with its many and varied paintings until the reached her door. Auntie Ko tapped on it lightly and Liling opened it she must have been waiting for their arrival.

Auntie Ko visibly relaxed once inside and she ordered Liling to lock the door and they entered Madame's boudoir. Aaryn Jong turned to see them and she looked so different. Gone was her white caked on make-up to be replaced by a more natural healthy glow that took years off her. She smiled sweetly and opened her arms, "Oh, Mai Lee, come, let me hold you." Mai Lee went willingly to be hugged by her foster mother. "We have been so worried. Ever since your young man was taken."

Mai Lee stepped back, "Why, what has happened?"

"You don't know?"

Mai Lee shook her head, "No, tell me."

"There was a huge commotion in the Temple when one of the Japanese guards spotted Yuan. They gave chase and he fled. Several items were broken and some sacred wall hangings were pulled down. We don't know where he is now or if he has been caught but the soldiers came and demanded to search the house. Fortunately, they didn't discover the steps to the storeroom. I had to hide Liling in a trap under the floor."

"Yes, they covered it with a rug and table," added Liling. "I am surprised you didn't hear anything."

Mai Lee shook her head in shock and Auntie Ko continued, "They took Manchu and arrested him. He was so high on opium he didn't realise what was happening to him."

"If they have imprisoned him he can stay there," said Madame. "I for one will not rescue him."

"What am I to do?" asked Mai Lee in a tiny voice.

"You said you had a plan?" pressed Auntie Ko.

"We were hoping that you would change your mind and stay here as my daughter and Liling's sister but it is just not safe to do that. I only hope that at some point when our land is at peace and no longer in turmoil that you will return." Aaryn Jong hugged Mai Lee again.

"Tell us your plan and we will do what we can to help."

Mai Lee fished in her bag for the messages, "As I remember I have to get to Raffles tomorrow evening where we will be met. Here, look at the map and read the message on the back, every third word," gushed Mai Lee.

Madame Jong nodded and skimmed through the message, "This must be destroyed. There must be no evidence of anything on you just in case you are caught although we pray that won't happen." Madame Jong took the message and blacked out the words with her brush and ink before setting it a dish and setting fire to it. She watched as it burned before tossing the ashes into a bin. "That's done!" she said, brushing her hands together. "You will stay here with us until the appointed hour. Auntie Ko will have a cart prepared, the gardener can drive it will attract least suspicion. I will don my travelling attire as if to go to out to visit my family."

"Madame visits her family once every month. So it will look normal," added Auntie Ko.

"Auntie, you will remain here with Liling. Mai Lee, you will hide…" she thought quickly. "I know, I will take gifts from my garden, some pots with flowers and shrubs. I will take a large ceramic pot and you can hide in that. We pass Raffles on the way to my parents' house. I always take them a flagon of rice wine. When I go inside, if the way is clear I will whistle, you will get out and then the rest is up to you."

"You never know, if Yuan is free he may make the rendezvous, too. If not you will be on your own," finished

Madame. "And now, let us enjoy these last few hours together. Auntie Ko?"

Auntie Ko led the way further into Madame's quarters where a table was laid with all manner of food. They sat around it together on cushions. Mai Lee thought that it felt odd to be having some kind of celebratory last supper with them all but she determined to make the most of this last night with her companions. Tomorrow would come quickly enough, of that she was sure. As she sat and ate she chatted as if free of all worries but she wondered what had happened to Yuan and prayed that he was safe.

***

Yuan had given the soldiers the slip and had run to Hobos' Alley. He lost himself amongst the down and outs, alcoholics, drug addicts and homeless in that notorious street. Sheltered under a makeshift tent with another young man, a self confessed thief, he shared a meagre supper with the man, Malik.

"The Japanese are no friends of mine. They raided my home and took my mother and sister," said Malik.

"They killed my widowed mother. My father died in the Great War."

Malik nodded, "You have suffered like me. But now you are on the run, what are you going to do?"

"I'm not sure yet. I will try and move ahead with my original plans."

"Which are?"

"That I can't tell you. I do not want to put your life at risk. You can't tell if you don't know."

"I understand. But a word of advice, if you intend on continuing to give them the slip you must change your ways and the way you look."

"How? How can I do that?"

Malik frowned and thought, "There may be a way. We have to teach you to walk and move differently. We must dress you in different clothes. What do you have on your feet?"

"Nothing," Yuan lifted up his sarong and revealed his feet.

"Hmm!" said Malik as he chewed on a piece of dried fish, "This could be fun. Do you have money?"

"A little."

"Good you will need it," and he smiled. "First thing we do is get you some shoes. You have any paper in that bag?"

Yuan nodded and pulled out a sheet of his student notepaper.

"A pencil?"

Yuan foraged again and withdrew a pencil.

"Right, lift your foot up." Yuan lifted his foot, "On the paper." Yuan did as he was asked and Malik drew around the shape of his foot, "Now the other one." The procedure was repeated with the other foot and Malik nodded in satisfaction. "That will do nicely. You wait here. I will get this done now."

"Wait! Where are you going?"

Malik winked, "It's best you don't know, if anything goes wrong what you don't know can't hurt anyone else."

Yuan nodded in understanding and managed his first smile of the day.

"I will try not to be too long, can you let me have some cash?"

Yuan pursed his lips. His mind was racing. Was this Malik person legitimate? Or was he going to run off with his money and leave him high and dry?"

"Well?" Malik stretched out his hand.

Yuan thrust his hand in his pocket and took out some notes. He passed them to Malik, "I hope I'm not kissing this goodbye."

"Trust me," said Malik and winked again before he ducked out from under the tent.

Yuan waited restlessly. He glanced at his watch; three hours had passed. He cursed himself for being a fool. He wondered if he had been betrayed and whether or not the Japanese would arrive in the alley at any minute. The tent flap lifted and Malik stooped and came in with an easy grin on his face. He was carrying some bags and he flopped down. He passed Yuan a handful of money, "Your change."

Yuan looked surprised and shook his head, "No, keep it."

"Are you sure?" Yuan nodded and Malik shrugged. He pocketed the extra cash. "I'd be a fool to turn it down. That'll buy me food for a week. Now look, look at what I have got."

Yuan looked interested as Malik delved in the first bag. He dug out a pair of shoes. "Here try these on." Yuan put them on his feet and grimaced, "They're all made wrong. "

"No, contradicted Malik. "They're perfect. The right shoe is built up. That will give you an uneven walk. We can even make it worse by popping a pebble inside, which will force you to hobble."

"And what if I need to run?"

"Bear with me." He reached into another bag, "Here, put these on." He took out some Western styled clothes, a shirt, trousers and jacket. "They should fit. You are about the same size as me." He emptied another bag, which contained a straw Panama hat.

Yuan changed into the selected items. He could see how different these clothes made him look.

"And now for the finishing touches. Here." Malik took a pair of scissors, "We need to trim your hair, give you a side parting." He began to comb Yuan's tangled locks and chopped and cut at his hair. "It's a bit rough but it will do, and now for the final piece of the disguise."

Malik took some cotton wool rolls of wadding such as a dentist might use. "Here stuff these in your cheeks." Yuan did as he was asked. "Good. Your own mother wouldn't recognise you now. Look."

He passed Yuan a small hand mirror and Yuan appraised his face. "I wouldn't have believed it," he murmured. The wadding even changed the way Yuan spoke, "Malik, you're a genius."

"I know. Let's hope that it works!"

CHAPTER TWENTY-FOUR

Raffles

The old gardener shook the reins and pulled the oxen to a stop outside the famous hotel and bar called Raffles in Seah Street. Madame Jong searched around her and jumped down. She tapped on the ceramic pot and whispered, "Wait for my signal."

Madame Jong wore a smart travelling outfit. But no more the thick white pancake that she had worn for years. She truly had abandoned her old style. She looked so much better and less likely to attract attention. Her hair was naturally styled and decorated with tortoiseshell pins and combs. She minced into the bar at Raffles and looked around. There were a few customers sitting sipping their drinks. She saw a young gentleman sitting in the corner munching on a pot of peanuts. He glanced at her and then quickly lowered his eyes and she peered again, still not quite seeing through his disguise. On the other side of the bar stood Hiroto, she gave the semblance of a nod before ordering a large flagon of rice wine to take away.

The bartender plonked the clay flagon in front of her and took the offered money. The young gentleman rose to his feet and hobbled toward Madame. He stood next to her at the bar as she waited for her change.

The paddle fans moved lazily in the warmth of the bar. Yuan nudged Madame, "Oh, I'm so sorry." His voice sounded strange. He whispered, "Is Mai Lee all right?"

Madame gasped, "Yuan?"

"Ssh. Yes."

"She's fine. She will be here in a moment." Madame collected her change and Yuan returned to his seat. Madame began to leave and she gave a bright chirpy little whistle. The bartender raised an eyebrow but said nothing.

Madame emerged from the building and saw Mai Lee

clamber out of the Ali Baba pot, hop off the wagon and move slowly toward her. Madame muttered quietly to her as she passed before getting back to the cart. "Yuan is in there. He's in disguise. So, too, is Hiroto. Be careful."

Madame swung up beside the gardener and with her eyes fixed forward the oxen were encouraged to move and plodded off down the almost deserted street. Mai Lee looked around her again before stepping up cautiously into the ground floor entrance to Raffles' bar.

She was swiftly met by Hiroto who swept her up into his arms. Mai Lee began to struggle and fight against him until he whispered into her ear. "Stop! This is all part of the plan. You have to look like you're my mistress."

Mai Lee relaxed and stared at the young man in the corner, scarcely believing her eyes. Yuan acknowledged her with a small flick of his hand and his lopsided grin. He affirmed with his eyes that it was all perfectly okay.

Hiroto crossed the bar floor with Mai Lee. No one gave them a second glance. They moved to where Yuan was seated. The paddle fans continued to waft and a couple squeaked irritatingly as they twisted and turned.

They sat down. On the seat next to Hiroto was a package, which he passed to Mai Lee. There was a bag under the table, which Hiroto moved with his foot toward Yuan.

Hiroto indicated the parcel and spoke softly, "Mai Lee, take that and change. Quietly now."

Mai Lee rose, picked up the package and headed toward the Restrooms at the back of the bar. She edged her way through and knocked shoulders with a Malay waiter who apologised. She brushed his words aside and entered the female toilet. She closeted herself in a stall and opened the package pulling out a sexy, tight fitting cheongsam with a keyhole cut to show off her cleavage and a high, thigh-revealing split. She quickly changed and dressed her hair over one side of her face. She placed her small feet into high-heeled strapped sandals and then touched up her make up with some pink cream rouge, green eye shadow, black eyeliner and crimson lips. She appraised herself in the mirror. She looked stunning and every inch the courtesan she was expected to be.

She wrapped her old clothes in the brown paper and stuffed them in the canvas bag before leaving the lavatory and walking back into the bar. Now, the place was filling up with people who had come in to unwind after work and as she wiggled back to the table, with a seductive sway of her hips, heads turned and she attracted many admiring glances. She sat next to Hiroto.

"You still have your student clothes?"

She nodded, "In the package in my bag."

"Good. You'll need them later." He jerked his head at Yuan, "Go on. Now it's your turn. Go."

Yuan slipped out of his seat and disappeared out to the back. Hiroto leaned forward and whispered again to Mai Lee. "You know what you have to do?"

"I think so."

"Play up to me. We'll act a little drunk when we leave; no one will care or pay us any attention. Then once we get into the base, I will pass you off as my comfort woman."

"I know the rest..." said Mai Lee.

They were interrupted by the return of Yuan who was now dressed as a Japanese officer. He stood stiffly to attention. Hiroto rose and saluted him.

The customers looked lazily at them and then turned away disinterested. Another Japanese soldier from Takagi's platoon entered the bar. He looked around and spotted Hiroto and gave him a swift wave. He eyed Mai Lee and gestured obscenely before going to the bar and ordering drinks.

Yuan, Mai Lee and Hiroto left. Hiroto made a show of walking unsteadily as he hung onto Mai Lee.

The soldier watched and laughed.

The trio stepped out into Seah Street. A vehicle drew up across the road from the bar. The driver stepped out and opened the passenger door. Polished boots hit the dirt road as Takagi stepped out. He narrowed his eyes as he recognised Hiroto. He then turned his attention to Mai Lee and a wave of recognition flooded across his face. This did not go unnoticed by Hiroto who urged the others to hurry to the parked military jeep, which waited on the corner.

Takagi was spurred into action. He shouted out and began

to give chase. They rushed across the street but the shouts from his commandant had alerted the soldier in the bar. He raced out and Takagi pointed at the escaping trio. They saw their quarry getting into the jeep and raced back to their own vehicle and went in pursuit.

Inside Hiroto's jeep they travelled in tense silence but kept alert at all times. Mai Lee watched the scenery flash by in child like amazement. She would have enjoyed it had they were not being chased. Hiroto took several twists and turns until they reached the country lanes.

They saw the signs to Tengah Airbase and Hiroto stepped on the gas and drove confidently to the gate and the checkpoint. The sentry on duty looked in and leered at Mai Lee, who had draped herself seductively over Hiroto, "I see you'll have fun tonight," the guard said crudely.

Hiroto smirked, "Want her? I'll send her to you later if you like?"

The guard grinned lasciviously, "Oh, yes. Do. I would love a piece of that."

"Consider it done," said Hiroto.

The sentry waved them through as he lifted the barrier, still chuckling to himself.

They drove on and approached the hangar where an aeroplane waited. Hiroto ordered, "Duck down now, Mai Lee. Hide." She crouched down and Yuan threw a cover over her so she could not be seen. "Are you ready, Yuan?"

Yuan asserted, "Hai."

***

Takagi's men in the moving jeep wove through the busy streets. Each soldier was on full alert looking for any sign of the military vehicle. Takagi thumped the dash in annoyance, "Damn! We've lost them. Where could they be going?"

"Maybe Madame Jong's," said one soldier.

Takagi nodded, "It's possible but unlikely."

They proceeded down the main street but had to pull up short to avoid a rickshaw and a flood of people who tried to cross the road. Takagi swore again in exasperation when an idea occurred to him. He rapped his baton on the driver's wheel and ordered, "Make for Tengah Airbase. Hiroto is scheduled to fly stores to Borneo. He may be going to try and fly her out. Hurry!"

The jeep screeched as it turned in the road leaving a doughnut trail of black tyre tracks. The pursuing party zipped off in another direction with smoking wheels and burning rubber.

***

At the airbase Hiroto has parked the jeep inside the hangar at the back of the plane. Mai Lee lay down low onto the floor and waited for her chance. A mechanic walked from the front of the plane. He wiped his hands on an oily rag and approached Hiroto who had stepped out with Yuan. "It's all ready for you," said the mechanic. "You just need to load the rest of the freight. Most of it's in."

Yuan began to remonstrate with Hiroto. "That's not my job, I am an assistant pilot not a skivvy to carry and load goods."

"You will do as you are ordered," regaled Hiroto.

The mechanic looked on in surprise as their voices became raised. An argument erupted and threatened to get ugly.

"I have had enough of your demeaning attitude and downright rudeness," yelled Yuan.

"And you will get off your high horse and stop being so arrogant and pompous. We all have to do things we dislike. We are soon to be at war," retorted Hiroto.

Yuan stepped forward menacingly. It looked as if Yuan was going to hit Hiroto. He dived at him. The stunned mechanic attempted to break up the beginning of a brawl and stood between them trying to keep them apart.

It was the chance Mai Lee was waiting for. She slipped unnoticed out of the jeep and carried her package and their bags. She scurried out of the jeep in the hangar, eased off the loose top of a crate waiting to be loaded. She threw in the bag and clutched her package and slid inside. She carefully covered herself with the straw packing after she replaced the lid and she sat quietly hardly daring to breathe.

Hiroto suddenly shouted loudly and stamped his feet. He waved his arms and called a halt to the row. "This is ridiculous. We are all tired. We will work together. It is stupid to argue."

To the mechanic's relief they appeared to make up. With great effort the crate that contained Mai Lee was lifted and loaded on board the plane. Hiroto dusted himself down and indicated the last packing case, "Can you manage that one?"

Yuan nodded and indicated the mechanic, "If he helps me."

Hiroto climbed into the cockpit and started the engine and the plane travelled out of the hangar and stopped outside whilst Yuan and the mechanic begin to move the second crate. They manoeuvred it to the back of the plane, which waited with its engine ticking over.

***

Takagi and his men raced down the leafy lanes toward the country airbase. They travelled in silence until they hurtled toward the gate and skidded to a halt at the sentry box. Takagi shouted out of the window, "Hiroto Sato. Have you seen him?"

The soldier started to grin and Takagi yelled at him, "Get that grin off your face, He's with a woman and another soldier."

The sentry stood to attention, "Sir, he's already gone through."

"Phone the hangar. Stop him from flying. That's an order." The soldier dithered and Takagi bellowed, "Now! And let us through, you blithering idiot."

The guard lifted the barrier and the jeep sped through. He dashed to the phone in his sentry box and dialled quickly.

***

Inside the hangar the phone began jangling for attention.

The mechanic stopped and looked up. Yuan urged the man to help him with the crate first. They struggled together to shift the packing case but the phone continued to ring. Its tone was persistent and annoying. Eventually, the mechanic shook his head and crossed to the back of the hangar where there was an office and the phone still rang shrilly.

Yuan looked worried and waited, uncertain what to do. The plane spluttered outside threatening to die. Hiroto shocked the engine into life once more. The propellers started to whir vigorously just as the telephone stopped its insistent ring. Yuan heard the mechanic shouting and sensed something was wrong. The man had dropped the phone, which swung on its cable and he ran from the office toward the plane.

Yuan dashed out and waved his arms at Hiroto and gestured that there was something wrong. At that moment, Hiroto spotted the fast approaching military jeep with Takagi and his men. He signalled wildly to Yuan to get on board. Yuan fled to the back of the plane with its open hold and he scrambled inside. The mechanic tried to catch Yuan and grabbed hold of his leg. Yuan kicked out but the man held fast.

Hiroto started to move the aircraft away from the hangar and he taxied toward the runway. Takagi's jeep veered off the road and chased after the plane.

The mechanic and Yuan were still locked in a struggle. A sudden burst of speed from the plane and the mechanic who was being dragged took a tumble. He lost his grip on Yuan's foot. The mechanic removed a pistol at his side and levelled it at the soldier impostor as Yuan fought to close the flap of the hold. Mai Lee pushed off the lid of the crate and stepped out struggling to balance. She shouted a warning to Yuan, who looked up and saw the danger, but Mai Lee had dashed to Yuan's side and pulled out his pistol from his holster. She aimed at the mechanic and let off a shot at the man, which winged his shoulder. The mechanic fell and grimaced in pain. The door flap finally closed with a sudden bang. Yuan bolted and secure it and turned to Mai Lee.

The plane gathered momentum along the runway with the

jeep still in strong pursuit. Hiroto revved the engine still further and spurted onward.

***

Takagi urged his driver to press on at a reckless, breakneck speed and the vehicle began to catch up with the plane. The Commandant barked his orders and the jeep attempted to overtake the plane. The Japanese chief instructed the driver to swing in front of the plane and stop it. The driver hesitated, Takagi bawled, “Do it. Do it now!”

The jeep drew level with the aircraft and the driver swung the wheel around to obey his commander and block the escape. But at that exact moment the plane lifted up from the runway into the air. It climbed safely into the sky.

***

In the back of the plane, Yuan and Mai Lee clung together in a tight embrace. Hiroto shouted above the noise of the engine, “Change back into your student clothes. Manila here we come.”

“Then what?” asked Mai Lee.

“We refuel and proceed to Hawaii to the American Airbase and onward to the U. S of A. Los Angeles and freedom.

Hiroto let out a whoop of joy as Mai Lee and Yuan kissed. They moved forward to the cockpit and saw the Japanese below who shook their fists and fired shots into the air, which were too far away to do any damage.

Hiroto turned to them both, “And now you will be truly free.”

And as the scent of jasmine surrounded her Mai Lee replied, “And I am me. I will belong to no one.”

The plane soared safely into the clouds, which cloaked them from below and flew the hopeful passengers to what they believed would be a new life.

The threat of another Japanese plane pursuing them was

minimal and the journey to Manila was to prove light hearted and enjoyable as the trio chatted together. However, Mai Lee turned the conversation to Hiroto.

"You realise you will be a considered a deserter and traitor to Japan?"

"I know and that makes me sad. I love my country. But all that was happening in Singapore was sickening and tore me apart. It was wrong and for that reason I became one of the activists. The country we are moving to are aware of my existence and my beliefs. I know we will be welcomed. Word has gone on ahead."

"My only fear is that with you gone there is no one to help those wrongfully imprisoned as you helped me," said Mai Lee.

"Have no fear, there are others who are of my opinion. In fact, they helped when we tried to cover up Rin's death."

Yuan spoke, "I don't regret killing him."

"Nor should you," said Mai Lee. "He was the most vicious, unpardonable brute…" She stopped, "Words fail me. It is wrong to call him an animal as no animal would do what he did."

Hiroto agreed, "You had better get comfortable it will take us eight hours to get there. Get some sleep. You will need to be refreshed on arrival."

"How do we know that the Japanese won't be waiting to arrest us in Manila?"

"They won't. I am going to Neilson Airfield and surrendering to the Americans. Wheels are in motion. They are expecting us. Remember Takagi doesn't know where we are headed. It could be anywhere, the islands, Borneo, anywhere. It will be fine," he said with more confidence than he felt. He knew that once he was clear of the coastline he would need to deploy evasion tactics and try to fly under the radar.

"We are lucky the weather is being kind to us. So many typhoons in one year. It has made flying difficult," said Hiroto.

They flew on into the night. Mai Lee and Yuan fell asleep. It seemed that they had no longer relaxed than Hiroto was calling out to them. "Not long now. You should prepare for landing."

Mai Lee stretched and sleepily rubbed her eyes, while Yuan was instantly awake.

"I've never flown before. This is a real experience for me. Exciting, too."

Hiroto was charmed by Yuan's enthusiasm, "First time for Mai Lee, too?"

"Yes, of course. This is all new to me."

"Sit yourselves down and brace yourselves. There are straps in the back to secure you. I shall be beginning my decent soon."

Yuan and Mai Lee did as they were asked. They were filled with trepidation. Neither of them knew what to expect.

They could hear Hiroto on the radio to the control centre but couldn't quite catch was being said. They felt the aircraft turn as it began to descend. They were going down to a new land.

CHAPTER TWENTY-FIVE

Conclusion or is it?

In spite of the early hour the airfield was bustling with activity. Hiroto taxied along the runway and was directed by a native air martial waving paddles, which guided him to the American hangar where a contingent awaited.

He brought the plane to a halt and stopped the engine. The propellers slowed and settled in their spin. Hiroto opened the cockpit door and jumped down. A smart lieutenant stepped forward and saluted Hiroto. The back flap of the aircraft dropped down and Yuan and Mai Lee stepped down onto Philippine soil. Yuan placed a protective arm around Mai Lee's shoulder and she smiled up at him.

They were being ushered away when a representative from the Japanese army presented himself to the Americans. Mai Lee looked fearfully at Yuan as the officer demanded their arrest and return to Singapore where they were wanted for murder, malicious wounding and treason.

The voices became raised and in translation voices were ferocious and angry. Mai Lee bit her lip and fingered her pendant. She was bewildered, frightened and did not understand what was being said but knew enough that the tone was one of rage.

A young airman presented to them and urged them to follow. He spoke in their language and reassured them, "You must not worry. No one here is going to give you up or send you back. You are safe. Come with me. We will fetch you some refreshment. Come."

They didn't need telling twice and with great relief they followed the young man from the hangar on route to another building.

"What about Hiroto?" asked Mai Lee.

"Yes, he is to fly us to Hawaii and to your glorious country," added Yuan.

Mai Lee stopped, “You are not going to let them take him, surely? He will be killed.”

“The soldier is no longer your concern.”

“NO! He saved our lives.” Mai Lee pulled away and ran back where the wrangling over Hiroto continued. She raced to Hiroto’s side, and shouted, “You can not send him back. He will be tortured and killed.” Mai Lee stood protectively in front of Hiroto and the surly Japanese Officer stepped up to her and spat in her face.

The action spurred the Lieutenant into action just as the first officer returned with Yuan. He ordered his man. “Take them all away, Baldwin. Take them *all* away to safety.” He indicated Hiroto, “Him as well.” He turned to the Japanese Officer and dismissed him. “You are trespassing on American soil, Sir. I suggest you leave now or we will be forced to detain you. You do not want to cause an international incident.”

The Japanese soldier was incensed but forced to accept defeat. He stamped his foot and marched away. Mai Lee took Hiroto’s arm and they followed Airman Baldwin as they were escorted to the other building.

Mai Lee and Yuan were kept in a holding area and identification papers prepared for them. Hiroto was questioned at length and proof given that he was indeed the activist who had been in communication with their intelligence network.

Mai Lee excused herself and she went to the Ladies’ Restroom to splash water over her face. She took her time, sweeping the water up from the basin and over her cheeks invigorating and refreshing her before she looked up. The water droplets dripped from her chin and she reached out for a paper towel to dab at her wet face. As she patted dry the delicate skin around her eyes the unmistakeable fragrance of jasmine filled the air.

Mai Lee stopped and gazed at the silvered mirror and Lily’s face shimmered before her, “Lily?”

“You are going to a good life,” whispered Lily. “But in time you are set to return to your own country.”

"Why?" asked Mai Lee surprised.

"Because there will be someone you will seek."

"There is no one I would wish to find," she said in a puzzled tone. "Well, maybe Ming Hua…"

"No, not Ming Hua although it is possible that you may see her again. But, I speak of your mother, Mai Lee. Your mother is still alive."

Mai Lee stared in stunned silence at Lily's reflection, which began to disintegrate. This moved her to speak again, "No, Lily. Don't go."

The image finally dissolved. But, Lily's words reverberated around her, "Your mother is alive, Mai Lee. You will search for her and I will always watch over you."

There was the sound of tinkling bells that Mai Lee was used to hearing when Lily's presence vanished. A steely glint manifested in her eyes and as she stepped out from the restroom, there was an air of determination in her step.

Yuan rose to greet her as she returned to the waiting room. "Our flight is ready." He smiled, "Hiroto is coming with us. We really are on our way to America."

Mai Lee nodded and smiled, she pushed her shoulders back and lifted her head proudly; "We are going forward to a good life; this I have been told. And I will be back."

"What?" Yuan stopped.

Mai Lee kept walking and called back, "My mother, Yuan, she is still alive and I will find her. When this Great War that is coming, the one you spoke of is over, then I will come back. It is my duty."

Yuan threw up his hands in the air and ran after Mai Lee and Hiroto to where an aircraft waited to take them to safety and freedom.